ECHOES AND OATHS

GUARDIAN SECURITY SHADOW WORLD

GUARDIAN DYNASTY
BOOK FOUR

KRIS MICHAELS

CHAPTER 1

The assassin, Jinx, settled into one of the deep leather chairs on the private jet waiting for him at the Colorado airstrip. The hum of the engines vibrated beneath his boots, a steady pulse like a heartbeat in the belly of the bird. He exhaled slowly, stretching his legs out as the aircraft's cabin lighting cast a dim glow over the polished wood and sleek, minimalist interior.

"We're waiting on two more passengers, sir. Then we'll be on our way. I was told they'd been delayed and to wait for them."

Jinx barely inclined his head, acknowledging the pilot's words with a flick of his fingers before closing his eyes. He already knew where they were headed. The place that had consumed over three years of his life. The place that had nearly killed him more times than he cared to count.

Venezuela.

The memory of that mission uncoiled in his mind. He could still smell the damp rot of the area where he'd lived. The bite of gasoline-stained, dusty dirt roads lingered at the back of his throat. He remembered the thick, oppressive heat clinging to his skin like an unseen second layer and the sweet scent of rotting fruit left out in the sun.

Jinx had set foot on Venezuelan soil for the first time three years ago. It had been a world he'd learned fast. Bloodstained currency, drug cartel murders, treaty betrayals, and unrelenting violence dominated the country.

Getting into Montoya's organization had been an exercise in extreme patience. No one simply walked into the inner circle of Venezuela's most powerful drug lord. Montoya was more than a kingpin. He was a choking presence that stretched over an empire built on drugs, dead bodies, and the need for relentless control. A monster wanted for decades of bloodshed, corruption, and ruthless gathering of intelligence through murder and intimidation. The Council had spoken. Montoya was targeted.

Numerous assassination attempts had been made

against Montoya by rival cartels, military units, and even the fractured remnants of his own government. Each failure had only made him more paranoid, more ruthless. He'd turned himself into a mirage. The man had slipped between safe houses, moving like dust through the cracks of a shattered nation.

Jinx's mission from his organization had been clear.

Infiltrate. Eliminate.

Guardian Security had given him no deadline, no restrictions. Take out Montoya. Whatever it takes. As long as it takes.

So, he started from the bottom, slipping into the underbelly of Montoya's empire. He'd become a mercenary-for-hire, a nameless trigger-man in a world that ran on blood and bullets. The street dealers, the enforcers, the small-time smugglers, they'd been expendable to Montoya. They'd also been Jinx's ticket in. He'd done his job. He'd become what he hunted.

His first job had been simple: escort a drug shipment through cartel territory to a safe house near the Colombian border. Montoya's enemies had been waiting. They had insider information. Leaks from someone close to Montoya. Jinx hadn't hesitated to use every resource he had. Brando's satellite feeds had given him the upper hand. His rifle had done the rest.

Two bodies had been left bleeding on the roadside. A third had been taken down with an impossible shot. The jungle had swallowed the man's guttural scream before he could radio a warning.

The cartel lieutenant overseeing the shipment had been impressed. That single job had earned him a promotion. Six months later, he'd no longer been just another disposable trigger-man. He'd been accepted, although not trusted.

Months later had come the test.

The man feeding information to Montoya's rivals had been caught. Montoya's lieutenants had demanded a public execution. A warning. A lesson. Jinx had been handed a gun, the cool rifle stock pressing into his palm like a brand.

Jinx was sure they thought he'd stall or fail. That, as an outsider, he wasn't made of the vengeance they needed at the highest levels. He was more. He was a Shadow. He was the personification of death and would not be stopped from completing his mission.

"Show your loyalty," Tomás Ortega had said, his dark eyes flashing with fear before becoming unreadable as he tilted his chin toward the kneeling man. Jinx hated Ortega with a passion that burned hotter than the sin-stoked fires of hell. The man was a weasel, spineless and utterly cruel. The man's façade of malevolence hid the weakness that Jinx saw in the man. The slime of his depraved and degenerate actions camouflaged Ortega's innate spinelessness. He only attacked the weak, the injured, and easy targets. How could he be the only one to notice the coward hiding in plain sight? The man's presence today was another swallowed helping of distaste and hatred he consumed in order to complete this assignment.

Ortega blinked and then narrowed his eyes. "Well?"

Jinx turned to stare at the traitor. The lines between necessity and morality had blurred long ago. The man had not been an innocent. He'd not been guiltless. He'd caused the deaths of many men. Granted, they'd been bad men, like those who'd surrounded him. But that day, the man had been a pawn in a larger game.

He'd lifted the rifle, pulled the trigger, and handed the weapon back to Ortega. The traitor had slumped forward, his blood soaking into the dirt. Ortega had given him a single nod. Jinx had passed the test.

From there, his ascent had been calculated,

methodical. Montoya's organization was a machine of power, and Jinx had been a part of its gears.

Montoya's lieutenants were hardened killers, ruling their piece of the empire. Everyone had watched him. The enforcers who made problems disappear tested him. The inner circle, five men who had stood beside Montoya through blood and war, had taken notice. Jinx had been under a microscope. But Montoya himself had remained untouchable.

Until Jinx had found a pathway forward.

His fingers flexed, remembering the moment everything had shifted. The moment the impossible became possible.

He opened his eyes, his gaze shifting to the darkened runway outside the jet's window.

The woman's name was Lucía Delgado.

Montoya had kept her hidden, a secret mistress tucked away in the shadows of his empire. She hadn't just been a kept woman. She'd been a liability. Lucía had said she was an afterthought he controlled with expensive gifts, whispered promises, and the ever-present threat of what would happen if she tried to leave.

Jinx had never needed to seduce or threaten her. He'd just listened.

In the rare, stolen moments when other guards

had been elsewhere and when the walls of her gilded cage had felt suffocating, Lucía had talked. The liquor in her glass had loosened her tongue, but he'd sensed an overwhelming sense of exhaustion that made her confide in him. The woman had grown weary of Montoya's paranoia, cruelty, and, recently, his lack of obsession with *her*.

She'd thought Jinx was just another enforcer. Another soldier in Montoya's war. She'd never realized the truth. And that was what had sealed Montoya's fate.

One night, as candlelight had flickered against the darkened glass of her half-drunk rum, she'd given Jinx exactly what he'd needed.

"He'll be at Hacienda Roja tomorrow night," she'd murmured drunkenly, running a finger absently around the rim of her glass. "No security cameras. No armored walls. Just him, his guards, and his paranoia. And if rumors are true ... a new selection of women. A new mistress. One to replace me."

For the first time, Montoya would stay in one place long enough to die.

It had been time.

It had been time to shed the life he'd built. To burn the persona of Mateo Rivas. To leave behind the woman he'd never meant to love. The one who'd wrapped herself around his soul so tightly that just the thought of walking away had felt like ripping himself apart.

Eira.

The one thing in Venezuela he'd wished he could keep.

She'd never been part of the mission. A woman who'd found him in the quiet moments between violence and lies. He'd loved her in ways he hadn't even realized he was capable of. She'd made him dream of something more. A small home in a forgotten Venezuelan town, where the air smelled like fresh rain and burning wood. A life that wasn't built on bloodshed.

It was the hardest thing he'd ever done.

He'd told himself it was for her. That killing Montoya would keep her safer and make her life easier. That when he walked away, she would grieve but survive.

Maybe that had been a lie. Maybe it had been the truth. He never thought he'd be going back to find out. He knew what his fate was in life. He was a killer. A decision he'd made long ago had set him on this path. He had no right to love a wonderful woman like her. He was filth, and she was purity. He was death, fear, and the worst nightmares imaginable. She was life, happiness, and the dream people like him couldn't touch or it would shatter into a million pieces. She was unattainable, and even if he wanted a life with her, which God knew he did, his very presence could be her death sentence.

That thought was the grounding force of his decision. One mistake or misplaced word was all it would take to shine a light onto *who* he was and *what* he did. Enemies would flock to see his execution or line up to help pay for the act. Then smugly smile if or when his family was wiped out in the process of taking him out. No, he'd made the only decision he could.

He stared at his shoes as he remembered the day he made his way to Montoya. Jinx had crouched in the undergrowth, his body a shadow amid the tangled jungle. Hacienda Roja had loomed ahead. It was an isolated estate, miles from the nearest city, swallowed by the rainforest. The thick canopy above had muffled the moonlight, casting the world in deep blues and shifting shadows.

Security had been tight but predictable. Jinx had studied the men for years, memorizing their patterns, weaknesses, and habits.

Jinx had waited until Brando let him know his exfiltration was on its way before he moved. The guard at the western perimeter had turned his head, just for a second. It had been enough.

A flash of steel. The sluicing sound of tendons and cartilage being severed. A gurgled gasp. A body slumping silently into the brush. His training and his work for Guardian had been his only focus.

Knives over bullets. No sounds. No warnings. No mercy.

Jinx had moved through the jungle. He'd moved silently. A breath over the land, a shimmer against the contours of the forest around him. Another guard. Then another. Each man had had a name. Each man had had a life. But that night, they'd been obstacles. They'd fallen where they'd stood, their flowing blood fed the earth.

He'd moved quietly after checking for cameras, alarms, or any electronic monitoring system. There'd been none. Why? Because Montoya had trusted the ones who knew he was there. That was his only mistake. Jinx had moved silently through the grand old home. Women's laughter behind the doors of several rooms had given credence to Lucia's belief she'd be replaced. Jinx had moved on with Brando guiding him through the hacienda.

Brando had given him directions to the study. That had been where Jinx found him. Montoya had been sitting in his private lounge, the rich scent of whiskey mingling with the slow-burning tobacco from an expensive cigar. An empire of blood and cocaine rested in the ledger on his desk. He hadn't been celebrating. He'd been too paranoid for that. He'd been counting his money, counting his enemies, and waiting for the next war he needed to survive.

He'd never even seen the Shadow approaching.

Jinx had stepped into the room, a silenced pistol raised.

Montoya had looked up.

And at that single moment, he'd known. Recognition had flickered in his dark eyes. No panic. No pleas. Just the quiet acceptance of a man who'd lived his life knowing it would end like this. Montoya had exhaled, his sigh carrying the weight of finality. His hand had twitched toward the pistol at his side.

Jinx hadn't hesitated. He'd fired two suppressed shots. Clean. Precise. Absolute. And fucking anticlimactic after almost three years of his life. A double tap. One to the brain, the other to the heart. Less than two seconds of effort after years of work. There had been no feeling of remorse, just a faint sense of relief the mission was over.

His bullets had hit true. Montoya had jerked, his

breath escaping in a wet, gurgled gasp. He'd collapsed back into his chair, blood blooming across the silk of his shirt and dribbling down his face. His fingers had twitched against the ledger he would never finish balancing.

The drug king had died.

With an exhale, Jinx grabbed the book Montoya had been working with and those in the open safe behind him before melting into the night. The laptop he'd shoved inside his shirt with the books and left the room. No alarms. No screams. Just a Shadow slipping into the darkness.

The fallout of his hit had come fast. Montoya's death had rippled through the underworld like a tsunami, shaking the foundation of his empire. No one knew who had done it. Some had suspicions, but the explosion of the organization was bloody and messy. Hundreds died in the when the turf war ignited. Disappearing at that time wasn't unusual. So many did. If he was noticed to be missing, people would assume he'd been killed.

Most whispered of a betrayal from within. Others claimed it was one of Montoya's lieutenants fighting for power. A few suspected foreign assassins, but no one had proof.

The lieutenants turned on each other. Blood ran

through the streets as Montoya's empire had split apart and shattered into pieces. Alliances broke. Old feuds ignited. And in the storm, one man had clawed his way to the top.

Tomás Ortega.

He'd taken what was left of Montoya's crumbling organization and rebuilt it. He was brutal and ambitious. But Jinx doubted he was ever feared like Montoya. There was an inherent weakness in the man. Jinx had seen it. Others had noticed it, too. But somehow, he'd covered it sufficiently to rise to thc top.

And now, a new force threatened the Ortega throne and the country's stability.

El Fantasma. The Ghost. A whisper in the dark. A name spoken in fear. Jinx had heard of him. Hell, all the Shadows knew of the cartel's assassin. He'd become bold and was building an army of his own. Jinx glanced down at the packet of papers in his hand. He had two targets. One known. One a mystery.

There was unfinished business. And this time, he wasn't just hunting. He was going to war.

"Your travel companions are pulling up."

Brando's voice crackled in Jinx's earpiece, snapping him out of his thoughts. He glanced out the tinted jet window, the late afternoon sun casting long shadows across the tarmac. A black SUV rolled to a stop near the plane, dust curling up in its wake. The vehicle's doors swung open, and two figures stepped out. Raven and Rook.

A slow grin tugged at Jinx's lips.

Raven looked exactly the same. She was a figure that was utterly unassuming. She wasn't the woman anyone would pick out of a crowd. Jeans, worn sneakers, and a faded T-shirt that had likely seen its fair share of laundromat abuse. Her dark hair was twisted up in a haphazard bun, a few rogue strands slipping free to frame her face. To the untrained eye, she was just a girl-next-door type, maybe a college student or an off-duty waitress. But Jinx knew better.

She was the same woman who'd once gutted a target with a paring knife in a hotel room in Prague, then walked out the front door, smiling sweetly at the doorman as she left. The same woman who could sever the balls off a wife-beating bastard and then bake cookies for an elderly neighbor in the same afternoon. Even Valkyrie, one of the deadliest assassins in Guardian's history, had admitted Raven impressed her. And that wasn't easy.

Then there was Rook.

Where Raven was a whirlwind of barely contained chaos, Rook was control incarnate. The man was a strategist, a thinker, and an executioner whose weapons weren't blades or bullets but something far more insidious. Poisons. Undetectable. Lethal. He was a walking chemistry set, capable of turning a sip of water into a death sentence. And because of that, he was never, under any circumstances, allowed to bring food or drinks to any party they had. It was a long-standing joke among the Shadows.

Jinx exhaled and stood as Raven sprinted up the steps, her sneakers slapping against the metal.

"J.!"

He braced himself just in time.

She launched at him, arms wrapping around his neck as her momentum forced him a step back. Her hands found his face, and she peppered his cheeks with rapid-fire kisses before he could stop her.

"Stop that, woman!" Jinx growled, dropping her unceremoniously.

She landed lightly on her feet, grinning like a lunatic as she wiped at his face. "You have lip gloss on you now."

He scowled, swiping at his cheek.

"They didn't tell us who we'd be flying with.

Where the hell have you been?" She crossed her arms, tapping a foot against the floor. "You missed Berserker's birthday."

Jinx shrugged, but his smile was knowing. "I was working."

"Bullshit. We knew you weren't on a job."

"I was tracking someone."

Raven narrowed her eyes. "Who?"

Jinx glanced left, then right, as if checking for eavesdroppers. "A lone wolf."

She rolled her eyes. "Why did I not think it would be an actual animal?"

Jinx didn't correct her. It wasn't a four-legged wolf he'd been tracking. It was Lycos. But that wasn't a conversation he planned to have.

"As for Zerk," Raven continued, arms still crossed, "he's gonna take a piece of you when he sees you again. Just a warning."

Jinx smirked. "He can try."

"You know he will," Rook said, stepping past Raven. The man was quick, yanking Jinx into a brief bear hug before smacking him in the arm with a solid punch. "You missed one hell of a spread. Raven and Phantom cooked, and Viper and Demon made some kind of cocktail from hell."

Jinx sank into one of the leather seats as Rook flopped into the one next to him.

"The Killer B," Rook continued, stretching out his legs. "Tequila, vodka, limoncello, simple syrup, and something fizzy. And by fizzy, I mean it barely counted because there was more tequila than anything else by the end of the night."

Raven laughed. "We had high cover from the elders, so we cut loose. It's been too damn long since we were all in one place at the same time."

Jinx didn't argue. It had been a while. Too long, maybe. But that was the nature of their work. They led fragmented, secretive lives lived in the shadows.

He fastened his seatbelt as the pilot stepped out of the flight deck.

"We'll be wheels up in five minutes. Do you need a refresher on the galley or your seatbelts?"

"Nah, we're good," Rook answered with a grin.

"Cool." The pilot disappeared back inside, shutting the door behind him.

Jinx turned back to the pair. "What are you two doing here?"

"I'm heading to Mexico," Rook muttered. He and Raven exchanged a glance, something unreadable passing between them.

"And you?" Jinx asked Raven.

"Venezuela." She smiled. "Backup. Not that you'll need any, right? Please say no. I brought three different swimsuits. No tan lines this time."

Jinx arched a brow. "I just found out, too," Brando muttered in his ear. The man was getting way too good at predicting his reactions.

"Why?" Jinx asked, focusing on Raven.

"Why do I want a tan, or why did they send me?" She smirked.

"Both. Sun damage doesn't suit anyone."

Raven flicked her hand dismissively. "I use sunscreen." Her expression sobered slightly. "The backup is because you were there before. If you're recognized ..."

Jinx's jaw ticked. "Almost three years. There are questions about my ability?"

"No." The response came from both Raven and Brando at the same time.

Raven leaned forward, tapping off her comms, and Jinx did the same.

"You were in deep," she said quietly. "You lived that life for years. If someone recognizes you, I'm there to finish the job. Your abilities aren't questioned. That's why they sent you. You know the players. You know how they think. But memories are long, and if your cover is blown or some bastard gets off a lucky shot, I'll be there."

Jinx studied her for a beat. Raven didn't hesitate. She wasn't there to question his skills. She was there to make sure the mission succeeded.

"And the voice in your ear?" he asked, knowing exactly who it was.

Raven rolled her shoulders. "Ring's an ass. You'd think he was my father the way he hovers."

Jinx smirked, glancing out the window as the engines roared to life. Ring cared for Raven. A bit too much, but that was her battle to fight.

It was good to have her along. Backup wasn't rare these days. The Shadows worked together. They always had each other's backs.

He'd once had Phantom appear out of nowhere, Specter on another occasion. Not to complete a hit, but to get him the hell out afterward.

And if the bosses were making sure he had everything he needed for this mission …

That meant things were about to get very, very interesting.

CHAPTER 2

The luxury of the jet was soon forgotten when they touched down in Mexico. He and Raven transferred to a small prop jet and took off not more than thirty minutes after they'd landed in Mexico. The plane ride was loud and turbulent. It lacked even the basic amenities lavished on the Guardian transports, but one of the Guardian jets couldn't land where this plane would. It touched down with the smooth precision of a pilot who had done this kind of job before. The event was silent, quick, and held zero desire for attention. When the wheels met the ground of the small, unregistered airstrip carved out of the jungle, Jinx unclipped his harness and stretched.

Beside him, Raven adjusted her duffel, eyes sharp. "We good?"

Jinx gave a slow nod, scanning their surroundings. The airstrip was just a clearing, an old CIA drop point repurposed for black-market transport. It was outside the cartel's direct control, but they'd still have to move fast. If the wrong people saw them, questions would be asked.

They stepped onto the packed dirt, the thick, humid air hitting them instantly. No lights, no control tower. One man leaned against a rusted truck. Jinx recognized him, an old contact who made it his business not to ask questions. They exchanged nods and a handful of money before loading their gear into the truck's bed.

Jinx slid into the driver's seat while Raven took the passenger side, rifle casually resting against her thigh. The truck rumbled to life, rolling toward a narrow trail that blended into the jungle.

"Where's the safe house?" Raven asked, her voice low.

Jinx glanced at her. "About thirty clicks east, near the foothills. Cartels don't like the area. There are too many damn caves, bad terrain for their convoys. Plus, a couple of years back, someone made it a habit of making their roads disappear." He made a gesture like an explosion.

Raven snorted. "You blew up their roads?"

"Maybe." Jinx shrugged.

The drive was long, the road twisting through dense vegetation. Jinx watched for checkpoints, armed convoys, or out-of-place vehicles, but they encountered nothing beyond the occasional stray dog or a lone farmer leading a mule.

As they neared Maracay, a larger city known for its military presence, Jinx made a call. He hung up and pulled down a dusty dirt road. "We're switching cars here," he told Raven. "Can't risk someone recognizing this truck. They could trace the truck back to my contact at the airfield and jeopardize our exfil."

Raven nodded and blew out a long breath. "Leaving is important."

Fifteen minutes and two wads of cash later, they were in a dusty Land Cruiser, a model common enough to blend in but sturdy enough to get them where they needed to go.

Raven tapped the window. "We're getting close, aren't we?"

Jinx nodded and exhaled as his fingers tightened on the wheel as they approached the outskirts of town. Memories flooded him. The town wasn't much. It was an old colonial-era village surrounded by jungle and mountains. It had a small clinic, a market that ran mostly by barter and trade, and locals who knew to keep their heads down. There was no cartel presence. The location was too inconvenient for their operations.

Jinx parked behind an abandoned mechanic's shop obscuring the Land Cruiser beneath a collapsed awning. He and Raven moved fast, taking a side route through an overgrown footpath. It used to be well-traveled. Now, vines pulled at Jinx's boots, and he had to duck through a tangle of branches. A few minutes later, they emerged on the other side, where there was a small house, which was hidden from the main roads.

He and Raven crouched outside with a view of the house and used infrared scopes to ensure no one had taken up residence. When he was sure it was clear, he tapped his comm device. "Assets have arrived at the safe house. Transfer Raven to our frequency. You'll be our control for this mission."

Brando's response was immediate. "Copy."

Raven smiled widely. "Thank you for that. Ring really is a pain in the ass."

"Figured you wouldn't mind a few weeks without him."

"Is that how long you think this will take? A few weeks?" she asked as they entered the house.

Jinx walked over to the fireplace and removed a brick from the side. He pulled a handle, and a trap door under the rug opened. He tossed the rug away before he answered her question. "If Guardian's intel on the Ghost is correct, yes. If it isn't, it could be longer." He pulled the handle on the door and lifted the heavy boards.

"Well, look at that." Raven whistled.

Jinx dropped soundlessly into the stronghold he'd built over the years in Venezuela. The fortified space was his sanctuary, hidden deep in the jungle, with everything he needed to survive and wage war. Weapons lined the interior. Rifles, handguns, and explosives were secured long before he'd made his move on Montoya's villa. He wasn't particular about his arsenal. If it could kill, he used it.

On the far side of the reinforced cellar, shelves held ammunition, MREs, canned fruit, soups, meats, rice, and beans. All the staples of a man who lived off-grid. He grabbed a few supplies and tossed them to Raven, who caught them effortlessly.

"Stock up," he muttered to himself. He'd fill his stores before leaving the country again.

Raven wordlessly took the weapons and ammo

first, then moved on to the food. While he hauled himself out of the storage space and secured the hidden entrance, she started cleaning up. Jinx methodically stripped and cleaned his weapons, ensuring every part was in perfect working order. The steady, rhythmic motions kept his mind focused, a necessity when his thoughts threatened to drift somewhere he refused to go.

Before long, the scent of cooking filled the air, and his stomach growled in anticipation. Raven set two plates on the small wooden table, which she'd dusted earlier, given the years of neglect. "Eat," she ordered.

Jinx sat, nodded his thanks, and dug in. He ate in silence but felt Raven watching him. She stayed quiet until he finished, then leaned back in her chair, arms crossed.

"When are you going to go see her?"

Jinx lifted his eyes, cocking his head. "Who?"

Raven's gaze sharpened, cutting straight through him. "Don't play dumb. When you came back from that mission, you were different. Everybody noticed. Some thought it was because you'd been undercover so long, climbing the cartel's ranks. But I call bullshit."

Jinx stiffened but said nothing.

"You were changed," she continued. "Withdrawn. Introspective. You didn't find joy in your friends anymore. You turned into a solitary person. The only reason I can see for that kind of transformation? You had a broken heart." She studied him, then tilted her head. "Did she break it, or did you leave her and rip it out?"

Jinx leaned back in his chair, assessing his friend. "You're a lot deeper than people give you credit for."

Raven smirked and carried their empty plates into the kitchen. "And you're dodging the question."

"No," he said simply. "I'm just not answering it."

She pumped the old hand pump at the sink, drawing water with strong, steady movements. "So, you did love her," she murmured, half to herself.

Jinx turned his head, staring out the window at the darkness beyond. *Love her?* Yeah, he'd loved her. He'd left his soul in Venezuela.

Eira was the only woman who'd ever made him consider walking away from Guardian. She was remarkable, unlike anyone he'd ever met. He still remembered the first time he'd seen her. It wasn't under grand or dramatic circumstances. No, it had been something simple that had told him exactly who she was at her core.

He'd been deep in cartel territory when he'd

found an injured dog. Its leg had been mangled, clearly broken beyond his expertise to fix. The men he'd been with at the time had scoffed at his concern.

"Shoot it," one of them had said as if the animal's life were meaningless.

Jinx had known right then that he despised those men. He hadn't said a word to them. He simply picked up the dog and started walking.

He'd been told that a veterinarian in town could help, and that had been where he'd first met Eira.

He'd always been better with animals than people. He understood them. Trusted them. He'd seen more compassion in a dog's eyes than in most men's. That belief had been ingrained in him since childhood.

His earliest memories were of working alongside his mother at an animal rescue. His father had traveled constantly, absent more often than not. But his mother had given him something more valuable than a traditional family. She'd taught him how to care for creatures that couldn't fend for themselves.

The rescue took in the injured, the sick, and the dying. It was a place of solace, of healing. Jinx had spent every afternoon after school cleaning cages, feeding the animals, and, on the worst days, he helped remove the ones who didn't make it. Those had been the hardest days. Those had been the days that had cut into his soul.

The shelter had struggled to survive. It had been twenty acres of prime real estate in California, land that developers salivated over. But his mother's best friend, Lana, had been the owner and fought tooth and nail to keep it running.

He remembered the night it had all changed. His mother and Lana had been working late to process a delivery from a hoarder's house packed with cats. He'd been in college at the time, buried in coursework. She'd told him to go home, study, and focus on his future.

He'd stayed as long as he could but finally relented and went home to study.

The cats had been in horrific condition. Malnourished and sick, their fur had been matted, and flea-infested skin had stretched thin over frail bones. Some had been too weak to stand, their wide, terrified eyes pleading for salvation. Jinx's mother and Lana had planned to spend the entire night triaging the animals. Triage consisted of cleaning them up, feeding them, administering medical intervention. Basically doing everything they could before the vet arrived in the morning.

But morning never came.

Not for the cats.

Not for his mother.

Not for Lana.

Fire had ripped through the shelter in the dead of night. After the investigators had combed through the smoldering remains, their conclusion was swift and devastating. The fire had been set from the outside. Someone had intentionally burned the shelter to the ground.

Had they known his mother and Lana were inside?

Yes.

The answer was yes.

Metal bars had been shoved through the latches of the doors, locking them inside. Even if they'd fought through the smoke and flames, clawed at the exits, screamed for help … there had been no way out.

Jinx had never made it to the college exam he'd been studying for that night. Instead, he'd started searching. Obsessively. Relentlessly. The police had no leads, but Jinx did.

Lana had been offered a substantial sum of money for the land. A corporation had sent representatives multiple times, pressuring her to sell, but she'd refused. The land had been passed down to her by her father, and the work she did at the shelter was her life's mission. At sixty-seven years old, she had no intention of selling or walking away.

So, Jinx had started there.

He'd used every skill he had, every trick he'd learned in college, to dig into the corporation. The internet had led him down a rabbit hole, a maze of corporate dealings that, at first glance, seemed legitimate. But beneath the surface, patterns had emerged. Ones that were impossible to ignore.

In Montana, ranchers had lost their water sources after someone had diverted the flow from their land. Unable to sustain their cattle, they'd been forced to sell.

In Florida, entire orchards had mysteriously caught fire. The land that just so happened to be part of a development deal the corporation had been pursuing.

And then, in California, an animal shelter had been reduced to ash.

Jinx had thought he was chasing a theory, but the deeper he'd dug, the more undeniable it had become. It wasn't coincidence. It was calculated destruction.

Then had come the biggest shock of all.

Lana had left the land to him.

Jinx had had no idea she'd named him her heir,

but she had. Which meant the corporation that had killed her wanted what was his.

When the offers started rolling in, he'd responded with interest. He'd told them he'd consider selling, if he could meet the person in charge of land acquisitions.

That had been the beginning of his end. Within three weeks, Jinx had an appointment with Dante Driver, the man who'd spearheaded the corporation's most controversial dealings. Every bit of research had led back to him. Every unethical land grab, every case of destruction in pursuit of profit.

Jinx had never showed up to the meeting. Instead, he'd followed Driver home. The man had lived alone. A fortunate thing, for him, at least.

Jinx had watched from the shadows as Driver had locked his front door for the night, completely unaware death had just arrived at his doorstep. Jinx had waited. Patient. Controlled. Then, under the cover of darkness, he'd moved. He'd secured the doors, binding them shut, trapping Driver inside. Then he'd set the house on fire.

The moment the flames had taken hold, and alarms had shrieked into the night. Jinx had known he was on borrowed time, but he didn't leave. He'd stood there, watching, waiting.

Smoke had curled from the windows, fire licking at the roof. It was the same nightmare his mother and Lana had endured, and for the first time, Driver had been forced to experience that same helpless terror.

Desperation had driven the man to action. With flames raging behind him, he'd thrown himself through a second-story window, crashing onto the ground with a pained, gasping wheeze. He'd coughed, lungs full of smoke, blinking up at Jinx in dazed confusion.

Jinx had walked toward him, slow and deliberate.

Driver had groaned, scrambling to push himself up on shaking arms.

"Are you all right?" Jinx had asked, voice almost gentle.

Driver had let out a raspy laugh, the kind only a man who'd cheated death could manage. "Yeah … yeah, I … I couldn't get the doors open."

Jinx had tilted his head. "That's exactly how my mom and Lana Masterson felt."

Recognition had dawned on Driver's soot-streaked face, his mouth opening to speak, but no words were uttered.

The knife had slid between his ribs before the

bastard could make a sound. Jinx had twisted the blade, watching the life drain from the man's eyes.

When the cops had found him two weeks later, the knife had still been in his possession. He hadn't run. He hadn't hidden. He'd done what he'd come to do. He'd been arrested and charged with murder.

Then Lycos had arrived. Lycos had been just as dangerous then as he was now. The eyes were the windows to the soul, some said. Jinx *knew* they were. He could still remember how the older man had looked at him, assessing him like a weapon someone had forged in fire. Jinx had been reminded of a bobcat they'd once saved. The animal's eyes had seen everything. Fear included. He'd treated Lycos the same way he had that wild animal, with respect and honesty. Something had told him it was the reason he'd been given the opportunity to work for Guardian.

"You have two options," Lycos had said, his voice cold, merciless. "You can rot in a cell for the rest of your life for killing a monster … or you can work for us and put your skills to use hunting them."

Jinx had only needed a second to decide.

He exhaled sharply, pulling himself back to the present. The past was the past. And yet, it wasn't because part of his past was still there.

And Raven knew it.

She dried her hands on a towel and glanced over her shoulder at him. “So, do you want to talk about her?”

He didn’t answer. But in the silence, they both knew the truth. He wasn’t avoiding talking about Eira because he didn’t care. He was avoiding it because he still did.

CHAPTER 3

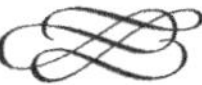

Eira Isaacson rocked gently back and forth on the weathered wooden swing that hung from the covered porch of her farmhouse. The creaking of the chains blended with the soft hum of cicadas and the distant rustling of cattle shifting in the pasture beyond. Dusk had begun its slow descent, painting the Venezuelan sky in hues of amber and violet. The scent of hay, sun-warmed earth, and distant woodsmoke lingered in the air, grounding her in the world she'd built with her own two hands.

Cradled in her arms, her son Teo dozed, one tiny fist curled against her chest. His weight was warm and reassuring, a steady heartbeat against her own.

Her gaze swept over the land. The rolling fields

of deep green, the modest barn with its fresh coat of red paint, the chicken coop alive with content clucks, and the dairy shed where her cousins were finishing the evening milking. It wasn't the animal hospital she'd dreamed of during long nights at veterinary school, but it was real. Tangible. A living, breathing thing she'd carved from hardship and heartache.

Dreams, she had learned, often clashed with reality in brutal, unforgiving ways.

As she rocked with her child nestled close, Eira wondered if the foolish dreams of a headstrong woman were always destined to teach humility.

When she'd returned from school, her heart had burned with purpose. She would save animals. She would build a sanctuary. Her affinity for creatures, wounded, wild, or unwanted, had never waned. There had never been a question of who she would become. From the moment she could walk, she'd tended to injured birds, bottle-fed abandoned kittens, and whispered to horses.

Her mother had once dreamed big, too. She'd married a foreigner swept into Venezuela by the booming oil business. They'd met in the city, fallen in love, and married within three months. But her father's promises had faded fast. Venezuela hadn't been for him. He'd left, first emotionally, then physically. He'd sent money, yes, but never returned.

Heartbroken, Eira's mother had retreated home to the small community tucked at the base of the Cordillera mountains. And that was where Eira had been raised, among strong women, hard workers, and the quiet resilience of people who didn't expect anything they hadn't earned.

Now, Eira was back in the same village. History repeating. The dream of a modern veterinary hospital had evolved into something more practical. More necessary. Since Mateo disappeared, she'd turned her animal rescue clinic into a functioning, self-sustaining dairy farm. She raised chickens for eggs and meat. Sold cheese and milk. Employed her aunts, uncles, and cousins. Every cent went back into the land, and into securing a future for Teo.

The man she'd fallen in love with had also vanished. Mateo Rivas.

But maybe he hadn't just disappeared. Maybe he'd died in one of the countless cartel wars that swallowed men whole. She didn't know.

The only thing she did know was that her son had no father.

She'd made the same mistake her mother had made. Trusted a man who didn't stay.

But Eira wouldn't make that mistake again.

She would raise Teo to be strong. To stand on his own. To avoid the cartels at all costs. To build something real, something enduring, something no man could take from him.

The cartels wanted everything. They wanted men for their wars. Women for their beds. But they needed food. And Eira provided it. Her dairy, her chickens, her eggs fed men who made war. And not surprisingly, due to Ortega's interest in her, she was paid a fair price. The arrangement bought her peace, for now.

Her gaze dropped to the black lab mix lying at her feet. The dog thumped its tail when her eyes met his, and she reached down to scratch behind his ears.

He'd been brought to her by Mateo. Horribly wounded, the poor creature had dragged itself halfway to death before being found. The leg had been too far gone to save. She'd had to amputate, but the dog had healed because Mateo had brought him to her.

Staying by its side, day and night, his gentleness had been undeniable. Mateo understood animals with a depth that seemed almost otherworldly.

He'd calmed a panicked bull with nothing more than a quiet presence and slow breaths. He'd haltered a wild horse that had thrown every man who dared approach it. Strays followed him like loyal disciples. And the first time she saw him holding that broken dog in his arms, she'd felt her world shift.

She closed her eyes and rocked slowly, letting herself remember him.

Mateo had been tall, at least six feet, with strong shoulders and a quiet intensity. His hands were calloused and rough, but his touch with her and the animals had always been gentle. Tender.

He'd lived with her, staying in her home whenever work didn't call him away.

And, of course, she'd known. Everyone in the region knew. Seventy percent of the men there worked for the cartels in some capacity. It was impossible not to.

But enforcer?

Her uncles had only told her after he'd left, or after he'd been killed. No one knew for sure.

They'd said he'd risen in the Montoya faction. That he'd been feared. That he'd had blood on his hands. That he'd been cold, calculated. Deadly.

She blinked hard, refusing to cry.

Murderer.

That word didn't fit with the man she'd known.

The man who'd whispered to her beneath the stars, who'd kissed her with reverence. She didn't know that man they feared. She'd only known Mateo. And she'd loved him with her whole damn heart.

Then, the Montoya faction had imploded.

It had happened fast. It was violent and chaotic. Hundreds had been killed in a matter of weeks. Montoya himself had been the first to fall, gunned down in his compound, his blood painting the marble floors he'd once ruled from like a king.

The scramble for power had been ruthless. Men Eira had grown up with were buried in mass graves or had disappeared into the jungle. Former allies turned enemies, and friends had become corpses.

Eventually, the Ortega faction had emerged from the carnage with bloodied hands and ruthless efficiency. They'd taken control, and the region had settled into a tense, uneasy truce, well…less peace and more submission under new rule.

When the dust had finally settled, it was no longer about loyalty. It was about survival. But Mateo was gone. Her world had crumbled, and so had her heart. Never again would she allow herself to hurt like that. She would never let another man break her like that again.

Eira had discovered she was pregnant with Mateo's child three months after he'd vanished.

Gone. Without a trace. No goodbye. No explanation. Just silence. She firmly believed he'd died. If he could've come back to her, he would have. She knew it in her heart. They were soulmates, destined to be together. She had wanted forever, a commitment and marriage, but he'd never made that promise. When she was with him, she never doubted he loved her, not once. But the commitment never came, making her wonder if she was enough for him. After he disappeared and she learned what he truly was, she understood why he couldn't. His life was always at risk.

She looked down at the boy in her arms, her heart aching and full all at once. Teo's soft lashes fluttered against his cheek as he slept, unaware of the legacy that stirred in the knowledge around him.

He was her only connection to the man she'd loved. The only proof Mateo had ever truly been hers. Her son would never know about the other side of his father. The whispered rumors of bloodshed, the name spoken in fear across cartel lands. No one in her family would breathe a word of it to him.

She would raise Teo on stories of kindness. Of quiet strength. Of how his father could soothe a wounded animal with a touch and calm a frightened mare with nothing more than a murmur. She would protect his memory the same way she protected her son, with fierce, unrelenting devotion.

A plume of dust rose in the distance, catching her eye. It twisted up from the dry road to her farm, curling in the hot Venezuelan air like a warning.

Vehicles.

Moving fast.

She stood up, gently shifting Teo against her shoulder, and walked to the front door, her voice firm but calm as she called through the mesh screen.

"Mom, come get Teo."

Moments later, her mother appeared in the doorway, wiping her hands on a flour-dusted towel from the kitchen.

"What's the matter?" she asked, her gaze already following Eira's nod toward the road.

"Vehicles," Eira said quietly. "And they're coming fast."

Her mother's breath caught. "Do you have your gun?"

Eira gave a single nod. "Always."

"Do you want me to get your Uncle Juan?"

She shook her head, eyes hard. "No. I'll handle whatever's coming."

Her mother reached out, took the sleeping child from her arms, and cradled him protectively. "Be careful, mi amor."

Eira stepped off the porch and watched as their converted milk truck, a battered, rusted-out military vehicle with a five-hundred-gallon stainless-steel tank welded to its back as it rumbled away from the dairy yard. The thing looked like it had survived three wars, and maybe it had. But it did the job, hauling milk to the nearby village where her uncle turned it into cheese in his shop.

After the painfully slow milk truck passed through the narrow front gate, three black SUVs skidded to a halt and lined up in front of the house. They hadn't come to barter. They hadn't come for cheese.

She didn't wait for an invitation.

Eira walked straight toward the middle SUV, full skirts swaying with every purposeful step. Her boots crunched over gravel and dry grass. She stopped as the vehicle door opened and one of Ortega's enforcers stepped out. Marco, the bastard. Oh, she knew his type. Clean beard, pressed shirt, combat boots. Dangerous in all the wrong ways.

He let his eyes rake over her body like she was property. Eira slipped her hand into the deep pocket of her skirt and curled her fingers around the grip of a small revolver. It was the only thing Mateo had ever left her. That and her son, who was now safe inside her house.

"What do you want?" she asked coldly.

The man sneered. "If it weren't for Ortega, you wouldn't be so disrespectful."

"If it weren't for Ortega, you'd be dead," she shot back, her tone like steel wrapped in velvet.

His face twisted into something feral, his upper lip curling to show his teeth.

She didn't flinch. Didn't blink.

"What. Do. You. Want?" she asked again, sharper that time.

He hissed something low in his throat but motioned toward the back seat of the SUV. The rear door opened, and inside was a beautiful Belgian Malinois. The dog was trembling violently, thick foam leaking from its jaws.

Poison.

Eira's chest tightened, but she didn't show it.

She turned her gaze to the driver, the quiet one, the one who hadn't spoken yet. "You," she said, pointing. "Pick him up. Carefully. And bring him with me."

Without waiting for a response, she spun on her

heel and headed toward the small stucco building beside the main house. A simple, two-room structure with whitewashed walls, tiled floors, and metal fans spinning lazily from the ceiling. It was small, but it was hers. It was enough.

The driver followed, carrying the dog as gently as he could manage.

"Put him on the table," she instructed, pulling gloves on and snapping the light above the exam table into place.

Her hands moved with purpose, her voice firm. She checked the dog's pulse, felt the trembling muscles, and lifted the dog's lips to expose the gums and check their color. Then she pried open the jaw to inspect the foam and vomit at the back of the throat.

"He's been poisoned," she said without hesitation.

The talkative enforcer scowled, glancing at the driver. "Are you sure?"

She didn't even look at him. "Yes, I'm sure," she snapped. "Now, get out of here so I can work."

They hesitated. She didn't.

Eira was already reaching for activated charcoal, drawing a syringe, and grabbing the saline drip. She didn't have time to suffer fools. Not when an innocent animal was fighting to breathe.

She worked on the animal and stabilized it. Giving it a sedative, she made it as comfortable as possible in her limited space. She stroked the dog's fur as she glanced around the small clinic. Her dream had been to help animals for as long as she could remember. She'd nursed squirrels that had fallen out of nests, tried to fix broken wings on birds, brought every stray animal she'd ever come across home, and loved and cared for them all. The biology of animals was an immediate curiosity for her, and it formed her path as an adult. Animals had no one to protect them. Man was the ultimate predator, and she was their guardian, at least in this small portion of the world.

CHAPTER 4

Jinx and Raven lay motionless on the rugged mountainside, their bodies pressed into the earth, blending with the scrub and shadow. The sun had long since passed its peak, casting the jungle in dusky gold and deepening shadows across the valley below.

It had taken them over a week of crawling through the dense terrain to find the military encampment rumored to house the man known only as *El Fantasma,* The Ghost.

At least, that was the intel Guardian had provided. But something about it felt … wrong.

The camp didn't resemble any cartel compound Jinx had ever seen. It lacked the usual chaos and swagger. No shirtless men were lounging in hammocks, no blaring music, no signs of idle hands or indulgence. Instead, the structures were sharp-edged and efficient, their construction military-grade. Tents were arranged in perfect grid formation, and their positions were clearly calculated to minimize exposure. Camouflage nets covered the entire area to maximize protection should an airstrike occur.

A perimeter was clearly defined, patrolled, and reinforced. No drunken guards stumbling on their watch. No mess. No weakness.

Through the high-powered binoculars, Jinx scanned the compound again, gaze lingering on details others might have missed. A long-range parabolic mic picked up scraps of conversation, streaming in low over their shared earpieces.

"It's not just a camp," Jinx muttered, voice low and tight. "It's a base. This wasn't thrown together. It was planned."

Raven lay beside him, her chin resting on her forearm, eyes sharp as they tracked movement below. "It's got a comms center, a proper chow hall, latrines, showers … hell, there's even a perimeter watch rotation. That's not cartel. That's paramilitary. Maybe ex-military."

"Yeah," Jinx agreed grimly. "But that doesn't mean

the Ghost isn't here."

For three days, they'd watched. Studied and mapped the routines and rhythms of the base. The man Guardian intel pointed to as *El Fantasma*. He was a brash officer in his late forties with a heavily scarred face, a nose like a hawk's beak, and a distinct limp. He carried himself like a man in charge. Loud. Commanding. Swaggering through the camp like a rooster in a henhouse.

But something didn't sit right.

"Something's off," Jinx said, narrowing his eyes as the man in question strutted across the compound.

Raven nodded. "I believe the Ghost is one of the men down there ... but I don't think Guardian has the right one."

Jinx tilted his head in agreement. "We're going to have to watch a hell of a lot longer to figure out the dynamics. Something's not adding up."

He adjusted the scope, tracking the scarred man's movements. Too flamboyant. Too visible. An assassin, especially one as feared and elusive as *El Fantasma,* didn't *want* attention. He existed in the shadows, invisible until the moment his target dropped. Every kill linked to the Ghost had been tight, clean, and untraceable.

This man strutted like a politician. He wasn't a ghost. He was a peacock.

"Assassins don't broadcast themselves," Jinx muttered. "And if this guy *is* the Ghost, then we've got the wrong file on the right man."

"Or the right file on the wrong man," Raven said as she set down the parabolic mic, rubbing her eyes. "No way a man with that limp and that face disappears into a crowd. And yet the Ghost? No one's seen him. That level of anonymity without our kind of tech? That takes skill."

"He needs to blend," Jinx agreed. "Disappear into a crowd, change appearance, walk into a place and out again without anyone remembering his face."

"This guy's too obvious," Raven said, voice flat. "The nose alone is memorable enough for a thousand IDs."

They both stared in silence for a moment, the forest whispering around them. Leaves rustling, insects buzzing in the thick, humid air.

"We need to restock," Raven finally said, pushing up to her knees and stretching her back.

Jinx nodded. "You didn't have to come with me," he said as they backed away from the ridge line, careful not to dislodge any rocks that might give away their position.

Raven dusted off her woodland camouflage BDUs and snorted. "And what would I do? Sit in that little cabin all by myself?"

"You could've rested. Waited for the next mission."

"Oh, please," she muttered, slinging her pack over her shoulder. "You know I don't get field assignments like this often. Just let me play a little."

"Play?" Jinx raised an eyebrow, smirking as he grabbed his own pack and followed her down the slope.

Raven grinned over her shoulder, her ponytail swaying with each step. "Okay, maybe not *play*. How about *camping*? I haven't done this since we went through training together."

"And you *miss* that?" Jinx gave a low, incredulous laugh. "Woman, you're insane."

"I am not insane," she shot back, eyes twinkling. "You *know* this. We were all tested."

Jinx chuckled as they descended the steep trail into the lower jungle, their boots crunching over roots and loose stone.

Sunlight slanted through the canopy, dappling their path in shifting gold and shadow. Birds called in the distance, and far below, the river glinted like a snake winding through the trees.

Raven moved like a predator. She was silent, sure, deadly.

So was he.

Together, they vanished into the wilderness, two ghosts hunting another.

“I think that guy’s a front,” Raven said suddenly, breaking the comfortable silence.

Jinx didn’t respond right away, his body mid-motion as he leaped from one rocky shelf to another along the mountainside. Gravel and loose stones scattered beneath his boots, tumbling into the deep ravine below with soft clatters.

He landed hard, crouched, then looked up and gave a curt nod.

“I agree,” he said, his voice low. “But he’s there. Somewhere.”

His gut had never failed him, not when it counted. And everything in him told him the Ghost was right under their noses, hiding in plain sight.

Only … not as the man Guardian thought.

The Ghost hadn’t just infiltrated the cartel’s structure, he had *rebuilt* it. What they were watching wasn’t a drug operation. It was a military unit. Disciplined. Coordinated. Trained. Dangerous.

It was more than any cartel stronghold Jinx had ever seen. It was something else.

And whatever the Ghost was waiting for, it was big.

"Ortega is a weak man," Jinx muttered as they descended the mountainside, picking their way through dense brush and slick stone paths.

Raven paused behind him, her boots crunching against a patch of dry earth. "How so?"

Jinx kept walking, his pace steady. Raven followed. "His eyes," Jinx said. "There's fear. Visible fear. I don't know how he's convinced people to follow him. I never would."

Raven was quiet for several moments, letting the sounds of nature stretch between them. She listened to the birds chirping, leaves rustling, the occasional crack of a distant branch.

"Some people buy allegiance," she said at last. "Could Ortega be one of those?"

"Maybe. But if he controls a cartel like this, there must be something else. Some angle we aren't seeing."

By the time they'd reached the narrow dirt road leading them to their vehicle, the midday heat had thickened, wrapping around them like a wet blanket. Raven fell into step beside him, sweat shining on her temples.

"So … why is the Ghost waiting?" she asked, pulling her canteen and taking a quick drink.

Jinx didn't answer immediately.

"He's looking for a weakness," he said finally. "A way in. Or maybe he's waiting for Ortega to show himself."

Raven arched a brow. "What do you mean, *show* himself?"

"I told you, he's afraid. Men like that don't leave their fortresses unless they're forced to. If he's holed up in Montoya's old stronghold … it's nearly impossible to breach."

Raven blinked. "You think that's where he is?"

"If I were him, that's where I'd be." Jinx stopped and turned to face her, his eyes serious. "No matter how trained that Ghost's camp is, it wouldn't stand a chance against that fortress unless Ortega comes out."

Raven blew out a breath. "So, what would draw him out?"

Jinx shook his head. "I don't know. Not yet."

They reached the hidden turnoff where their old Land Cruiser was camouflaged beneath palm fronds and netting. Once inside, they both sank into the dusty seats with audible sighs. Raven pulled off her cap and ran a hand through her damp hair.

"So. Showers. Food. Sleep. Then we hit Ortega's camp?"

"*Hit?*" Jinx glanced over as he shifted into gear, backing the vehicle out of its hiding place.

Raven smirked. "Okay. *Observe.*" She drew out the word like it was a joke. "We *observe* Ortega's camp."

"Yeah," Jinx said, eyes on the road ahead. "We need to know what he's up to. And why the Ghost isn't making a move."

She leaned her head back against the window. "Seems to me like the situation's just as messed up as the one you left almost three years ago."

Jinx grunted.

"Speaking of which ..." Raven turned her head slightly. "Are you ever gonna tell me about her?"

He exhaled through his nose. "No."

Raven didn't push, and he was grateful. Because he couldn't. His memories of Eira were sacred. Too raw, too tender to voice.

How could he explain how her presence had settled the chaos in his mind? The way her laugh had made his chest ache? How her skin had felt against his, warm and soft like silk?

How did you explain *peace* to someone who'd never tasted it?

Her voice. Her smile. The way she moved through the world…healed it, cared for it, *understood* it. The way she'd *seen* him, not as a killer but as a man. A man worth loving. He couldn't tell anyone about that. Not Raven. Not Guardian. Not anyone. Because what he'd had with Eira … wasn't a memory. It was a part of him. A sacred part. And it belonged to him alone.

Granted, he didn't expose her to his real self, to the assassin he'd become. However, when he was with her, he was himself, or at least as close to himself as he could remember. With her, he was the college boy who cared for animals at the rescue. The young man with a future and a dream. He'd relaxed around her. He'd laughed, played, and flirted. He'd made the mistake of becoming attached and then, without knowing it, of falling in love.

He kept driving, silence settling between them again. The jungle blurred past in streaks of green and gold as they picked up speed. For the next hour, they traded theories. They were, basically, half-hearted guesses about who the Ghost could be and what his endgame might involve. None of it brought them closer to the truth.

And the truth felt further away than ever.

The peaceful silence shattered as they rounded

the bend toward the small mountain village where Jinx's hidden safe house was tucked between the trees. Three matte-black SUVs roared past them in a blur, kicking up a wall of dust.

"What the fuck was that?" Raven twisted in her seat, watching the taillights disappear around the curve.

"Ortega's crew," Jinx muttered, tightening his grip on the wheel.

"How do you know?"

Jinx's jaw flexed as he pressed harder on the gas. "No one else would've had that kind of money," Jinx muttered, voice low and bitter as he accelerated, tailing the SUVs from a safe distance.

Raven turned toward him. "Fuck," Jinx swore again, his jaw tightening as he suddenly eased off the gas.

"What? What's the matter?" she asked, brows pulling together in concern.

"They're going to Eira's."

"Eira's?" Raven blinked. "Who's Eira? What's an Eira?"

Jinx didn't answer. Instead, he swerved hard off the dirt road, cutting into the underbrush and bringing the vehicle to a jerking halt beneath the thick canopy of jungle vines. Without missing a beat, he threw open the door.

"Come on. Bring the mic."

Raven was already out, her boots hitting the ground before the words finished leaving his mouth. She grabbed the parabolic microphone and followed Jinx as they pushed through the brush. Vines tugged at their clothes, and insects buzzed around them in a humid cloud as they jogged downhill through the trees.

They dropped to their bellies at the ridge just beyond the clearing, crawling forward until the scene below came into full view.

An old truck, rusted and groaning beneath the weight of its steel tank, had slowed the caravan. The narrow driveway had forced the SUVs to stop, bottlenecked by the massive vehicle. If the vehicle moved faster than three miles an hour, it was only because it was going downhill.

Jinx raised the mic and aimed it toward the scene. That's when he saw her. His breath caught in his throat, sharp and painful.

Eira.

Her long, black hair flowed freely down her back, moving like silk in the breeze. Her body, soft, curvy, and breathtaking hadn't changed at all.

And there she was, walking down the stairs of the farmhouse like she owned the earth beneath her feet, straight toward Ortega's enforcers.

She didn't flinch. Didn't cower. Her spine was straight, her chin high.

God, yes. That was *his* woman.

Raven handed him the headphones silently. He slipped them over his ears, every sound sharpening. The crunch of boots, the quiet growl of idling engines, the distant clucking of chickens. Raven slid in beside him and listened through her own set.

"She's a tough one, isn't she?" Raven murmured with a grin. "I think I could like her."

A small cry from one of the SUVs caught Raven's attention.

"Oh shit. The puppy's sick," she said, lifting her binoculars. "Look at that girl go. Man, I *like* her."

Jinx stayed silent, eyes locked on the woman he hadn't seen in years. Her voice filtered through the mic. It was sharp, fearless, and unwavering as she confronted the enforcers, challenged their delay, and barked orders like a general in her own right.

He couldn't breathe.

His gaze drifted to the land around her. She'd done everything they'd talked about. Every dream they'd dared to whisper in the darkness. It was all there. Or at least the beginnings were there.

The small dairy herd was healthy, being turned out into the twilight pasture, their dark bodies shifting through golden light. Hundreds of chickens flapped and clucked inside a massive coop off to the right. Fences were mended. Outbuildings freshly painted. The old clinic, still standing proud, looked like it belonged there more than ever.

She'd done all of that.

Without him.

His chest constricted. It felt like someone had shoved a knife between his ribs and twisted. Night after night, they'd lain in bed, dreaming that place into existence. And now, it stood. Real. Thriving. And he hadn't been part of a single second of it. Pride in what she'd been able to accomplish warred with the anguish of not being a part of it.

Raven elbowed him gently. "She must've kicked them out."

Jinx blinked back to the present. The two men who'd taken the dog into the clinic had just exited, looking frustrated. They stormed back to their SUVs, slamming the doors and kicking up gravel as they spun away down the drive.

From the house, an older woman, Eira's mother,

if memory served, hurried toward the clinic, her apron flapping as she ran.

"I'm glad someone was there to check on her," Raven said quietly. "I didn't hear any gunshots, but that doesn't mean those assholes didn't try something."

Jinx shook his head. "She would've shot them before that happened."

Raven paused, her entire body stilling. Slowly, she turned her head, staring at him.

"She's the one," she whispered, her voice different now. Serious. Almost reverent. "Isn't she?"

Jinx didn't answer.

"You don't have to say yes," she said quickly, her eyes narrowing in realization. "How else would you have known where they were going? How would you have *known* she would've shot them before they hurt her?" She shook her head slowly. "You couldn't have unless you *knew* this woman. Intimately."

Jinx stared out at the clinic, a shadow of a smile tugging at his lips as pain flared through his chest.

Raven exhaled like she'd been hit. "Holy hell. Why did you leave all this?"

He reached for the binoculars and brought them to his eyes again, the lenses trembling slightly in his grip. He focused on the clinic door just as Eira emerged into the golden hour light, her hair caught by the breeze, her expression composed and resolute. She hugged her mom and sat down on the rocker in front of the clinic. Her mom went back to the house. He stared at the woman he dreamed of and who haunted him in quiet moments. She'd done well without him. That was the answer. That would always be the answer.

His voice came low and raw, the ache in it undeniable. "How could I not?"

CHAPTER 5

The punch to his shoulder jarred his entire arm, knocking into him with surprising force.

Jinx snapped his head toward Raven. "What the fuck did you do that for?"

"That's bullshit, and you know it," Raven snapped, eyes flashing with anger. "You should've fought for her. You should've stayed. Hell, we've all got enough money to walk away and never have to work again. Why didn't you stay?"

Jinx narrowed his eyes at her, voice dropping low. "That's none of your business."

Raven rolled her eyes with a scoff. "'Right. *As if.*'" She mimicked his earlier words with biting sarcasm. "'How could I not?'" She shook her head and jabbed a finger at his chest. "Let me tell you how you *could have not.* You could've kept your damn cover. You could've stayed. If you loved her enough … you *could have stayed.*"

Jinx's eyes blazed. He moved closer, his voice a low, dangerous growl. "Don't you *ever* doubt the love I have for that woman. I don't care how close of a friend or teammate you are. If you *ever* say that again, you'll be in danger."

Raven raised an unimpressed brow, undeterred. "So, instead of staying and protecting her, you left her in a drug-infested, war-torn country. Alone."

"She's not alone," he bit out. "She has her family. A huge family."

Raven crossed her arms and gave a sharp laugh. "Yeah? Like that's going to warm her bed at night?"

The statement hit Jinx like a light-armored anti-aircraft rocket to the gut. He visibly flinched, his body tensing, and Raven saw it.

She followed his gaze, both of them staring through the binoculars at the small, whitewashed clinic where Eira had disappeared earlier. She was sitting on the porch in front of the building.

"Yeah. That one gotcha, didn't it," Raven said softly, then looked back toward the hacienda with a quiet exhale. "You know … she's got a lot here. I mean, compared to everyone else in this region. Every farm we passed and homestead we saw on our way in is smaller. Run-down. But not this one." She looked over at Jinx and nudged him with her shoulder. "You *can't* be mad at me. And if you are, you can't stay mad at me. So, stop pouting and answer my question. Have you noticed that her farm is ... more?"

Jinx gave a tight nod. "That detail hasn't gone past my observation."

"That's because Ortega's protecting her," Brando's voice came over their comms, crisp and certain.

Jinx and Raven exchanged a look.

"What are you basing that on?" Raven asked.

"The parabolic mic," Brando said. "I played the audio back. One of the enforcers said, and I quote, 'If it weren't for Ortega, you wouldn't be so disrespectful.'"

Raven's expression sobered as she turned toward Jinx. "He could be right."

"I *am* right," Brando replied, smug.

Raven groaned. "You're starting to sound like your cousin."

"Is that a bad thing?" Brando asked innocently.

"In my opinion? Yes," she muttered.

Jinx ignored the banter and stared hard through the binoculars. "Why would Ortega protect her?"

Raven snorted. "Look at her. She's gorgeous."

Jinx shot her a sidelong glare. "Don't go there."

Raven's eyes widened with mock innocence. "I'm *not* going there. But Ortega obviously *is* or wants to. Otherwise, she wouldn't still have all this. An operational farm. Land that hasn't been razed or stolen. Healthy animals. A working clinic. Why hasn't her livestock been slaughtered for cartel consumption? Why hasn't her home been ravaged like so many others in the area?" She turned toward him fully. "You have to ask yourself that, Jinx. Because if you don't, you're ignoring the obvious. Ortega, or someone else, is *taking care* of your woman."

"I agree with Raven," Brando chimed in again. "If someone, namely Ortega, is protecting her, there's a reason."

"And we don't know the reason. But I'm sure *she* does." Raven pointed toward the porch, where Eira was sitting. "Then we can use that. We can use *her* to get to Ortega. To take down the Ghost."

Jinx's head snapped toward Raven. "*No.* I will *not* use her. I will *not* use her to hunt these people." His gut clenched at the idea. There was no way he'd allow that to happen. He'd fall on his sword and die on that hill.

Raven sat up, face tightening. "Then how the hell are we supposed to get eyes inside the cartel, figure out where Ortega is, what his weaknesses are, and what the Ghost has planned? Because *obviously* the guy Guardian thought was the Ghost isn't."

"I know how to do it," Jinx said, standing suddenly, jaw clenched. "Mateo Rivas."

Raven blinked and looked up at him. "Well, don't keep it to yourself. Who the hell is he?"

Brando groaned. "No way, man. You can't."

"Can't what?" Raven asked.

"That was my persona when I was down here." His voice dropped like gravel. "I go back in as the enforcer I was."

Raven gaped at him. "Just walk back in after what … years of being gone? You don't think that'll look suspicious?"

"I can handle suspicion." It would be easy. He'd claim to have been overseas working as a mercenary.

"Wait, we need permission to bring him back to life," Brando said. "I'm making a call."

Raven crossed her arms. "Does she think you're dead?" She tossed her head in the direction of the clinic.

He shook his head. "I don't know what she thinks. I just disappeared."

"Okay, well, that sucks, but what about Eira, then? If you return as an enforcer, you'll be *seen*. And if her family is as big as you say, it won't be long before they'll tell her you're alive. Where does that leave her?"

A screen door slammed in the distance, followed by the unmistakable cry of a baby.

Both Jinx and Raven froze.

The sound clutched at something primal in Jinx's chest.

He lifted his binoculars just as Raven did the same. They watched as Eira's mother walked the fussing child over to her.

"Oh shit," Raven breathed out slowly. "Dude … you got a kid."

Brando's voice cut in immediately. "Wait. *What*? What did you say?"

"Standby," Jinx said, silencing Brando.

Eira stood and gently took the baby from the older woman who'd stepped out with him. Then she returned to the swing and began to rock with the calm of a practiced mother, pulling a shawl over the baby. She started singing a lullaby.

But Jinx had already seen the child.

His body went still. Then he exhaled. The breath was long, shaky, and...stunned. *Dear God, could it be?*

Raven nudged him again. "You've got a *kid,* man."

He lowered the binoculars and rubbed his face with both hands as if trying to wipe away the thought. Trying to force his brain to catch up with what his heart already knew.

"That can't be," he said hoarsely.

Raven huffed. "Do the math, Einstein. Unless this woman was cheating on you."

The glare he leveled at her could've shaved splitters off diamonds.

She raised her hands. "What? If she were cheating, sure, it could be someone else's kid. But if she loved you, and you were the only one for her, then it's *your* kid. You need to make that determination." She tilted her head, softer now. "Personally? I think it's yours."

Jinx stared at her, blinked once, then stood.

Raven's eyes tracked his movement. "Where are you going?"

He didn't answer.

"Jinx ..." she started.

He turned just slightly, his voice ironclad. "Raven, I'm giving you two words of advice."

She arched a brow.

“Shut. Up.”

Then he dropped the binoculars and walked into the darkness toward Eira’s farm. He was being pulled toward her by forces stronger than he could fight. If that were his child … he swallowed hard. He had a child. He knew Eira was true to him. Their love was a once-in-a-lifetime love. He didn’t doubt her love or loyalty to him. Leaving her was his way of showing her how much he loved her. Taking death, blood, war, and all the brutality of an enforcer from her life made sense. Or at least it had then.

Raven let out a long sigh and crossed her arms. “I’ll wait right here.”

Jinx didn’t bother responding.

He didn’t even hear her.

His focus was already locked on the woman he’d never stopped loving … and the child he never knew he had.

BRANDO’S VOICE crackled over the comms. “I have Fury online.”

“Well, that’s awkward,” Raven muttered, settling onto a rock at the edge of the overlook. She watched as Jinx melted into the darkness, disappearing like smoke around the perimeter of the small ranch... no, farm ... or whatever the hell you called a place like that. She wasn't exactly a country girl.

"How is it awkward?" came Fury's voice, cool and direct over the channel.

"Yeah, well, not *awkward* awkward. Just a pain in my ass because now I get to explain shit," Raven replied with a sigh. "Jinx has personal complications down here in Venezuela."

"Define complications."

"If I have my guess right," Raven said, dragging out the words as she lifted the binoculars again, "I'd say about twenty pounds, a kid, I suck at ages for munchkins... but a total cutie, for sure."

There was a beat of silence on the line.

"What the fuck?" Fury finally said. "English, Raven."

"A baby," she drawled, clearly enjoying herself. "His *woman*. And his *baby*, to be exact. And we think Ortega is protecting the woman."

"Jinx wants to bring Mateo Rivas back," Brando cut in. "Go in as an enforcer."

"Why?" Fury asked, his tone sharp. "We know who the Ghost is. Why would he want to do that? Ortega is coded. We only act if the opportunity arises." Fury spoke like the mission was already wrapped up in a nice tactical bow. It wasn't. Not even close.

Raven exhaled and shook her head. "Yeah, not so much, O fearless leader. Or handler. Or whatever your latest job title is. See, we were on our way back to report when we got sidetracked by Ortega's men."

She adjusted the focus on her binoculars. "Anyway, the person Guardian believes is the Ghost? Yeah … no way. Jinx and I both agree. Our instincts say the same thing. It's not him. We need another way in. We need to get closer to Ortega and to whoever the real Ghost is."

The night vision flickered to life as she zeroed in on the far side of the little hospital. Jinx was there, half in shadow, standing completely still. Probably listening.

"Stay on the line. I'll be back," Fury commanded.

Raven tilted her head and smirked. "Yes, *Ahhhhr-nold.*"

"I heard that," Fury growled.

"Whoops," she said with a laugh that held zero remorse, then lifted the binoculars again.

"He's muted," Brando said.

"Copy. Jinx, you're in the clear. She's alone," Raven reported as she tracked the movement in the courtyard.

"His kid?" Brando asked.

"Yep. Think so."

"Him going back as Mateo will be hard for her," Brando said, the weight of his voice changing. "Fucking life never gives the breaks we need, does it?"

Raven took a deep breath, voice turning resolute. "We *make* the breaks, Brando. Life passes by the people who sit on their asses waiting for the world to roll up with a silver platter and a billion bucks. You want something, you fight for it. You build it. You bleed for it."

"Still sucks for them," Brando muttered. "I know he loves her. I was his comms officer for the years when he was under. Hang on … Fury just came back online."

After a pause, Brando said, "You're up, sir."

"I've talked to Lycos and Archangel," Fury said, voice firm. "If Jinx believes he can pull this off, let him. But, *and I cannot stress this enough,* if he thinks that woman or the child is in danger, Raven, you're to get them the hell out of there so he can do his work."

"And if she won't go?" Raven asked, eyes still on Jinx as he inched closer to the farmhouse.

Fury sighed. "Shit. Then punt."

Raven snorted. “Punt it is, sir. You don’t know what she’s built down here. She’s a strong one.”

“Great. Keep me apprised. Brando, daily updates.”

“I copy.”

“Raven, take care of yourself. And Jinx.”

She laughed. “Ha! Like *he’d* let me.” Then, quieter, she added, “I’ll do whatever it takes, sir.”

“As long as it takes,” Fury said before the comm line clicked off.

A beat of silence passed.

“Raven,” Brando said quietly, “I have a feeling this mission’s about to get long … and messy.”

She lowered the binoculars just as Jinx approached his woman, stepping out of the jungle’s edge and crossing the clearing toward her.

Raven didn’t lift the lenses again.

Some things were too sacred to spy on.

“And I only packed three swimsuits,” she muttered with a smirk. “What a shame.”

CHAPTER 6

Eira rocked Teo gently as the little boy slept against her chest. The soft creak of the porch swing beneath her mixed with the distant calls of night birds and the rhythmic chirping of insects that filled the warm Venezuelan evening.

Inside the small clinic, the dog rested comfortably on the exam table, sedated but stable. He would be okay. Whatever poison he'd ingested, it had been potent, but the quick thinking by Ortega's men had given the animal a fighting chance. She couldn't identify the toxin yet, but she would.

Still, the thought of Ortega made her skin crawl. She shivered despite the warm air and tightened her hold on her son.

She'd been to his compound twice now to treat his animals. And both times, she'd felt the weight of his gaze. She recoiled at the memory of his slow, appraising look. She'd heard the honeyed tones of his voice, the too-smooth way he'd spoken to her.

He was interested.

She didn't need him to say it. She could feel it. Every look, every lingering word, had been soaked in intention.

And every time, it was all she could do not to shiver in revulsion.

In that part of the world, Ortega *was* the law. His word meant safety, or annihilation. Eira knew the only reason her small farm had survived, the only reason her family's businesses continued to operate, was because Ortega allowed it.

Because Ortega wanted her.

She'd turned him down, politely but firmly, several times. She'd declined dinner invitations and cited Teo as her reason. When Ortega had pressed to know who the father was, she'd looked him straight in the eye and told him the truth.

"Mateo Rivas."

The name of Teo's father had shaken him. The flash of fear in Ortega's eyes had been swift, but she'd seen it. It had disappeared in a blink, replaced by his usual cold confidence. But the reaction had been real. No one knew if Mateo was alive or dead. And Ortega wasn't willing to take the risk that he was still out there.

But how much longer would that bluff last? How long would Ortega allow her to deny him? She knew what he wanted. And she hated the thought. Because what she wanted and what she *needed* was Mateo. She needed his strength. His love. The steady, silent way he'd always made her feel safe, even in chaos.

She'd grown up in a country that was tearing itself apart at the seams. The same thing that happened to many nations. Greed, profit, power, and zero empathy for anyone standing in the way of those goals had fractured the land around her. Cartels killed, drugs were moved, people took cover when they could, and when they couldn't, they prayed. Her family had suffered losses. Mateo had come into her life when she was at her lowest point. She'd lost her father. He left them, and she knew her mother's depression warred with the woman's desire to take care of her daughter.

The practice she thought would flourish brought in bartered bits of food or stock animals that were too thin and needed medical attention or feed. She took the payments and worked every day to build something she and her mother could continue to sustain.

Then Mateo walked into her life. He was massive, strong, and yet so undeniably gentle with the poor injured dog that he'd brought to her for care. She'd used the last of her medical supplies to amputate the dog's leg. Two weeks later, Mateo brought her a backpack filled with vet supplies. "As payment for taking care of a stray."

"You or the dog?" She smiled up at him. She saw the surprise in his eyes at her flirtatious comment, but the smile that spread across his face was beautiful.

Over the following months, Mateo showed up routinely. They connected over the animals and her desire to build something. When he was with her, she felt safer than ever. The undeniable certainty that he would protect her wrapped around her in a comforting warmth she could still feel. They moved from friends to lovers. The progress was slow. He let her choose when to move forward and never pressured her. Their relationship was natural and so… easy. She'd fallen in love.

But he was gone.

She was alone. And she'd stood on her own two feet. She and her mother had scratched a life out of dust, sweat, and perseverance. She'd built this place. A working, sustainable farm. True, Ortega's protection meant the cartels didn't touch her livestock or her products. Her chickens were left alone, her milk undisturbed.

But it was only a matter of time. Ortega's power wouldn't last forever. Whispers carried through the villages. The rumors of a rising military faction, of the Ghost, a killer who wanted the drug trade. A war was coming. A war was always coming.

When that happened, she and her mother would take Teo and flee. The old car was gassed and waiting under a tarp. She started it and drove it around the farm every week. The car was their emergency exit. The city was far but reachable. If they could leave in time.

Sighing, she leaned back and looked up. The sky stretched wide and star-flecked above her, as brilliant as she'd ever seen it. The heavens were endless. Indifferent. Beautiful. She wondered if Mateo was looking up at the same stars. Was he alive? Or among them?

If he were alive … why hadn't he come back? Why hadn't he reached out?

The questions came every night. Each one a fresh cut to the soul. And the answer was always the same. If he were alive and hadn't come back, then he either *couldn't …*

Or he *didn't want to.*

She shook her head, angry at herself. *No.* She refused to believe that. Mateo hadn't left her because he didn't want her. What they had, it had been real. Strong. Unshakable. He wouldn't have just left. He would *never* leave her alone.

The night creatures sang their soft music around her, weaving a lullaby with crickets and tree frogs, the rustling of palm leaves in the breeze …

Then…

Steps.

Soft, deliberate.

Behind her.

She froze.

Her heart stuttered in her chest.

That gait. That rhythm.

She knew those steps.

She'd dreamed of those steps.

Inhaling sharply, she looked up at the stars.

"Why are you still haunting me, Mateo?" she whispered. "Why do I still hear you? How long will our love haunt me?"

A low voice answered from the shadows.

"I will love you forever."

Her entire world imploded in that one moment.

Eira shot to her feet, clutching Teo protectively against her chest. She stumbled backward, reaching out with her free hand and grabbing the frame of the clinic's outer wall to steady herself.

And then he was there.

Mateo.

His arm came out, catching her just before she could fall. He stood before her, solid and still. Eyes searching hers. Her body shook violently. She stared at him, lips parting, breath catching in her throat. Her vision swam. Panic clawed at her chest. She started to hyperventilate.

Teo stirred and began to fuss, woken by her distress. His small cries pierced the stillness, grounding her, tethering her to the moment.

She pulled him closer, trying to soothe him with gentle pats to his back, her hands trembling.

"Shhh," she murmured. "It's okay … It's okay …" But Teo felt her emotions, and his crying grew louder. From the main house, her mother's voice rang out.

"¿Necesitas ayuda, mi amor?"

Eira forced herself to breathe, to find her voice. "No, Mom! We're fine. *We're fine!*"

Her voice shook. But she said it again. Because even though the past had just walked out of the darkness and shattered her world, she had to believe it. They were fine. They had to be.

Mateo nodded silently, gesturing for her to go inside the clinic.

Eira hesitated, her legs heavy with shock. The sight of him, *really him*, had left her stunned. For so long, she'd dreamed of this moment. She'd prayed for it. And now that he was there, real and solid and standing just feet from her, her mind couldn't seem to catch up with her heart.

She walked slowly ahead, her knees weak, her heart thundering in her chest, while Mateo followed closely behind, stepping into the clinic and shutting the door behind them.

Without a word, he reached for Teo. Eira clutched her son tighter for a beat, then released him.

Mateo lifted the child gently to his shoulder, supporting Teo's head with ease, his large hand cupping the back of his son's head like he'd done it a thousand times. He bounced him slowly, tapping his back with calm, practiced movements. Teo settled almost immediately, tucking his head under Mateo's chin and closing his eyes.

Eira stared.

"We have a lot to talk about," Mateo said, his voice rough.

He helped her to a nearby chair, and she sat down stiffly, then held out her arms. "Give me my child back." Without hesitation, Mateo passed Teo into her waiting arms. She clutched her son to her chest, pressing her lips to his temple.

Mateo knelt in front of her, his eyes never leaving her face.

"You're not dead," she whispered, her voice cracking under the weight of disbelief. "If you're not dead ... why did you leave us?"

"I didn't know it was *us*, mi amor—"

"*Do not* call me that," she snapped, her voice shaking. "Do not call me *your love*. If you loved me, you would have come back."

"I left because I loved you," Mateo said quietly.

Eira let out a bitter laugh, her head shaking as tears rolled down her face unchecked. "I know what you were. They told me you were an enforcer. A murderer. But I defended you. I *refused* to believe it. There was no way the man I knew, the kind, gentle, loving man I knew, was a killer."

Mateo's eyes closed for a moment. When he opened them again, his gaze was heavy with truth.

"I'm far worse than anything anyone has told you," he said. "I came here on a mission. My job was to kill Montoya. I did. And then I left. I went back to America."

She stared at him, heart pounding. His words didn't register. Not at first. "So, I was nothing?" she asked, her voice cracking. "I was a diversion? A part of your mission?"

"No." His answer came sharp and quick. "You were not part of that. You were *never* part of the mission. That's why I kept everything, my work, the cartel, separate from you."

He looked at Teo, now asleep again in her arms, and gently reached out, tracing the curve of the baby's round cheek with his finger.

"What did you name her?" he asked softly.

Her?

"Him," Eira corrected sharply. "I named him Teo. After his father."

Mateo's eyes snapped up to hers. His lips parted, and then a smile, soft, broken, and reverent, spread across his face.

"A son," he whispered. "*My son.*"

Eira's expression turned cold. "You gave up any right to me, or to this baby, when you left us here."

Mateo sank to the floor, crossing his arms over his knees. He steepled his fingers, a familiar gesture she remembered from long ago. It was something he always did when he was trying to choose his words carefully.

"Eira," he said, voice low and even. "When I left you, I did it because I loved you. I thought I would bring nothing but danger into your life. I thought I'd cause you more pain. I realize now … I was probably wrong."

Her eyebrows shot up. "*Probably*? Mateo, I'm going to say this very clearly. I loved you with *everything* I had. I gave you *all* of me. And now, after almost three years of silence. Years during which I thought you could be *dead*! You show up and tell me you left me because you loved me?" She let out a hollow laugh. "Do you have *any* idea how insane that sounds?"

Mateo scrubbed his hands down his face and sighed deeply. "I'm beginning to," he admitted. "At the time, it made sense. If I'd come back, if the war had followed me, it would've found you. It would've found your mother. It would've found our unborn child."

"Bullshit." She snapped at him.

"You didn't know about who I was, Eira. You had no idea what I was involved in. The evil that moved in my wake would have consumed you. I couldn't risk coming back. I couldn't risk anyone knowing about you and how damned important you are to me." His voice cracked as he continued. "You know as well as I do the factions in this war don't care about collateral damage. They don't care about women. Or children. They would've burned this place down with you inside."

Eira's mouth dropped open. She snapped it shut again, eyes narrowing.

"Or conversely, Mateo … you could've come and gotten us. Taken my mother and me and left *with* us. But you didn't."

He dropped his head and nodded slowly. "That was an option."

"One you didn't choose," she whispered. "You left. You made the decision for *all* of us."

Mateo's voice was quiet. "Yes. I did. I own that. That's on me."

She stared at him, holding Teo closer. "So, why are you back?" she asked, her voice hard now. "It isn't for me, is it? It isn't for Teo?"

He hesitated. "No," he said. "My employers sent

me back. I've been tasked with eliminating the Ghost … and, if possible, Ortega."

Eira flinched like he'd slapped her. She blinked in disbelief, her heart lurching as his words settled over her. She'd said it to hurt him. Had thrown the accusation like a dagger, praying, *begging* him to deny it.

But he didn't.

Her voice broke. "Did you ever love me?"

Mateo's head shot up, his eyes locking on hers. "With all my heart," he said fiercely. "And I *still do.*"

"And yet …" Her voice trembled. "You left us here. Alone. While you went where? Back to America? What kind of life did you live, Mateo?" Her voice was rising now, bitter and raw. "Do you live in a nice house? Do you have air conditioning? Do you walk into a grocery store and buy anything you want? Do you have neighbors you can talk to without worrying the cartel will gun you down in the road? Do you sleep safely in your bed at night?"

She paused.

"Did you feel safe … in America?"

Mateo stared at her for a long, heavy moment, his eyes searching her face for some crack in the wall she'd raised.

"I don't know how else to tell you that I'm sorry," he said finally, his voice hoarse with emotion. "I made the wrong decision. Every accusation, every truth you've thrown at me tonight, *all of it*, is on me."

He struck his chest once, hard, as his eyes filled with unshed tears. "I made the mistake. *I'm* the one who screwed up, Eira. I should've brought you and your mother back with me. I should've taken you out of this hell. I thought I was protecting you ... but I was only doing what *I* thought was best. And I was wrong."

Eira let out a bitter laugh and gently hushed Teo, who squirmed in her arms. The baby let out a soft cry, picking up on the tension in the room.

"You tell me you're back here because of a mission," she said, her voice tight. "Not because of *us*. You say you love me and that you left me *because* of that love. What kind of twisted logic is that? What kind of organization employs a man to kill others?" She looked at him, accusing and exhausted. "Are you part of another cartel? A rival faction?"

Mateo shook his head quickly. "No. No, nothing like that. My government sent me. Not just mine. Multiple governments. I'm tasked with finding and eliminating high-level threats. Montoya was one of them. Now, the Ghost and Ortega are next. I've never told anyone that truth. It would seal my death if it got out, but you deserve to know." He looked at her, and the honesty in his eyes shocked her. "I've never stopped loving you. I left because of what I do. I thought it would be safer for you. I thought I was protecting you."

She stared at him, stunned. His eyes dropped to the child in her arms, and his expression softened.

"I didn't know about Teo," he whispered. "Not until thirty minutes ago when your mother brought him to you. That's when I saw him."

Eira's brows drew together. "Then why were you even here?"

"I saw Ortega's convoy heading in this direction," he said. "I followed them. I was worried." He hesitated, then added quietly, "I heard what you said to his enforcer." He paused for a moment. "Is Ortega protecting you?" he asked. "Are you … involved with him?"

Eira's expression twisted in disgust. Her words came like blades, and the thought he could believe that sickened her. "How *dare* you ask me that?" she spat. "How could I *ever* be involved with a monster like him? Did you *never* know me at all?"

Mateo flinched. He looked around the clinic as if searching for something solid to hold onto. "And yet … he's protecting you," he said softly.

She lifted her chin. "Yes. He's protecting me.

Because he *wants* me. The only reason he hasn't taken me, hasn't ripped all this away from me, is because I told him Teo and I are yours."

Her eyes narrowed as she locked her gaze to his.

"I saw the fear in his eyes, Mateo. I *saw* it. At that moment, I knew what my uncles told me was true. That you were an enforcer. A killer." She exhaled a shaky breath. "Which you've confirmed tonight."

"I will make this right, Eira," Mateo said, his voice steady but pleading. "If you give me the chance, I'll make *all* of it right. Please allow me to do this."

Eira shook her head, overwhelmed didn't even come close to what she was feeling. "Don't ask me to make a decision. Not now. Don't ask me to process the shock of you being alive, the fact that you're *back* and that you're after the Ghost and Ortega…*and* decide what to do based on what we *had* versus what we have now."

Mateo nodded. "I understand the shock."

"No," she snapped, laughing bitterly. "No, you *don't*. You have no concept of what I'm going through right now. You should *leave*." She wanted him gone as much as she wanted him to pull her into his arms and swear he'd never leave them again. God, how could he be alive? How could he just drop all this on her lap?

He looked between her and the sleeping child, then nodded slowly.

"I will leave," he said quietly. "But I'm *back*. And I will return for both of you. I'll come back in a way that doesn't bring danger to you, him, or your family. I will protect you as I do what I need to do to get rid of the men who prey on this country." Mateo stood and looked down at her. "I know I've told you a lot tonight," he said. "And you can go to Ortega. You can tell him everything I said. That's your right." He paused. "But I *will* take out Ortega. I will find the Ghost. I will kill them both."

His voice dropped, quiet and absolute.

"Then I will return. For you. For my son. For your mother."

Eira stared up at him, her breath caught in her throat. "I would never warn Ortega. But what makes you think we'd go with you?"

Mateo met her eyes, unwavering. "Then I'll *stay*. I'll stay with you. I'll protect you. I'll give you a life you can be proud of. A husband you can be proud of. A father *he* can be proud of."

He didn't give her a chance to respond. He turned and walked to the door, pausing only to look at her one last time before quietly closing it behind him. The silence that followed was deafening. Eira leaned back in the chair, still holding her sleeping son, and closed her eyes as the tears finally fell…hot, silent, and unrelenting.

She'd begged for this in her dreams. For *him* to come back. And he had. But now, with the weight of truth pressing down on her chest like a stone, she couldn't help but wonder …

Had her dreams turned into a nightmare?

CHAPTER 7

Jinx waited in the shadows, crouching beneath the veil of darkness until Eira and Teo disappeared inside the small farmhouse. The soft click of the door locking echoed faintly in the humid Venezuelan night. Crickets sang in the distance, and the low hum of cicadas pulsed through the heavy air.

Blowing out a slow breath, he dragged a hand down his face. He'd screwed up. Big time.

Telling her what he was there to do … that was one of Guardian's cardinal rules. Never reveal who they were, what they did. No one was supposed to know the truth. They were Shadows that lived between the lines of war and peace. But tonight, he'd shattered that rule.

He hadn't told her anything about Guardian Security, but he'd given her enough. Enough to end him. To blow his cover and send this entire mission spiraling into hell. And maybe … maybe that was why he'd told her. A part of him wanted her to have control. To take back the narrative of a story that had started with love, burned down to ash, and left a child in its wake.

She'd promised she wouldn't tell Ortega. And he believed her. Once her house lights dimmed, Jinx turned and made his way back toward the ridge line where he'd left Raven. The darkness pressed close, but the moon carved thin silver lines over the distant rolling hills and the jagged silhouette of the jungle beyond.

He tapped on his comms as he approached.

"Well? How'd that go?" Raven's voice crackled in his ear when he was still a couple hundred yards away.

"About as well as you'd expect," Jinx muttered, his boots crunching over the brittle brush and gravel as he closed the distance.

Brando cut in. "Fury says Mateo's authorized."

Jinx grunted at the update. "Acknowledged."

Raven lifted her chin when he finally stepped into the clearing. "And how exactly are you going to work that? How's Mateo supposed to magically materialize after years off the grid?"

Jinx kept walking, cutting a path toward where their truck waited, half-hidden beneath the twisted branches of a ceiba tree. The thick scent of wet earth lingered in the air.

"Relatively easy," he said without missing a step. "Brando, I need you to get with the powers that be. Build me a cover. A mercenary, contracted overseas for at least the last two years. Make it airtight. Enough to stand up to Ortega and the Ghost's scrutiny."

"And then?" Raven asked, matching his stride.

Jinx's jaw flexed. "Then I come back. Mateo returns. I'll make my presence known to Ortega and the Ghost … and see which bites the hook first."

He strode past Raven, snatched the parabolic mic from where he'd left it, and kept going toward the truck.

"You think it'll be that easy?" Raven asked, hustling to catch up, her footfalls light but hurried on the dirt path.

Jinx climbed behind the wheel. "These men are soldiers. Men of war. They remember Mateo as a stone-cold killer. If they have questions, Mateo will answer them in blood."

Raven slid into the passenger seat, shutting the door quietly behind her. "And what about Eira? And your baby?"

There was a beat of silence as Jinx shoved the keys into the ignition but didn't start the engine. His fingers tightened on the steering wheel.

"Boy or girl?" she asked quietly, without looking at him.

"A son," Jinx said. "His name's Teo." Jinx's breath caught, a subtle hitch he tried to hide. He swallowed hard. The sight of his son in the arms of the woman he loved would be forever imprinted in his mind.

"She still loves you, you know," Raven added, her voice softer now. "She gave your son your name. Or at least, the name you gave her."

Jinx didn't answer. He just started the truck, pulling it out from beneath the cover of the trees and onto the narrow dirt road that led back toward the hills.

Brando's voice came through the comms again. "There's a problem."

Jinx nodded grimly. Yeah, he knew there was. The man was going to be one hell of an issue. "Ortega," Jinx provided.

"Yeah," Brando agreed. "If he's protecting her and knows you're back … is he gonna fight for her?"

"She told him she and Teo were mine," Jinx said, voice clipped.

Raven let out a low whistle. "That's not good. That means he knows you've got a weakness."

Jinx exhaled heavily, staring out at the empty stretch of road ahead. The sky was ink-black, and stars splattered like broken glass across the heavens.

"Unless I convince him otherwise," he said quietly.

Raven's head snapped toward him. "And how the hell do you plan on doing that?"

Brando spoke before Jinx could reply. "By not claiming the kid, denying her?"

"No." Jinx's voice was sharp, cutting through the air like a blade. "By proving that if anyone fucks with them, they'll be obliterated." If anyone hurt them, he'd cover the country in blood. No one would be able to stop him.

Raven shook her head, her dark ponytail swaying. "Which would require someone to actually fuck with them so you can make your point." She glanced at him sideways. "Would she understand that? Would she understand you were making a point to keep her safe?"

Jinx was quiet for a long beat, the tension winding tight between them.

"If she doesn't know about it," he finally said, "what can she do?"

Raven arched a brow. "And if you're not here to protect her, and somebody decides to mess with her?"

Jinx smiled then, slow and lethal, turning his head just enough to look at her. "You'll be there."

Raven blinked, her lips parting. "Say what now?"

"You're going to stay with Eira," Jinx said, his voice brooking no argument. "At the ranch."

"And how's that supposed to help you find and kill both the Ghost and Ortega?" Raven asked, folding her arms across her chest as she shot him a skeptical look.

Brando's voice crackled through the comms, his dry chuckle slipping through the system. "It'll allow him to focus."

Jinx gave a short nod, not bothering to add more. Brando had hit the mark.

He guided the truck down the winding dirt road, weaving past sleeping goats curled alongside the road and stray dogs slinking through the shadows. The faint glow of lanterns from the small village ahead shimmered like stars trapped between the trees.

They drove in silence until he pulled the Land

Cruiser into a thicket on the edge of the village, camouflaging it behind the deserted wreck of a house. The humid night pressed down on them, sticky and thick, the scent of earth heavy in the air.

Together, they made their way on foot through the maze of twisted trees and brush. They stopped at the small cinderblock house Jinx had used while he was in country during his mission. Its faded stucco walls blended into the darkness.

"I'll wait outside," Jinx said quietly when they reached the door. "You can bathe."

Without waiting for her answer, he slid down the rough exterior wall and dropped to sit on the hard-packed ground. His legs stretched out in front of him, arms resting on his knees as he stared at the moonlit street.

Too much rattled around in his head. Eira, Teo, Ortega, the Ghost, what he'd told Eira and why, plus the emotion of seeing her and his baby. Raven's relentless questions wouldn't let him sort through it all. He needed quiet and space.

Raven lingered in the doorway, watching him like she wanted to say more. Finally, she nodded once.

"I'll take care of your woman and child," she said

quietly. "If you need me, I'll do it. But this probably isn't the best use of my talents."

Jinx's gaze flicked up to her, the corner of his mouth twitching in something close to a smile.

"But it'll allow me to make the best use of mine," he replied. His voice dropped lower, edged with something fierce. "Keep her safe, Raven. That's all I ask."

She inclined her head, something almost soft flashing across her face. "When will you introduce us?" she asked.

Jinx exhaled heavily, his eyes drifting back to the empty field. "I don't know yet," he admitted. "I need to formulate a plan."

Raven leaned against the doorframe, folding her arms as she watched him in the moon's dim light. "When you do, run it past me first," she said. "Before you take it to the big dogs. You're too close to this, emotionally involved. We don't want them questioning our methods … or the mission."

A muscle ticked in Jinx's jaw, but he nodded. "Thank you for watching out for me."

Raven nudged his boot with the toe of her shoe. "It's what we do. Whatever it takes."

A low chuckle rumbled in his chest, the first real

sound of humor he'd made all night. "As long as it takes," he echoed.

Raven slipped inside the house, the soft creak of the door closing behind her and echoing in the stillness. Jinx drew a long breath, letting his head tip back against the rough wall as he tried to untangle the emotions coiling like barbed wire in his gut.

The humid night wrapped around him, heavy and close, filled with the distant hum of insects and the faintest pulse of music drifting from somewhere deep within the village. The sharp scent of earth, sweat, and smoke clung to the air.

A faint rustle in the tall grasses nearby snapped his attention back to the present. His muscles tensed instantly, every sense sharpening as he focused on the sound. There it was again. A soft, hesitant shuffle.

From the shadows, a small, thin dog emerged. Its body was gaunt, ribs visible beneath a patchy coat, tail wagging low and tentative. The animal crept toward him, belly nearly brushing the ground, posture submissive but hopeful.

Jinx's hand lifted slowly, palm open and still. The dog hesitated, then crawled closer, inch by inch, until it reached him. It sniffed his fingers, nose quivering, before inching forward to press against his thigh.

"Hey, little one," Jinx murmured, his voice rough with something that wasn't entirely fatigue. He gently stroked the animal's scruff, feeling the brittle, matted fur beneath his fingers. As he scratched behind the dog's ears, his touch skimmed something tight around its neck. A length of twine, crude and biting into the skin. "Shit," he whispered under his breath.

Carefully, methodically, he worked at the knots, using his pocketknife to slice away the twine without hurting the animal. The dog whimpered when the cord finally fell away and immediately rolled onto its back, paws lifted in surrender.

Jinx ran a hand over its skinny belly, offering the only comfort he could at that moment. Another refugee, he thought grimly. Just like the others. Left behind in the wreckage of drug wars, corruption, and violence.

The dog nosed at his boot, then settled quietly beside him, its head resting against his leg, knowing it had finally found somewhere safe. Jinx stared out into the darkness, his hand absently stroking the dog's fur. The night stretched long and quiet, but his mind roared with noise. He would become Mateo again.

The man, the menace, the killer.

He knew that man intimately. Every scar, every cold calculation, every sin. Sliding back into Mateo's skin would take no effort at all. It was like slipping on an old, battered jacket. One that had never really stopped fitting.

He would return once Brando secured his cover and Raven was settled at the ranch with Eira and Teo. His fingers moved gently over the dog's mangy fur as he closed his eyes, listening to the muffled sounds of Raven moving around inside the house, The creak of the old floorboards and the splash of water from the hand pump.

But his mind drifted back to Eira in the quiet spaces between those sounds. To her fierce, furious eyes. To the curve of her smile when she'd trusted him. To the little boy with dark hair who didn't even know his father existed.

If Eira refused to leave … if she wouldn't come back to America with him … Then Mateo would have to stay. By staying, he'd give up the advantage of Guardian's technology, of their weaponry, and of their money. All things he'd used to make his way for the years he was undercover. He'd give up his team, which was the only family he had left. He'd be cut off, by himself, left with his savings, strong back, and the innate training of an assassin. It would have to be enough. He'd *make* it enough.

This country wouldn't change. The cartels would shift faces, and the power struggles would realign, but the violence would remain. The war would continue. And if that were the case, then Mateo would remain, too. He would stay in the darkness, sharp and dangerous, feared by all the men who preyed on the innocent.

CHAPTER 8

Eira laid Teo gently in his bed, her fingers brushing over the little boy's back in slow, soothing circles. His soft breaths evened out almost immediately, the weight of sleep dragging him under, oblivious to the storm raging inside his mother.

Her mind spun relentlessly. Her thoughts, fears, and memories collided like shards of a broken dream. She couldn't put them together in any sort of sensible way.

She stood quietly, staring down at her son, brushing a curl away from his forehead before slipping from the room and pulling the door closed behind her. The house was dark, the only light filtering through the thin curtains from the moon outside. She crossed to the small living room and sat down heavily on the worn sofa, folding her arms tightly around herself as if she could hold her emotions in place.

The night outside pressed close, filled with the distant sound of night birds and the rhythmic chirping of crickets. Somewhere far off, a dog barked once, sharp and lonely. Jasper, Mateo's dog, groaned and flopped over onto his side, sleeping in the corner of the room.

Her mother's bedroom door creaked open, and a moment later, she padded barefoot into the kitchen. Without a word, she filled the old kettle and set it on the stove.

"I'll make tea for us," her mother said quietly as she moved through the familiar motions. She sat down next to Eira, studying her daughter's face in the darkness. "What has you so upset? Was it something Ortega's men said?"

Eira's eyes snapped toward her, startled. "No," she said quickly, shaking her head. "No, it wasn't anything Ortega's men said."

Her mother frowned, her gaze sharpening. "Did the dog die?"

Eira exhaled a slow breath, her shoulders slumping. "No. He'll be fine. I checked on him before I came out here. He's sedated, sleeping in his cage. I'll keep him a few more days just to be sure, but I don't think he got too bad of a dose. He was lucky."

Her mother shook her head, a faint scowl tugging at her lips. "Who would want to poison an animal? Do people not have better things to do with their lives?"

"It could've been accidental," Eira murmured. "He might've gotten into something on his own. Antifreeze is a common poison. It's sweet, and dogs will lap it up." She rubbed her arms absently, trying to shake off the lingering chill threading through her veins.

Reaching over, her mother rested her hand gently on Eira's knee. "Sweetheart, if it's not the dog, and it's not something Ortega's men said … then what is it?"

Eira closed her eyes for a heartbeat, sucking in a shaky breath. "Mateo," she whispered.

Her mother stilled beside her. "Oh, mi amore," she murmured, her voice softening. "You know he would've come back if he were able."

Eira shook her head, a bitter sound breaking in her throat. "He was able, Mom," she said quietly, her voice cracking under the weight of it. "He was able. He came back tonight."

Her mother gasped sharply, her hand flying to her chest. "What are you saying?"

Eira turned toward her, her heart pounding. "He left the country," she said. "And now he's back. He confirmed tonight that he was, in fact, an enforcer for Montoya."

Her mother stared at her, stricken, her expression shuttered as her mind raced. Eira could almost see the questions forming behind her eyes. The same ones she'd wrestled with.

How could he be gone for so long without a word?

Where had he gone?

What had he been doing?

Why had he left?

Before her mother could voice them, Eira lifted a hand. "I don't know," she said quietly. "I don't have the answers to the questions you want to ask. All I know is ... he's back. He sought me out tonight. I told him Teo was his."

Her mother blinked, her lips parting in surprise.

"And he said he's going to stay ... if we don't leave with him."

Her mother's brow furrowed. "You'd leave me?" The question was thin and worried.

Eira shook her head quickly. "No, Mom. That's

not what I'm saying. He said he wanted all of us, you, me, and Teo, to go with him. After he finishes whatever it is he's doing here."

Her mother's frown deepened. "What work?"

"I don't know," Eira admitted softly. "I don't know exactly what he's involved in, but ... he said he still loves me."

Her mother scoffed bitterly, the sound sharp in the quiet room. "Then why did he leave?"

Again, Eira shook her head, her throat tight. "He said it was for my safety. That he left because he loved me ... because he wanted me to be safe."

Her mother stood abruptly, moving into the kitchen without another word. She busied herself with the tea, filling the silence with the clink of mugs and the soft whistle of the kettle heating on the stove.

Eira watched her, knowing her mother's need to occupy her hands when her mind wouldn't stop racing. When the tea was ready, her mother returned and handed Eira a chipped ceramic mug. They sat in silence, the weight of everything hanging heavy between them.

Finally, her mother spoke, her voice quiet but firm. "Do you still love him?"

The question landed like a punch to her chest.

The pain she felt roared to the forefront of her mind. Tears formed and fell as Eira stared into her tea, the steam curling upward. "Mom …" she began, her voice raw. "When I saw him tonight, I thought my prayers had been answered. I love him. I've *always* loved him."

She paused and swallowed hard, the ache in her throat sharp and deep. "But now I know … without question … that the kind, gentle man I knew is also a killer. And the question I have to ask myself is, do I want Teo to grow up with a killer for a father? Do I trust a man who left without a word? How can I trust again?"

They sat together in the darkness, the faint glow of the kitchen lantern casting long shadows across the small living room. The night outside pressed close, a symphony of distant crickets and the occasional low call of a dairy cow echoing beyond the walls.

Eira cradled her mug between her hands, the tea now lukewarm, but she barely noticed. Her mind leaped from one thought to the next in a vicious, relentless cycle.

Across from her, her mother cleared her throat and set her empty cup down on the scarred wooden table. "I should ask you something, Eira," she said quietly.

Eira glanced at her, bracing. When her mother said she "should" do something, it was impactful and usually uncomfortable.

Her mother's eyes were steady but soft, her voice careful. "I should ask you … did Mateo ever treat you badly?"

The question lodged like a stone in Eira's throat. She swallowed reflexively, trying to dislodge the emotion. Her mother continued, her tone gentle but pointed. "Now that you know for certain who he *really* is … when you look back at the life he gave you, those years you were together, do you think he would ever treat you the way a killer treats his enemies? Would he raise a hand to you? Hurt you in any way … other than leaving you without knowing what happened to him?"

Eira frowned, her heart clenching painfully. She didn't even have to think. "No, Mom," she said quickly, shaking her head. "Never." Her mother nodded, her gaze never leaving Eira's.

"But I have to think of Teo," Eira whispered, the words catching in her throat.

Her mother leaned forward and reached out, resting a warm, steady hand on Eira's knee.

"There are so many children in this world without fathers," she said softly, her voice growing rough with emotion. "Because of those damn drugs."

Her voice cracked, and Eira's eyes snapped to her in shock. She couldn't remember the last time she'd heard her mother curse. Her mom swallowed hard and kept going. "If Mateo is the man you knew … if he is willing to take you and Teo and me away from all this death and devastation … then we go."

Eira's breath stuttered, her pulse thudding in her ears. "But, Mom, what about the aunts and uncles? What about our family?"

Her mother gave a tired, weary shrug. "They'll take over the dairy here. They'll understand. They'd say the same thing I'm saying now. If there's a chance to leave … if there's a chance to prosper … and if there's even the smallest chance at love for you, Eira … we take it."

Eira let out a shaky breath, her heart twisting painfully. She murmured. "But, Mom, I feel so *violated*. I feel like he walked away from something I never would've walked away from. How do I trust him again?" She shook her head, the emotion rising sharp and hot in her throat. "I don't know if I can allow him to redeem himself. How can he possibly fix what he did? How can I ever know that once he has us he won't leave again? How can I ever be sure?" Of all the things that screamed through her mind right now, that was one of the loudest. He'd left them. By choice. He'd walked away and stayed away until he was sent back. Would he have returned without that direction?

Her mother stood without answering, gathering their teacups and carrying them back into the kitchen. The faint sound of running water filled the silence as she rinsed them and set them on the drying rack.

Then she crossed the room and turned down the lantern, casting the house in deeper shadows.

When she came back, she stopped in front of Eira and looked at her daughter, her voice soft but certain. "I suppose I should ask you one more question," she said quietly. "How will you live if you don't give him the chance?"

"How will I live if he leaves us again?" The whispered words dropped between them. Forgiving him? She could do that. Eventually. Trusting him? She may never be able to do that again. Trusting him with not only her heart, but Teo's, too? She closed her eyes, and a tear dropped over her cheek. "How, Mom?"

"I can't answer that. It is a question for you only."

Her mother quietly slipped back into her room, the soft click of the door closing sounding louder in the stillness of the house. The faint light beneath the door disappeared, leaving Eira alone in the darkness.

She exhaled shakily and let her head fall back against the worn cushion of the couch, her eyes closing as the weight of everything pressed down on her chest.

"I don't know," she whispered into the silence, her voice fragile, breaking at the edges.

And she didn't. She didn't know how she would live if she sent him away without giving him the chance to prove he loved her, or without letting him show that his leaving had been an act of protection, not abandonment. What he'd done, the choices he'd made, had been born from love and not neglect. Her throat tightened, her heart aching under the storm of doubt and hope swirling inside her. *Dear God ... what was the next step?*

CHAPTER 9

The old wooden door creaked as it swung open, revealing Raven stepping onto the small porch. The heavy evening mist rolled over the green hills, and the humid air clung to everything like a second skin. Raven's lips curved in a grin as she glanced down and crouched, scratching behind the ears of the scruffy little dog glued to Jinx's side.

She shook her head and chuckled. "Jinx, how the hell do you keep finding animals?"

Jinx leaned back against the doorframe, a lazy, amused glint in his eyes. "They find me," he said simply. "They always do."

The small dog shoved himself closer to Jinx's thigh, tail wagging furiously, his tiny body vibrating with uncontainable joy.

Raven snorted. "You've got that damn animal magnetism even with strays." She reached down, scooped the mutt into her arms, and cooed at him. "Oh my gosh, you're such a cutie."

The dog's tail whipped faster, spinning like a helicopter rotor about to lift off, while his big brown eyes stared up at her like she was the best thing in the world.

Raven glanced down at Jinx, her eyebrow raised. "This one just might come home with me."

Without waiting for a reply, she turned and disappeared back inside, cradling the little dog like a baby. Jinx pushed off the doorframe, stretching his long frame before following her into the small house. The safe house was tucked deep in the Venezuelan hills, far enough from prying eyes but close enough to danger.

Inside, Raven rifled through a crate and pulled out a can of meat, feeding the dog straight from her fingers while Jinx splashed cold water over his face at the rusted basin in the corner. Outside, the cicadas hummed, the damp jungle pressing against the house like a living thing.

Giving him the time to finish washing in private, Raven had taken the dog outside to let him relieve himself. When she returned, the puppy practically glued himself to her heels.

No question about it, the damn thing was going home with her.

Jinx dropped into one of the battered wooden chairs at the small table. Together, they cracked open several cans of food, making do with whatever supplies he'd stockpiled. Raven, for her part, continued to sneak the puppy bites from her fingers like a doting mother.

It should've felt like a simple camp meal, but Jinx's mind churned beneath the surface, locked on things far deadlier than their quiet meal.

He tapped the comm device in his ear. "Brando, are you there?"

"I'm always here," Brando replied, a chuckle rolling through the line. "What do you need?"

"I need information on every single one of Ortega's enforcers. I want to know who's in his inner circle. I want names, faces, ranks, and how long they've been with him. I want to know everything."

"Already working on it. Figured you'd want a full dossier before you walked into that hornet's nest."

Raven tapped her earpiece, her voice smooth and purposeful. "Can you get that intel on the military unit?"

Brando sighed. "I might be able to scrape together some information, but those people are ghosts. They keep to themselves. Getting pictures or matching names to faces won't be easy without it."

"I can get pictures," Raven said without hesitation. "I can go back to the same spot we were yesterday. I can get close enough with the telescopic lens."

She glanced over at Jinx, a brow lifted in silent question.

He gave her a nod. "Do it tomorrow. While you're snapping shots, I'll get things situated here and talk to Eira about what's coming the following day." He had to clean his weapons; take stock of what ammo remained; find his other stockpiles throughout the area; and refresh, clean, and ready those stashes.

Raven grinned, sharp and confident. "Child's play." She looked down at the small dog and talked to him in baby talk, which got her the helicopter tail wag.

Brando's voice returned. "Fury wanted you to call once you were able to talk."

Jinx flicked a glance toward Raven. "Call him now."

"Hold the line."

Thirty seconds later, Fury's voice grated over the comms. "Jinx, what's your initial plan?"

Jinx rubbed his chin, staring out the cracked window at the stars populating the heavens. "I need to make a statement," he said quietly. "A clear one. Something that leaves no doubt about my lethal tendencies. I've asked Brando to get me a full rundown of Ortega's enforcers. I'll choose wisely." Someone was going to die to make his statement. He'd try to pick the one who deserved it the most.

A pause stretched over the line. Then Fury's voice came back, sharp as ever. "Are you planning on joining forces with Ortega immediately?"

Jinx shook his head, even though Fury couldn't see him. "No. If we're bringing down Ortega and the Ghost, I plan to stay rogue until both come to me with offers. Playing one against the other as much as I can to draw out the two bastards." A thought sparked in his mind. "A third contending for dominance in the area would stir the pot. Have Brando fill the time between with financial success and ties to as many people they would admire as possible. People we can manipulate or alter communications to show I'm a force to be reckoned with. A small army allegedly coming back to Venezuela after me wouldn't hurt."

"That'll put you in a dangerous spot," Fury

warned. "Not having an allegiance to one of them is a death sentence in their world."

Jinx nodded grimly. "It will. But I know these people. I know how they operate. The fact that I won't immediately pledge loyalty will make them nervous. That uncertainty will ripple through both factions. I want them watching me, questioning me. The pressure may force them to show their hands."

"We need to come up with a name for those military assholes," Raven muttered. "They're not military, no matter what they call themselves."

"Fine. Those assholes work for me." Fury scoffed.

Brando chuckled in the background. "That'll look great in my reports."

Jinx glanced over at Raven and smiled. She was sitting cross-legged at the table, the tiny black-haired mutt curled up in her lap, licking her fingers as she slipped him bits of food from her plate. One small ear was pointed up, the other dipped down. Its only coloring was a white splotch of hair on the tip of his nose. For a moment, despite the looming danger, despite the weight of the plan spinning in his head, there was something almost peaceful about the scene. Raven could be the girl next door. Not in a million years would anyone believe she was an assassin … and that thought brought him back to the problem at hand.

"I need to protect Eira and her family," Jinx said quietly, his voice rough with the weight of responsibility pressing on his chest. "And to do that, I might have to make more than one statement." If someone messed with her, he'd have to show his possession.

"You have authorization to get this mission done. You know the requirements." Fury's voice came back over the comm, cool and precise. "Minimal collateral damage. Get it done."

Brando interjected without missing a beat. "For what it's worth, Fury, I've been digging. Not one of the people working for Ortega qualifies as innocent. Most have multiple murders under their belts. Some of them are sadists, pure and simple. If any of these bastards were operating in the United States, Guardian would seriously consider letting the Shadows loose on home soil."

"I don't doubt it for a second," Fury replied. "The world's changed in the last twenty-five years, but bad people are still seeping up through the pits of hell. The monsters of this world have evolved … and so have we."

Raven's voice cut in dry and sharp. "Yeah, that's why working alone isn't always the best way to eliminate these assholes anymore. It's not like back in the day."

Fury's evil laugh echoed over the line, gravelly and amused. "Back in the day? It seems to me I'm still *in* the day. Anytime you want to haul your ass back to the Rose and try your hand, just say the word."

Raven snorted. "Like I'm that stupid? No, thank you very much. I'll stay right here in Venezuela with my puppy."

A beat of silence stretched over the line before Fury's voice dropped, tinged with dry amusement. "You already starting a menagerie, Jinx?"

Jinx sighed, rubbing the back of his neck. "Hey, I've been here almost a week. I was just sitting outside, minding my business. He came to me."

"And I'm keeping him," Raven said firmly, scratching behind the dog's ears. "He's the cutest damn thing."

Fury snorted. "You do realize we're not an animal transport service, right?"

"Why no, I hadn't," Raven replied sweetly, her tone full of snark. "Thanks for the update."

Fury's voice turned serious again. "Jinx, good luck with her and the puppy. Keep me informed.

Daily reports. And I'm not talking about the number of animals you accrue. The Rose is clear."

"I'm still online," Brando said. "And just so you know, you really shouldn't mess with him. My brother Con tried that once. It wasn't pretty. They still don't get along, but they tolerate each other."

Raven's eyebrows shot up. "Not pretty? What kind of not pretty?"

"Mothers were involved. As in both of their moms." Brando chuckled darkly.

"That's never good."

Raven nodded her head in agreement. "No doubt."

Jinx steered them back to the mission, his voice hardening. "Brando, when can you get me that information?"

"I should have it all compiled by morning. And I'll forward the request about the cover story. You need to get some sleep."

Raven leaned back in her chair, the puppy still curled contentedly in her lap. "I'll get as many pictures as I can tomorrow. Then I'll meet you back here tomorrow night." She was looking straight at Jinx as she spoke.

"Upload those photos, and I'll process them as soon as I get them. It'll give me more time to scrub the not-so-useful Venezuelan government's databases for matches."

"You got it," Raven confirmed.

"Don't forget the airport and points of entry for those pictures, Brando. I don't think many of the people we saw in that camp were homegrown," Jinx added. "The day after tomorrow, we'll head to Eira's place. I'll explain everything to her, and you'll stay with her."

Raven lifted her gaze to his, reading the tight lines around his eyes. "You sure she'll want me there?"

"She will," Jinx said quietly, his throat tightening. "She will if she believes Teo is in danger." Which he would be. Fuck, he hated the situation. "I'll ask her to leave the country before this starts. Brando, prepare a transport out of here in case she agrees."

"Do you think she will?" Raven asked.

"No." Eira didn't have a reason to trust him or anything he told her at that point. She was a proud woman who'd built a business during a drug war, which was difficult in a country filled with patriarchal and misogynistic stereotypes. She wasn't a fainting flower, and she'd only leave to ensure Teo was safe. He'd repeatedly play that card when he took Raven to her place. If they were out of danger, things would be easier … for him.

When Brando cleared the comms, the quiet hum of the Venezuelan night settled over the house. Both Raven and Jinx tapped their earpieces, muting them.

Raven spoke first, her voice softer now, carrying weight behind the words. "You know I've got your back on this."

Jinx glanced at her, nodding once, the jungle night pressing around them, heavy with the scent of rain and distant woodsmoke. "I know. And that's the only reason I'm going forward with this mission."

Outside, the crickets started their night song, unaware of the war quietly brewing.

CHAPTER 10

Eira brushed her hands off on her jeans, her fingers rough from a morning's work. The scent of hay and dust clung to her skin, mixing with the faint, sweet tang of the dairy cows she'd just finished turning out to pasture after their morning milking. The sun blazed overhead, burning through the hazy blue sky, and the dry breeze carried a cloud of dust swirling up from the road below.

She paused at the top of the hill, her eyes flicking back toward the small farmhouse nestled in the fold of the valley. Inside, without question, her mother would be with Teo. It was naptime by now. The soft lull of the afternoon seemed almost peaceful, but tension coiled in Eira's stomach like a tightened spring.

Today, Ortega's men were supposed to come to pick up the dog she'd nursed back to health. It was a simple transaction on the surface. But nothing was simple anymore.

The sound of approaching engines drew her attention, and she frowned when the convoy of sleek, black SUVs didn't appear as expected.

Instead, an old, battered Land Cruiser rumbled around the bend and rolled to a stop before her, dust billowing around the tires.

Her heart stopped.

The driver's door opened, and Mateo stepped out.

Eira's knees nearly buckled beneath her.

For the last two days, she'd convinced herself that night had been a fever dream. Or maybe a nightmare conjured by old memories and fear. But no, there he was, solid and real and impossibly larger than life. The sunlight fell across his face, carving sharp lines across his cheekbones and jaw. His broad shoulders, thick thighs, and lean, powerful frame seemed even more imposing than she remembered. He radiated danger and control like a weapon honed to perfection.

How had she not seen the danger etched in the man? He towered over most Venezuelan nationals, but then again ... so did she. Her father's Scandinavian blood had given her height, which had always set her apart, but she felt small standing before him.

The passenger door creaked open, and Eira's eyes shot to the movement. Her stomach dipped unexpectedly when a woman stepped out. Tall, lean, graceful, and beautiful. Immediately, Eira's guard went up. She felt something sharp sliding beneath her skin. Competition. It was ridiculous. She barely had time to register the woman's presence before her brain threw that word into her head.

Why would she even think that? But the thought clung to her. Why was *she* there?

Mateo stopped in front of her, close enough for her to feel the heat rolling off his body. She tilted her chin back, staring into eyes that had haunted her for years.

"So, you weren't a dream," she murmured, voice low and brittle.

He shook his head once. "I told you, I'm back." His voice still had that same smooth edge, the one that cracked something open inside her. He glanced around. "Is there someplace we can talk?"

Eira swallowed hard, nerves prickling beneath her skin. "Ortega's men will be here sometime today to pick up the dog," she said quietly, nodding toward the hospital building. "If you can make it quick, we can talk there."

Without hesitation, Mateo moved to open the door for her, and she brushed past him, the woman following a step behind.

Inside, the cool dimness offered a moment's reprieve from the relentless sun. "Eira, this is Raven," Mateo said simply. "She's a coworker of mine."

Eira folded her arms across her chest and focused on the woman. "Coworker?" She arched a brow, suspicion tightening her mouth. "Do you do what he does?"

The woman smiled. The gesture was sharp, cool, and not at all friendly. "Someone might say that's not a nice thing to ask." When she looked directly at Eira, the woman's eyes sent a shiver down her spine. They were cold. Dead. Like nothing behind them could be saved. "I'm here to protect you," Raven continued. "And to protect Teo. Mateo's going to do what he has to do to ensure this mission is complete."

Then, like flipping a switch, Raven's face softened. She blinked a few times and offered Eira a smile. It was calculated but friendly. "Unless, of course, he can convince you to leave the country with me."

Eira's breath caught in her throat. She looked from the woman to Mateo, her heart thudding painfully. "Leave?" she echoed. "Why would I leave?"

Mateo growled at his coworker, "I thought we would let me broach that subject?"

"Meh, I can't keep a secret. You know that." Raven sighed.

He ignored the woman and turned to her. "You can leave now to protect Teo," Mateo answered quietly, stepping closer to her. His presence was a wall she couldn't get around. "There's going to be a war soon. One I'm going to start … and finish. It'll be dangerous. You, your mom, and Teo should leave."

Before she could stop him, he reached for her hand, wrapping his fingers around hers. His grip was firm, unyielding like he feared she might disappear if he let go.

Eira tried to pull her hand away, but he didn't release her immediately. The warmth of his touch scorched her skin, spreading up her arm and settling deep in her chest. She finally managed to tug free, stepping back. Her hands rubbed her arms as she turned away from him, needing distance, needing air.

"How do you think you'd react if you were in my situation?" she asked quietly, voice sharp and brittle around the edges. Her entire world was brittle around the edges right now. As if one more surprise could splinter her reality further than it had already been fractured.

Raven cut in before Mateo could answer, her tone flat. "Hopefully, with some semblance of intelligence. He's telling you it's not safe, for you, your child, or your mother. Let that sink in."

Mateo made a small disapproving sound in his throat and glanced toward Raven. Without speaking, he nodded toward the door. Raven rolled her eyes dramatically, sighed, and flounced out without another word.

The air between them felt heavier when she was gone.

"I don't want you in danger," Mateo said, voice softer now. "I don't want your mother or Teo to be in danger. I've arranged a way for you to leave."

Eira shook her head, her throat tight, her arms folded protectively around herself. "I can't trust you," she whispered. "You'll abandon us in some other country ... somewhere we know nothing, with no one to help us."

Her heart pounded, the weight of everything unsaid hanging like a storm between them.

"You know I wouldn't do that," Mateo said quietly.

The audacity of the statement struck her so hard that Eira barked out a bitter laugh. It echoed too loud in the quiet space between them.

"You don't know what I know, Mateo," she snapped, shaking her head. "All I know is that I thought we had something perfect. And then you left. No warning. No message. No indication whether you were alive or dead. You disappeared." Her voice cracked, but she powered through. "You left. And I can't, no, I won't trust you."

He sighed and tried to change her mind using her son. "Even with Teo's welfare on the line?"

Oh, hell no. He didn't get to play worried dad. "Especially with Teo's welfare," she bit out and planted her hands on her hips, her stance defiant, a warrior mother staring down the man who'd broken her. "Don't you understand?" she said, her voice trembling beneath the anger. "For the last two years, that child, the child who grew in me, who I bore and raised, has been my entire life. I've poured every ounce of myself into this place. Every waking hour, every drop of sweat and blood to make this farm something. Something Teo could be proud of." She took a breath, swallowing the lump in her throat.

"Am I worried about what's coming? *Of course*. Am I worried that your damn war will affect us? *Yes*. But this farm matters. My milk makes cheese that feeds the people here. My chickens lay eggs, and they're slaughtered to feed the people around us. Are those people cartel? *Yes*. Do they pay me? *Yes*. Is it because Ortega's watching over me? Probably. But at least someone was watching over me." Her voice broke then, her fury finally bleeding into pain. "Where were you, Mateo?" Her anger filled the room, heavy as the humid air pressing through the thin windows.

Mateo hung his head, rubbing the back of his neck as if the words physically struck him. "Eira … you can't know how my heart bleeds, how sorry I am for the mistakes I've made."

She threw her hands in the air. "Oh, well, that makes everything better! An apology. That's all it takes, right? Of course, I'll do whatever you tell me because I'm still the same girl you left. I'm still the same innocent idiot who believed you loved her." Her voice dropped, hardening into something jagged. "But I'm not *that* girl anymore. I'm *not* trusting. I don't know you. You've proven beyond a shadow of a doubt that I don't know who you really are." She sucked in a shaky breath and met his eyes. "You say you want to protect me? *I don't know that.*

Maybe you just want to get rid of me so you and that woman can do whatever you want. I saw her eyes. She's a killer. Just like you."

Mateo sat heavily on the edge of the examination table, the years and weight of his decisions etched into the lines of his face. "I'm going into town today," he said quietly. "I'm going to start a war. It might not reach you, but I won't take that chance. Raven will stay here. She'll protect you. She'll protect Teo and your mother."

Eira crossed her arms, her eyes burning into his. "And what if I say no?"

He met her gaze without flinching. "Then she'll wait in the shadows. She'll watch the edges of this place. And if you need her, she'll be here."

From the other side of the door, Raven's voice floated through, dry as ever. "I don't think I'd like that too much."

Mateo shook his head and pinched the bridge of his nose, frustration riding him hard. "Eira," he said, voice rough. "If you ever loved me, let Raven stay here and protect you. I'm not asking as a soldier. I'm asking as the man who loves you and never stopped. If you ever felt anything real for me, please let me protect you, your mother, and my son."

The sheer gall of the man hit her like a slap. "If *I*

ever loved *you*?" she repeated, incredulous. "The unmitigated nerve—"

Before she could unleash the storm building inside her, Raven opened the door and stuck her head in. "Dude, that was absolutely the wrong thing to say," Raven announced as she stepped inside and shut the door behind her. She leveled her gaze at Eira. "Look, I know Mateo is complete shit when it comes to relationships. And no, not because we have one." She waved a dismissive hand. "He's like a brother to me. I don't find him sexually interesting at all. He's just a big, broody hunk of muscle who's not nearly as smart as he thinks he is."

Eira's lips twitched despite herself at the shock of the woman's words.

"But here's the sitch," Raven continued without missing a beat. "He loved you so much … he left you. I know, stupid. I told him so. And for the record, none of us knew about you. Not one of us. Not until last week."

Raven crossed her arms and lifted her chin.

"I'm the only woman on his team. And no, I'm not involved with any of them, sexually or romantically. They're my family. They keep me alive, and I keep them alive. Big lunk-headed brothers." Her gaze softened for a brief moment. "But I've known this man for ten years. I've seen him kill without hesitation. I've seen him walk through hell without flinching. But when he returned from that mission … something in him had been broken. A part of him was ripped away. *You*." She glanced at Mateo, then back at Eira. "He's been suffering every damn day since because he wasn't here with you. Because he thought it would protect you if he stayed away."

She paused, and when she began speaking again, her voice was quieter, razor-sharp. "Yeah, I know it sucks for you, too, sweetheart. But he stayed away because he loved you. That's the bare truth. What he does, this war, the violence, that's his job. And he's damn good at it. But it's not who he is when it comes to you." She turned on her heel without waiting for a reply, slamming the door behind her as she left. Silence filled the room like a vacuum.

Eira blinked, staring at the door, then slowly turned back to Mateo. "Okay," she said finally, her voice quieter. "I believe you don't have a relationship with her. That's obvious."

A small smile ghosted across Mateo's mouth, the tension easing from his shoulders.

"She's …" Eira added, unable to stop herself. "Loud. Ballsy. And pretty damn obnoxious."

He laughed, and the sound slipped past her

defenses, making her stomach twist in ways she didn't want to acknowledge. After a long moment, she breathed and looked at him, her heart still raw.

"She can stay," Eira said softly. "If things start to get bad, if this war you're about to declare starts creeping toward us, I'll send Teo and my mother with her."

She paused, her gaze locking with his.

"But understand this, Mateo. When you returned, you said you were here to stay and never stopped loving me. Prove it. Show me the truth in your words, or leave now and never come back."

Before he could answer, she turned on her heel and marched out the door back toward the barn. Her steps were stiff, her hands shaking as she grabbed a pitchfork and began shoveling manure and straw out of the milking area like her life depended on it.

Tears burned behind her eyes, hot and angry, blurring her vision. She didn't hear his footsteps until his boots were beside hers. Without a word, Mateo wrapped his arms around her from behind, folding her against his chest like he could somehow hold her together.

Dear God, the warmth. The strength. The protection. The scent of sweat, hay, and the man she'd loved and sometimes hated in equal measure broke her.

Standing there in the middle of a cow barn, Eira let herself fall apart. All the pain. All the anger. All the confusion. Her loneliness and fear fell in each crystal drop of tears. Tears she hadn't shed when he went missing. Tears she hadn't shed when Teo was born without his father. Tears she refused to shed because she'd had to be strong. For too many reasons, she cracked open and let all the emotion out. And the man she had never stopped loving held her while she did.

CHAPTER 11

Jinx held Eira close as her body trembled against him, each sob slicing through him like a thousand knives. He hadn't known pain like that. Watching the strongest woman he'd ever met unravel in his arms and knowing he was the reason.

When she finally pushed away, wiping at her tear-streaked face, his arms instinctively twitched to pull her back in, but she turned away, her shoulders hunched and tense, her shame thick in the air as if she couldn't bear to let him see her broken. As if he hadn't already seen the cracks he'd put there.

Jinx closed the space between them, the wooden floor of the old barn creaking beneath his boots. He placed both hands gently on her shoulders, feeling the fine tremor in her muscles.

"Will you ever be able to forgive me?" His voice was low, rough, and edged with desperation. It wasn't a question he wanted to ask, it was one he needed to.

Eira took a shaky breath, her shoulders rising and falling as she let it out in a shuttering sigh. She didn't look at him when she whispered, "How can I answer that question?"

Slowly, she turned to face him. Her eyes shimmered with unshed tears, her cheeks blotched and wet. The rawness in her expression gutted him.

"When you didn't come home, I thought you'd died," she said softly. "I grieved you, Mateo. I mourned you like a widow. And then … I found out I was pregnant."

Her voice cracked on the last word, and Jinx felt something sharp and cold wedge into his chest.

"I went through all the emotions again," she continued, her voice brittle. "Damning fate for being so cruel. Cursing myself for not making sure we were more careful. And then cursing myself even more for thinking that. Because if I'd been more careful … I wouldn't have Teo."

Her gaze dropped, her fingers brushing over the

frayed hem of her shirt like she needed something to anchor her.

"It took me months after I found out I was pregnant to come up with a plan," she said. Lifting her chin, she looked around the barn, her eyes lingering on the worn wooden beams, the rusted tools hanging on the wall, the faint shafts of light slanting through the gaps in the planks.

"This place ... This was the plan. This was how I was going to survive, how I was going to keep Teo safe. This was going to be my legacy to him."

Her lips parted in a bitter laugh.

"And then Ortega took over."

Jinx's jaw tightened at the name. A sour taste filled his mouth as he listened.

"It was about nine months ago that everything settled down," Eira continued, her voice turning distant like she was recounting a nightmare. "By then, I had Teo. Ortega brought one of his dogs here. Before he locked himself away like the coward he is. He's in Montoya's compound now. He's untouchable. Even Simón says he rarely sees the man."

Her fingers curled at her sides, her voice dropping to a whisper.

"But one time was enough for Ortega's obsession to start again."

Jinx's eyes narrowed. His gut twisted.

"Again?" he asked, his voice low and dark.

She nodded, giving him a sad smile that didn't reach her eyes.

"I went to school with the Ortega boys," she said, her voice turning distant with memory. "That was back when this area was still breathing. When the fields were alive, and the villages bustled. Well … as much as Venezuela could thrive under the weight of corruption."

Her gaze drifted past him toward the green hills rolling beyond the barn, shadowed by the humid haze of the lowland jungle.

"Ortega's brother was older than us, but those two boys, they always found ways to pick on me, to be near me. My mother used to say boys didn't know how to tell a girl they liked her. They pulled your hair because they didn't know how to ask for your heart."

Her lips flattened.

"Well, he knows now."

A pulse of jealousy, hot and unwelcome, flooded Jinx's veins. He clenched his fists to keep from punching the barn wall.

"Was he ever inappropriate?" His voice was carefully measured, but he couldn't hide its edge.

Eira glanced up at him and let out a dry, humorless laugh.

"No. The one time Simón was ordered to bring me back to the compound, whether I wanted to or not, was when I told him Teo was your son."

The words slammed into Jinx like a fist to the ribs. His heart stuttered.

"That shocked Simón so much he risked going back to Ortega empty-handed," she said, her gaze locking on his. "Because no one ever saw your body, Mateo. No one knew for sure if you were gone."

The barn felt suddenly colder, the humid air pressing against them, but there was no comfort from the warmth.

"The others, the other enforcers, you remember them. Ortega hunted them down. He made them choose: join his crew or die. Most stayed because they'd followed Montoya and liked the money."

Jinx shook his head, disgust twisting in his gut. "He's not a leader. He's weak. He doesn't command loyalty. How the hell did he rise to power?"

Her lips quirked in a humorless smile. "He's cruel. Not as cruel as his brother was, but cruel enough. And I knew I'd never leave if I set foot inside that compound. That's why I told them the truth about Teo."

Jinx swallowed hard, stepping closer. "I'm glad you did."

Eira's eyes glimmered with something between sadness and resignation. "Except now it puts us all in danger, doesn't it?"

He nodded once. "To a degree, yes. They'll see my love for you and Teo as a weakness they can use against me."

She stepped toward him, her voice sharp with the fear and fury of a mother backed into a corner. "That's why you want us to leave the country."

Jinx met her gaze, something raw flashing in her eyes. "I want you safe."

"And where would we go, Mateo?" she asked, her voice tight. "What would we do? We'd be in a foreign country without papers, visas, or a way to survive. My government won't give us the documentation your country needs. You're here to do this job you told me about. What happens if you don't survive?" Her voice broke at the end, a tremor cutting through the steel. "We'd be alone. Teo and me. In a world that wants to swallow us whole."

Jinx took her face gently between his hands, forcing her to look at him. "I'd make sure you were taken care of," he said quietly. "No matter what."

The doubt in her eyes was immediate. She

stepped back, putting a small distance between them. Jinx could feel his frustration boiling beneath his skin like lava. His jaw ticked, and he ran a hand over his neck, trying to control the rising storm inside him. She didn't believe him. The frustration wasn't with her. It was with the decisions *he'd* made. If he could turn back time, he would. But he couldn't. "I have plenty of money," he said quietly, deliberately, his gaze locked on Eira. "More than enough for you, Teo, and your mother to live comfortably if I don't survive this mission. But I have every intention of surviving." His voice softened, but the steel never left it. "I have every intention of coming back to you."

Eira folded her arms across her chest and lifted her chin defiantly as the warm Venezuelan breeze stirred her hair. The humid air pressed heavily against them, thick with the scent of damp earth, sunbaked grass, and cattle. "And I have every intention of taking care of my mother and my child the way I always have," she replied. "You stand here and tell me you're about to start a war. But I've been surviving through this war my entire adulthood, Mateo. I know the dangers. And now you're back, you bring another layer of protection, your name." Her eyes shimmered with determination. "Now that you're back, why would anyone try to harm us?"

The question punched him in the chest because he knew the answer. "Ortega has an army," he said quietly. "The militia in the foothills has another. You've lived in this battlefield for too long not to see the cracks forming. Please, Eira, let me send you out of this country."

She shook her head, her arms tightening around herself like armor. "I'll consider it," she said after a pause. "But it's only a consideration." Her eyes flicked back to him, sharp and assessing. "The war you're about to start … when will it happen?"

Jinx shook his head, the shadows shifting across his face as the late afternoon light slanted through the gaps in the barn walls. "I'm not sure. It could take time. I don't know the inner workings of Ortega's cartel anymore. I don't know what the militia intends. Everything is a guessing game right now."

Eira's gaze didn't waver. "Then give me time," she said softly but firmly. "Give me the time to adjust to the fact that you're back. Give me time to know what you're telling me is the truth."

His brow furrowed. The weight of her words settled heavily between them. "Why would you think I'm not telling you the truth?"

She laughed hollowly and shook her head, her expression crumbling. "Withholding facts is lying, Mateo," she said, voice sharp as a blade. "You never told me you were an enforcer. You never told me how high up you were in Montoya's cartel. You didn't tell me you were a killer. You didn't tell me you were working for your government."

"There were things I didn't tell you to protect you and myself."

Her eyes locked on his, fierce and wounded all at once. "You lied to me by omission. Why would I think you're telling me the entirety of the truth now?"

Jinx scrubbed a hand over his face and exhaled roughly. He stepped back, pacing, breathing in humid, heavy air. He felt like he'd just taken a hit to the gut. Stopping, he met her gaze and spoke, his voice stripped bare. "This is the absolute truth," he said quietly. "I loved you, Eira. I still do. I tried to shield you from the ugliness I had to become. I didn't want you to see the monster I had to be to survive, to do what needed to be done." His throat worked as he swallowed hard. "I walked away because I thought none of my deeds would ever come back to haunt you. I thought leaving would protect you."

He let out a bitter breath, shaking his head. "I didn't know about Teo. I had no idea Ortega had taken over. I didn't know you were caught in this hell." His voice dropped, rough and low. "I walked away, and I tried so damn hard to forget you. I told myself it was the only way to keep you safe." He paused, voice softening. "Yes, I'm a killer. But I don't eliminate people for the joy of it. I take out monsters. I work for governments of this world, and I'm here to remove two of the biggest monsters on this continent."

His gaze bore into hers, steady and unwavering. "But I can't do that if I'm worried about you. About Teo. About whether you'll survive the war I'm about to start. I need you safe, Eira, so I can concentrate on finishing this … so we can both walk away." He took a step closer. "If you want to stay here afterward, I'll stay. If you want to leave, I'll take you anywhere. America, Europe, any country you choose. I'll follow you."

His voice broke with the next words. "I can't imagine my life without you." Eira released a shaky breath and walked away from him, her footsteps echoing in the quiet barn. She rubbed her arms, her fingers trailing over the goose bumps on her skin, then leaned back against the rough wooden wall.

"I've changed, Mateo," she said, her voice soft but steady. "I don't know if the woman I am now is someone who can still love you."

Her words hit him like a sledgehammer to the chest. He crossed the distance between them and stopped a few feet away, his hands flexing at his sides.

"That doesn't matter, Eira," he said quietly. "If I've ruined our love, it doesn't change anything. I will still take care of you. Of Teo. Of your mother. I'll never abandon you again."

She glanced at him, her lips curving in a small, bitter smile.

"Words are cheap, Mateo."

Outside, the oppressive heat of the Venezuelan lowlands clung to the air, thick and suffocating. In the distance, the distant boom of thunder rolled across the horizon, a storm gathering over the jungle just past the foothills. But between them, the storm had already arrived.

"Not mine," Jinx said, his voice low but unwavering. "My words are filled with absolute truth. I will never lie to you again, by omission or otherwise."

Though Eira's gaze softened, the shadows of doubt still lingered in her eyes. She glanced toward the door, her expression guarded. "Your friend can stay. But where will you be staying?"

Jinx closed the distance between them slowly and carefully as if approaching a wounded animal. He took her hands in his, cradling them gently in his. "I would like to stay here," he said quietly. "With you and Teo."

Her big brown eyes lifted to his, and he saw the flicker of old memories, the wariness tangled with longing.

"Things can't return to how they were, Mateo."

He shook his head. "I'm not asking for that. I'm asking for a chance to get to know you again. To know my son."

The afternoon light slanted through the barn's wooden planks, casting stripes of gold across her face, across the dust motes dancing in the humid air between them. Outside, a cicada hummed loudly, a sharp, electric buzz accompanying the tension in the air.

"When things start to happen," Jinx continued, "I need you to trust me. And I need you to trust Raven."

Her brow furrowed at the mention of his partner, but she didn't speak.

"I need you to understand something," he added softly. "It might take months before I'm able to finish what I came here to do, perhaps longer. But maybe ... during that time ... I can show you that my love never stopped. And maybe you'll let yourself trust me with your heart again."

Before she could respond, he leaned down and brushed his lips against hers. A kiss so light and tentative it felt like a question. Because it was; he was begging for a chance. One more chance. He wouldn't screw it up this time. When he pulled away, her eyes fluttered open, wide and uncertain.

"I've missed you so much," she whispered. "And I'm so confused, Mateo. I don't know what to do, feel or what to think. One minute, I'm so angry. The next, I'm crying, and I miss you so much. I don't know how to feel."

His thumb traced gently over the back of her hand.

"Until you do," he murmured. "Until you trust me again, we'll protect you. I love you, mi amor. Just give me a chance."

Eira's lips curved slightly, almost reluctantly. "A chance? A chance to prove you are here for me because you love me, not just because of your mission? That will take a lot of work. Nothing in this life is easy, and gaining my trust will be the hardest thing you've ever done. Prove your words, Mateo," she said. "*That* is your only chance."

As a weight lifted slightly off his shoulders, he nodded, swallowing past the knot in his throat.

"That's all I ask."

She stepped back, her smile sharpening with a hint of mischief.

"Now," she said, "you need to go talk to my mom."

The relief that had settled in his chest vanished like smoke in the wind.

Jinx groaned. "So much for relief."

CHAPTER 12

Eira stood in the front room, her arms crossed protectively over her chest as her gaze flicked between her mother and Raven. The tension in the air pressed against her skin like the oppressive humidity outside. Through the open window, the distant sound of cicadas buzzed in the background, mingling with the faint rustle of the Venezuelan jungle beyond the rolling hills of their cattle farm.

Her mother's eyes narrowed, pinning Raven with suspicion, her voice sharp and clipped. "What do you mean she's going to protect us? Why didn't Mateo say something when he talked to me? She doesn't look like she could protect anyone. Mateo said he would do that now."

Eira answered evenly, trying to keep her mother calm. "Mom, I told you. Mateo still has some work he needs to do. We both know who Mateo was, and what he does. What he's going to do now will cause waves in the cartel. He wants her here in case someone tries something." Despite the heavy heat, she rubbed her arms as a chill skated down her spine. "I can't risk someone trying something against you or Teo. If Mateo believes this woman can protect us, I believe it, too."

Her mother frowned, her gaze sweeping toward Raven, unimpressed. "We don't have a place for her to stay. Mateo has the small room. You're sleeping with Teo. I have my bed."

Before Eira could answer, Raven replied casually, her tone firm but easy. "That couch is fine for me. Or even the floor. Doesn't matter."

Both Eira and her mother turned sharply toward her, surprised she understood.

Raven gave a little shrug, the corner of her mouth twitching. "I know three or four languages."

Her mother narrowed her eyes further. "Do you even have a weapon?"

The woman Mateo had left to care for them smiled. It was a sharp, predatory smile that had nothing soft or comforting about it. "I'm armed right now. I have at least five weapons on me. And I don't need a weapon to kill. I've been trained by the best. I promised Mateo I would take care of you, your mother, and your son. No one will get through me to reach you."

Eira's mother shook her head, her jaw tight with disapproval. "How are we supposed to explain her presence here? The cartel is suspicious. They'll want to know who she is and what she's doing here."

Raven shrugged again, her voice light but unwavering. "That's simple. I'm your niece. Your father's brother's daughter."

Eira blinked, startled. She tilted her head. "How do you know my father had a brother?"

Raven rolled her eyes. "A simple internet search. Look, I'm not here to complicate your lives. I'll stay out of the way or help when I can. I don't know anything about cows, except they're huge, and they stink. But I can help around the farm if it doesn't take me away from my main mission, which is protecting you."

"She's staying, Mom." Eira's voice left no room for argument. "There's no point in fighting about it."

Her mother's lips pressed into a thin line. "She doesn't take care of Teo. She doesn't stay alone with him."

Raven chuckled darkly. "Yeah, not really my thing either. I'll leave the nappy changes and feeding to you and his mom."

A sharp bark from outside sliced through the room. Eira glanced toward the window and immediately stiffened when she spotted her dog and the small puppy Raven had brought with her, both yapping wildly at the front gate. Dust curled in the air beyond them, stirred by the black SUV slowly creeping up the access road.

She didn't need a closer look to recognize the vehicle.

"Mom," she said quietly.

Her mother didn't hesitate. She turned and disappeared down the hallway toward Teo's room.

Eira's heart raced as she peered out the window. Dust swirled around the SUV's wheels as it slowed in front of the house, the midday heat shimmering off the black paint like liquid fire.

"It's Ortega's enforcers," she muttered under her breath. Raven stepped up beside her, her expression unreadable. "What's your name?" Eira asked quietly, keeping her gaze on the vehicle.

"Let's stay with Raven," she replied smoothly. "That'll save us all some confusion."

Together, they stepped onto the front porch as

the SUV's engine rumbled low, the scent of motor oil and dust wafting toward them on the hot breeze. Eira took a steadying breath, bracing herself as the door opened and Simón climbed out.

Simón was a monster by anyone's definition. He was tall, broad, and cold as a loaded gun, but he'd always treated Eira with something close to respect. If monsters could have favorites, she was his.

"The dog's ready?" he asked, his voice gruff.

"Yes," she replied, forcing her shoulders back. "Make sure you clean up the motor fluids wherever the dog sleeps. It was probably antifreeze."

Simón grunted, his gaze flicking past her to Raven. His eyes narrowed slightly.

"And her?" he asked, switching to English. "Who are you?"

Raven cocked her head at him, feigning confusion, then glanced at Eira, speaking in Spanish. "What did he say?"

"He wants to know who you are," Eira replied dryly in the same language.

Raven smiled sweetly at Simón, though nothing was soft in her eyes. "I'm her cousin."

"From where?"

"Sweden. Do you know it?" Raven said in fluent Swedish, or at least Eira assumed it was Swedish. It sounded European. Simón's gaze sharpened, lingering, but he said nothing.

Eira looked at Simón and in Spanish said, "My father is from Sweden," Eira added. "Everyone knows that I have family there."

Simón narrowed his eyes. "Why would he send her *here*?"

"Because I caused too much trouble at home," Raven said in Spanish. "I'm being taught a lesson. Working with the cows and the chickens."

The other men stepped out of the SUV now, moving like shadows, each falling into place with unsettling ease. Ortega's enforcers came in many shapes. Simón was the professional, all-cool calculation. Marco, who slithered forward last, was the chaos.

His smile was oily and predatory, his gaze sliding over Raven in a way that made Eira's stomach knot.

Simón shifted his stance to Eira. "Get the dog. We'll wait here." His order was barked, but Eira believed it was intended for Marco, not her.

Eira nodded, motioning for Raven to follow her into the small hospital. The moment the door shut behind them, she leaned in close, her voice low. "Stay away from Marco. He's dangerous."

Raven's chuckle was soft, almost pleased. "I

almost want him to try something. I saw him yesterday, and I heard what he said to you." Her smile faded, her voice dropping to something harder. "But don't worry, Eira. I won't do anything that will endanger you. You need to believe that."

Eira gave a tight nod and crouched to clip the leash onto the dog's collar. The animal came out of the kennel with his tail wagging, and together, they stepped back outside, the heat pressing down on them. She handed the leash to Simón, and the dog immediately sat obediently at his side.

Simón's face was unreadable as he spoke again. "Ortega asked me to extend an invitation. One I would recommend you take."

A cold knot tightened in Eira's stomach even before he finished, and she shook her head slowly, her jaw tightening. "Simón … Mateo came home."

Simón's reaction was almost imperceptible. There was a flicker of surprise that vanished as quickly as it appeared. But Marco wasn't nearly as disciplined. He let loose a string of curse words in rapid succession, his voice sharp in the heavy afternoon air.

Simón silenced him with a single cutting glance. The weight of command in his stare brokered no hesitation. Then Simón looked back at Eira, his eyes sweeping the farm's landscape, taking in the swaying grass, the dust-coated fence line, and the distant line of cattle clustered beneath a thin stand of trees.

"Where is Mateo now?" he asked quietly.

Eira uncrossed her arms, anchoring her fingers through a belt loop of her jeans. "I believe he's in town." Her gaze flicked to Marco, pointed and cold as she drove the point home. "My man is back."

Marco's lip curled in a snarl, his eyes narrowing dangerously, but he said nothing.

Simón opened the back door of the SUV, and the dog jumped inside without another word. He motioned sharply to the other men lingering nearby, and one by one, Ortega's enforcers filed back into the vehicle.

Simón lingered, closing the door gently before turning back to Eira. "Ortega will not be happy." His gaze slid once more over the farm, lingering on the small farmhouse, the rusted swing set in the distance, the freshly painted barn. "If he can't have what he wants, he might not protect you anymore. It's not safe for you or your family." He glanced briefly at Raven. "For any of you."

Eira's spine stiffened. She hooked her thumb through her belt loop again and met his gaze without flinching. "It's never been safe for us here,

Simón. Not since the drugs started coming through this area." Her chin tilted defiantly. "But Mateo will protect us now. And I pity anyone who thinks this is the right time to make a move."

A faint smirk tugged at Simón's mouth. "You might want to express that to Ortega. Or maybe I will. I haven't been threatened lately." He scratched his chin absently, his attention drifting toward the cattle grazing lazily beyond the fence line, flies buzzing around their ears. "I don't think you understand how deep Ortega's obsession with you runs."

Eira gave a bitter laugh. "Oh, I understand. I've understood since we were children. He needs to learn he can't have everything he wants."

Simón's expression sobered. "I've tried to warn you, to watch out for you."

"And I've always been grateful. Mateo will be told of your help." She dipped her head slightly. "But we all choose our path, Simón. Mine has nothing to do with cartels."

A bark of laughter left him rough and humorless. "As Mateo's woman, your life has everything to do with cartels. Don't bother telling Mateo anything about what I've done. It wasn't for him."

Without waiting for a reply, he turned and climbed back into the SUV. The engine rumbled to life, and the vehicle slowly pulled away, tires kicking up a slowly spreading cloud of dust as it disappeared down the pitted access road.

Raven stood beside Eira, arms folded, her gaze following the SUV as it vanished into the horizon. The distant sound of cicadas and the lowing of cattle filled the silence between them.

"So, tell me about Ortega," Raven said casually, her voice low.

Eira exhaled slowly, her shoulders heavy as she watched the dust settle over the dry road. "He and his brother grew up not far from here. Back before the cartels dug their claws into this area." She glanced at Raven. "We went to school together. Both of them were … different."

As she continued, her voice dropped, the words heavier. "Tomás is a bully, but only when he's in a gang. Esteban, his older brother, was always quiet. Violent. He used to hurt animals because he enjoyed it. I've seen what he'd do. He was sick. Everyone knew it. His parents were afraid of him. Tomás thought he walked on water, though." Raven arched a brow but didn't interrupt. Eira met her gaze. "You understand Esteban's type?"

Raven nodded once, her mouth tightening. "All too well. The things serial killers are made of."

"Exactly. There were a couple of murders. Old people who lived alone. A woman whose husband had died a year earlier. Everyone thought it was Esteban. But he disappeared not long after the woman was murdered ... when he was thirteen or fourteen. No one knows what happened to him. Some say he ran off. Others say worse. They said his father made sure he wouldn't hurt anyone again." Eira shook her head, her voice softening. "I went to university shortly after that. My father sent money so I could go to school. It was guilt money, my mother said. She sent me to the university in Maracay. I worked full time because the money wasn't enough, and it took longer to graduate, but I became a veterinarian."

A bitter chuckle slipped from her lips. "I thought this area could use one. I have an affinity for animals, and once, there were many farms in this area."

"Mateo attracts animals," Raven murmured, leaning against one of the porch posts, her arms still crossed casually. "It doesn't matter where he is in the world. They find him. The strays, the neglected, those looking for a safe home. He takes them all in. He has a place back in the States. I don't know how many acres, way over a hundred. Rescued horses, donkeys, livestock, and a pack of dogs that just won't quit expanding. I can see why he likes you. That guard dog was putty in your hands."

Eira internalized the information. A hundred acres … about forty hectares. A vast amount of land. Perhaps his claim of wealth wasn't an exaggeration. She drew a deep breath and spoke, recalling how optimistic she was when she graduated. "When I came home after school, I thought I could make a good life as a vet. But by the time I returned, the cartels had buried themselves in the soil." Eira's gaze swept over the fields, her mouth tightening. "There's a route not far from here. Highly contested and heavily guarded by Ortega's men. It's one of the main arteries that funnels drugs north to Central America, the United States, even Europe."

Her voice dropped lower. "That route cuts this area off from any government help. It's the line the authorities won't cross because their pockets are already lined with cartel money. Ortega pays well to ensure he's left alone."

Raven nodded, her expression unreadable. "I noticed the damage and neglect when we passed through."

Eira gave a hollow laugh. "It's not neglect. Neglect implies someone cared at some point. What we live under is control. Ortega's control." She sank onto one of the old rockers on the porch, her fingers brushing over the worn wooden arm. "Everything I've built here, this farm, the animals, the small life I carved out, could be taken away in an instant. The only reason I have eggs to sell, milk to deliver, is because Ortega allows it." Her voice cracked slightly. "And now that Mateo is back, the only question is how long before Ortega decides he won't protect us anymore."

Tomás was greedy and a bully. She didn't understand why he'd waited, but she thanked God he had. And that Mateo had come back. She let that thought sit on her heart for a moment. She was *glad* Mateo came back. She'd never stopped loving him. Trusting him would be harder.

Raven's gaze softened as she studied her. "Even if Ortega has an army, Mateo and I would never let him take this from you."

Eira's laugh was soft, almost broken. "Two people against two thousand?" She shrugged. "The odds aren't in your favor."

A faint, amused snort escaped Raven. "No. You have that backward. The odds aren't in their favor."

Eira shook her head, her eyes distant.

"What happened when Montoya was killed?" Raven asked quietly.

Eira puffed out a heavy sigh. "Chaos. The cartel imploded. The people tore each other apart, scrambling to claim territory and control."

"And what would happen if Ortega fell?" Raven asked, voice careful.

"Probably the same thing," Eira admitted. "A power vacuum. Blood running freely in the streets."

Raven was quiet for a long moment before speaking again. "So, if getting to Ortega would solve some problems … it would also cause many more."

Eira closed her eyes, her foot gently nudging the old rocker into motion. The sound of creaking wood filled the heavy air. "Problems are the way of life here."

"Then, maybe," Raven said softly, "you should consider Mateo's suggestion. Let me take you, your mother, and Teo out of here."

Eira nodded once, her gaze fixed on the empty road stretching beyond the fence line. "I'm not stupid. When the time comes, I won't endanger us needlessly." She glanced at Raven. "But until that time, I need to understand the man Mateo is. What he showed me before was a mirage."

"He showed you the best of himself," Raven said,

standing away from the post. "The other side is just his job. Some people are stockbrokers, and others clean up the messes that society won't or can't handle. Show me the chickens? They're about my speed."

Eira stood up and frowned. "You *actually* believe that?"

Raven looked at her. "That the chickens are my speed? Yeah, totally. They're kind of cool."

Eira shook her head, stunned at the woman. "No, that what you do is just a job."

"With all my heart," Raven said, skipping down the stairs. "So does Mateo."

Eira watched Raven grab her pup and stroked the other dog's scruff. Her joy and laughter were real. It was almost as if Raven were two different people. The dangerous one and the one in front of her now. Could it be Mateo functioned the same way?

CHAPTER 13

The drive into town was one Jinx didn't want to make.

Violence for the sake of chaos had never been in his nature. But this wasn't about chaos. This was necessity. To rid the world of two of the most heinous monsters walking the earth, war was coming whether he wanted it or not.

His hands flexed around the steering wheel as his mind replayed the moment he'd held Eira in his arms, her body trembling against his, her grief spilling out in angry, broken sobs. The weight of her tears had gutted him, carved him hollow with guilt and regret. He had done that. He had caused that pain. If he had stayed … if he'd walked away from

Guardian, maybe he could have spared her the heartache.

But deep down, he doubted it. She would've had to come with him. And he wasn't sure she could've been convinced to leave her family.

However, once a man stepped into the cartel world, there was no walking away. Not unless he lived in the shadows like Jinx did, slipping through cracks, existing between worlds.

Jinx had pledged his loyalty once, a lifetime ago, to Guardian. He'd never renounce that loyalty or do anything to harm the organization. Integrity was something each Guardian had in measures that didn't exist elsewhere. Law enforcement worked damn hard to weed out the offenders, and the courts worked to keep them off the streets, but when they failed, when the world needed an entity wiped from existence, he and his teammates were called into action.

Loyalty to organized crime, cartels, factions, and crime families usually ended in bloodshed, death, and destruction. When the enforcers and factions went to war over Montoya's crumbling empire, he knew the outcome would've been the same. He wouldn't have bent the knee to Ortega's regime. They wouldn't have pulled him in, so they would have eliminated him and anyone he cared about. Probably slowly and loudly to ensure others fell in line. That was what you did to the strongest of your enemies in that region of the world. *And that's why you left.*

Ortega … Jinx's jaw tightened as he wound through the cracked streets, the sun beating down on the rusted rooftops and faded paint of the small Venezuelan town. Tomás Ortega was weak. A man like him didn't rise to the top without someone propping him up. Someone with power, connections, or an agenda. How the hell had that piece of shit climbed the ladder? That was a question Jinx needed to answer before this was over.

The town hadn't changed. The same cracked pavement, the same buildings leaning into one another like tired old men. A hardware store stood abandoned, its windows boarded and sun-bleached. Paint peeled from the stucco walls lining the narrow streets, and the scent of exhaust, dust, and humidity clung to everything like a second skin.

Jinx knew exactly where he was going.

The cantina at the end of the road sat in the same sagging structure, its faded sign swinging in the afternoon breeze. Right now, it was probably empty. That would change in a few hours, once the cartel boys shook off their hangovers, rolled out from under whatever woman had kept them warm, and came hunting for the hair of the dog that bit them.

His comms crackled in his ear. Brando's voice came through. "I've identified most of the pictures Raven took. Sending them to your cell."

"Copy," Jinx replied, pulling into a dusty parking space across from the cantina.

The inside of the small building was dim and cool, shadows stretching across the cracked tile floor. Behind the bar stood a woman he didn't recognize. She was in her late fifties, maybe early sixties, with dark eyes that gave him a once-over like she was sizing him up for trouble.

"What can I get you?" she asked, wiping down a spotted glass with a rag that had seen better days.

"One beer," he replied, laying cash on the scarred wood of the bar.

Her eyebrows lifted ever so slightly, but she took the money without question and filled a dusty glass with beer, sliding it across to him.

Jinx carried it to a table in the far corner, his back against the wall, a clear line of sight to both the door and the grimy windows. He leaned back, tipping his chair just enough to balance, and pulled out his phone.

Brando's pictures with faces, names, and sparse information flicked across the screen. Too sparse. The men on that hill weren't the average cartel scum. They were military-trained bastards from other countries, ghosts in their own right. And ghosts were hard to kill.

When the bartender disappeared into the back, Jinx spoke low. "There are four pictures without any information."

"I know," Brando replied. "I'm working on it. I dumped all the images into Interpol's system. It's scraping for hits. Most of these guys aren't locals. I thought it was a good place to start. Raven said there were a couple of the brown-nosers who she couldn't get a good picture of. I'm having AI recreate the full face from the partials she took, and I'll be scraping those, too."

Jinx grunted in agreement but didn't reply. When the bartender returned, he shifted his focus back to the pictures, memorizing faces, names, nationalities, and known connections.

Forty percent of Ortega's men, he recognized. The other sixty percent were new, fresh meat drawn in by promises of power and money. It was the way of the cartel. Loyalty meant nothing. Life expectancy meant even less.

He drained the last of his beer, warm now and bitter, when the sound of fast engines shattered the stillness outside. Black SUVs rumbled to a stop in front of the cantina, their exhaust fumes curling into the air like snakes.

Jinx rose, moving to the bar just as the woman glanced toward the street.

"If you want to avoid trouble," she murmured, her voice low, "you should leave now. There's a back door."

"I know. Another beer, please," Jinx said calmly, placing more cash on the bar.

She gave him a long, measuring look. Something flickered in her dark eyes, recognition, maybe, or wariness, before she shook her head and turned to the tap to pour him another drink.

The door creaked open behind him.

A mangy dog slunk in off the street, ribs sharp beneath matted fur, tail wagging nervously. It made a beeline for Jinx like it recognized one of its own. Jinx crouched, scratching behind the animal's ears as two SUVs' doors slammed shut outside, followed by crude laughter and the sharp, grating sound of men who thought they owned the world.

The dog tucked itself behind Jinx's legs as the men filed into the cantina, swaggering and loud.

Until they saw him.

The room shifted, voices dying like someone had sucked the air out of the place. Jinx smiled to himself and lifted his beer, taking a slow sip.

It was always good when the wolves recognized there was a viper in their midst.

One of the men pushed through the crowd, muscling his way toward the bar. Jinx slanted a glance his way and felt recognition flash cold and sharp through his veins.

Newer enforcer. Fresh blood. A bastard, if Brando's files were to be believed, and they always were. That one had a reputation. A video, even. He'd made his bones on the dark web, carving a family apart with a machete. He forced the wife to watch as he mutilated her husband and sons before killing them. A coward with a taste for violence only when his victims were already broken.

Jinx met his gaze over the rim of his beer, his smile sharp and cold.

The bastard would do.

The man squared his shoulders, hitching up his jeans like he thought it made him bigger, meaner. His eyes locked on Jinx at the bar. Jinx could feel the fucker zero in on him. He couldn't have scripted it any better.

"Hey, you! This ain't your bar. You need to leave."

Jinx didn't even glance his way. He set his beer down with a quiet clink, staring at the glass like it had more of his attention than the fool running his mouth.

"I said, leave," the man barked, stepping closer. "Do you not hear me?" The man's hand clamped down on Jinx's shoulder.

Mistake.

Jinx reacted in a split second, faster than breath. He spun, automatic in hand, and pressed the barrel to the man's temple. Before anyone could process what was happening, Jinx pulled the trigger.

The man's body crumpled to the floor in a heap.

Without hesitation, Jinx drew his second automatic, leveling it at a man he recognized. A messenger boy from back in the day, before Jinx had walked away from this nightmare.

"Tell them to back the fuck off," Jinx ordered, his voice low, razor-sharp.

Recognition flared in the man's eyes. "Mateo? Holy hell … Mateo, is that you?"

"Mateo? What? Who?" another man said, gaping at the corpse on the floor. His voice shook. "Ortega's gonna order us to kill this bastard." The man motioned toward Jinx.

Jinx's revolver shifted instantly, pressing hard against the second man's forehead. He stepped close, invading the man's space like death itself. "One more word," Jinx said softly, dangerously, "and you're dead."

Behind him, the stray dog whimpered and then yelped. "Move, fucking mutt." The bastard had kicked the defenseless animal. Jinx's instincts flared. His revolver snapped to the side and fired without hesitation.

Another man dropped like a stone.

He was back on target with his forty-five before anyone understood what happened. "Anyone else care to test me or kick an innocent animal?" Jinx asked, voice dripping ice.

The first man, the one who'd recognized him, threw his hands up, palms wide in surrender. "Mateo, yo … we're cool. We're cool! Ain't nobody gonna bother you or the dog. Right, guys? This is Mateo Rivas. Enforcer from Montoya's time. *The* Mateo, man. You've heard stories about this guy, and they're all fucking true."

As one, the men seemed to back off. Hands moved away from weapons, and tension eased. Jinx's gaze narrowed on the young man in front of him.

"I know you," Jinx said finally. "You were a messenger when I left."

The man straightened his shoulders, puffing up like he wanted to prove himself. "That's right. My name's Diego. I'm an enforcer now." His fingers hovered near the weapons strapped at his waist as if Jinx couldn't tell who he was pretending to be.

Jinx stepped back toward the bar, holstered one of his revolvers, and reached for his half-finished beer. He took a long, casual sip, then nodded toward the bodies cooling on the tile floor.

"Get your trash out of here."

Diego repeated the command without hesitation, and the others moved quickly, almost too quickly, dragging their fallen companions out the door. Jinx watched and noted each man's face. The one who'd talked to Eira yesterday wasn't present. Several older men were missing from what he could see, but then again, so was an SUV. They were probably going to get Ortega's dog from Eira. He thanked God that Raven was there. Not that he doubted Eira could take care of herself, but Raven would ensure she wouldn't have to do so.

Jinx pulled a wad of cash from his pocket and dropped it on the bar without looking at the woman behind it. "For your troubles. And the cleanup."

The woman didn't say a word. She took the money and wiped the stained countertop, her gaze flicking nervously toward the door as if she were expecting someone else. He was, too. The third SUV hadn't arrived and with all the junior people in this bar now, the older, more deadly people had yet to make their presence known.

Diego lingered beside Jinx, voice low. "Where've you been, man?"

Jinx cast him a sideways glance, his mouth twisting into something that wasn't quite a smile. "Other countries. Other wars."

The man's expression tightened. "Ortega will want to see you. Maybe bring you into the fold. You'd be one hell of an asset."

"Ortega?" Jinx snorted, the sound more lethal than amused.

Diego nodded slowly. "He's El Jefe now."

Jinx watched as the remaining cartel men quietly claimed their seats, their bravado stripped bare. None of them moved fast. None of them reached for weapons. That might've had something to do with the revolver still resting loose and easy in his hand. One held a cell phone and was pointing it toward him. He lifted his automatic. "Delete the fucking picture now, or I'll do it after you're dead."

The man dropped the phone, and it clattered on the wooden tabletop. The guilty look and hard swallow that followed told Jinx he'd been right. "I said delete the fucker."

"Andres, give me the phone," Diego said, walking across the room to snatch the phone away. "I've warned all of you. This man will kill you, and he won't lose any sleep doing it." The man held up the phone so Jinx could see it as he deleted the picture of him. "Done." He tossed the phone back. "I'm done trying to keep your asses alive."

Diego walked back to him and leaned against the bar, facing away from his coworkers.

"How'd Ortega become king?" Jinx asked.

"It was a bad war, man," the enforcer replied. "Lots of killing. Somehow, Ortega came out on top."

"Yeah?" Jinx's tone dripped with disbelief. "And who funded his ass? No one I knew would've backed him."

The man's eyes darted around, checking if anyone had overheard. He edged closer, lowering his voice. "Mateo, don't start that. Not here. I'll talk to you later when nobody's around. Don't trust anyone." The kid lifted his fingers, and the woman returned, handing him a beer.

Jinx fought the urge to roll his eyes. It hadn't

taken long for Ortega's men to start turning on him. That was the thing about tyrants, they never inspired loyalty.

He shifted, watched the woman leave, and kept his voice low and quiet. "What about the faction in the low foothills?"

The enforcer damn near jumped out of his skin, grabbing the glass he'd almost knocked over. *Damn, did that hit a nerve?* Diego swallowed hard and shook his head. "I don't know anything about them."

The answer came too quickly, too defensively. Jinx sneered to himself, sharp and discerning. The kid knew more than he was revealing. Things were stirring beneath the surface. Alliances, betrayals, secrets that hadn't yet seen the light of day. The environment remained the same. The players had changed, but Jinx would uncover the answers he sought. It was merely a matter of time.

Within thirty minutes, the third black SUV rumbled to a stop in front of the cantina.

There were no revving engines, no laughter, no shouting that time. The doors opened and closed silently. They were sharp, efficient sounds that carried weight. Three men entered the dim, sweltering bar, their steps measured and deliberate.

Trailing them on a taut leash was the Malinois

that had been recovering at Eira's. The sleek, muscular dog's sharp eyes scanned the room like a soldier trained for war. The scrappy stray that had claimed Jinx earlier skittered toward the back of the cantina, tail tucked tight, sensing trouble and wanting no part of it.

The man in the middle peeled off his sunglasses with slow precision. His gaze swept the room once before locking onto Jinx like a laser sight.

That one, Jinx knew.

Simón.

They'd worked together in Montoya's cartel. Simón was a bloodthirsty, batshit crazy bastard and, ironically, one of the few men Jinx knew who hated Ortega more than he did.

The man at Simón's left was the bastard who'd threatened Eira.

And the third...Jinx's gaze flicked to him. That was the driver Eira had asked to bring the poisoned Malinois to her hospital. Jinx knew all of them. Knew what they were capable of and what atrocities they'd committed. Brando's intel had painted a clear picture.

Simón didn't waste time. His sharp voice cut across the quiet like a blade. "What the fuck did they do, and why did you kill them?"

The question was directed squarely at Jinx.

Still hovering near him at the bar, Diego started to speak, but Jinx halted him with a glance and a slight shake of his head.

"They were stupid in public. You found out quickly." Jinx said coolly. "Isn't that still a death sentence around here?"

Simón's eyebrows rose, and a slow, dangerous smile crept across his face. "Fuckers are laid out on the street. Kind of obvious. Everyone said you were dead."

"Everyone was wrong. Again." Jinx took another sip of his beer, letting the statement hang heavy between them. "You aren't training your men to use their manners."

Simón snorted, shaking his head, and strode to the bar with the Malinois at his side. "Beer," he barked at the woman, who hustled to comply. He turned back to Jinx, one brow lifted. "It ain't my job to train them. And who the fuck uses manners anymore?" His eyes flicked to Diego. "Give us some space."

Diego moved quickly without question, wisely fading back toward the far wall.

The Malinois sat obediently at Simón's side but

stared unblinkingly at Jinx. Its muscles were tight, poised. Jinx slowly extended his hand.

The dog leaned forward, sniffed, then licked his fingers.

Simón's laugh was a rough bark of sound. "Fuck, man. I would've bet a hundred American dollars that bastard would've taken your hand off instead of licking it."

"I've got an affinity for animals," Jinx murmured, scratching behind the dog's ear before shifting his attention back to Simón. "You one of Ortega's officers now?"

Simón rolled his eyes and grunted. "Pretty fucking obvious. Did you get dumber while you were gone?"

"No. Richer," Jinx replied without missing a beat. "But I've got unfinished business here."

Simón's eyes gleamed darkly. "Eira. And your bastard."

The smile slid clean off Jinx's face. He straightened, the sharp edges of his posture radiating lethal energy. His voice dropped low, a blade in the air. "If her name comes out of your mouth again, I'll cut your tongue out, cook it, and eat it." It wasn't a threat. It was a promise. Jinx closed the distance between them in a blink, their faces inches apart, the tension in the cantina so thick it could've been cut with a knife. The air felt heavier than the suffocating Venezuelan humidity pressing against the cracked plaster walls.

Simón let out a sharp, dry laugh and took a long drink of his beer, unfazed. When he set the glass down, he shook his head. "There's the cold-hearted bastard I knew. Thought maybe you'd gone all soft and squishy on us. How the hell did we not know you were fucking her?"

"What I do, or don't do, isn't your business," Jinx shot back. Every muscle in his body vibrated with the need to put Simón on the floor, but he forced himself to stay still. He needed this man as an ally, not a corpse.

Simón's gaze shifted, voice dropping low again. "Well, your business didn't used to be my concern. Now, it is. She told me you were back. Now I have to fucking tell the spineless bastard I work for." His words slowed, each one a loaded bullet. "Ortega wants your woman. She's held him off so far, but he's … anxious to have her."

Jinx's blood froze in his veins. He turned his head slowly, very slowly, to look at Simón. His voice came out like death itself. "That will end in Ortega's death."

Simón said nothing, taking another long pull from his beer. He stared out the dirty window behind the bar as if he hadn't just delivered his boss's death sentence.

"How did he take the helm?" Jinx asked just as quietly.

Simón shrugged one shoulder. "No idea. He's keeping it with money. Lots of money."

"Loyalty?" Jinx asked quietly, taking another sip of his warm beer. The Malinois leaned subtly against his leg like it sensed the storm brewing.

Simón chuckled darkly. "About as loyal as that fucking dog."

Jinx's gaze flicked to the group in the far corner of the cantina. The cartel's low-level enforcers pretending to mind their own business, but their eyes tracking every movement. They couldn't hear the conversation. No one could, except Brando, and no doubt it was being recorded to be dissected after Jinx finished.

"So, the military faction will be taking over soon," Jinx said flatly. It wasn't a question.

"Not so sure about that," Simón murmured, his gaze cutting sideways toward him. "Be careful, Mateo. There's shit happening around here that I don't understand. There's someone else, and I have no idea who the fuck it is."

"The military assholes." Jinx filled in the name of the entity.

Simón glanced around. "Not them. Something is brewing." He glanced at Jinx. "Are you staying at Eira's?"

His defenses flared again. "I am. Why?"

Simón lowered his voice even further. "We need to talk."

Jinx nodded. "Where?"

Simón drew a deep breath. "Meet me at the abandoned farm west of Eira's tomorrow night. I won't be missed for a while. They'll think I'm fucking my woman."

"You have a woman." Jinx leaned forward. "Are you going to take her out of here?"

"I'm working on it. If she disappears, it'll be noticed. But I have to figure something out. I'm not sure any of us will be alive this time next year." Simón held his beer in front of his lips as he continued in a whisper, "You picked the wrong time to come back, my friend." He finished his drink before pushing off the bar and tugging on the Malinois's leash, guiding the dog away from Jinx.

Before Simón reached the door, he glanced back

over his shoulder. His voice was sharp and clear, leaving no room for misinterpretation.

"This man is off limits. You fuck with him, you answer to me. That is, if he doesn't kill you first."

The weight of the statement settled over the room like a cloud. It shocked the hell out of Jinx, and judging by the stiffening of shoulders and the glances traded among Ortega's enforcers, it had rattled them, too. They shifted uneasily, casting nervous looks between Simón and Jinx like they weren't sure which one of them had just become more dangerous.

Across the room, Diego met Jinx's gaze but didn't move to approach. Smart kid. Smarter than Jinx had initially given him credit for.

Simón's warning had just bought Jinx something unexpected.

Protection from Ortega's officers. And that was a double-edged blade. It might keep some cartel dogs off his back in the short term, but it also tangled him tighter into their web. Yet it was a snare that could unravel everything he was trying to do.

He took a slow sip of his beer, scanning the room, memorizing every face, every reaction. The whisper network would already be spinning. By nightfall, the entire area would know he was back, alive, and under Simón's protection. And once the military faction caught wind of it … well, they'd reach out.

And if they didn't?

He'd make sure they had no choice.

The weight of the room pressed on him, the stale air heavy with sweat, smoke, and barely concealed fear. Brando's voice crackled in his ear, dry and laced with dark humor. "Can't we just take a bomb and blow up the military assholes? Let God sort them out."

It took everything Jinx had not to smile at Brando's feigned exhaustion. Instead, he dipped his head slightly, speaking low into the mouth of his beer glass.

"Not certain, but I don't think He wants to deal with them either."

However, a move that grand would shake the entire region to its core. It could be useful if things didn't pan out the way he anticipated. A statement. Jinx was already calculating how best to do exactly that.

CHAPTER 14

Eira glanced at Teo, who stood on the framed stool she'd made for him. It was a standing playpen that was needed. Teo wanted to do everything she did, and she didn't want him to fall, so she used scrap wood to make the contraption. He played with his wooden spoon and small pots as she worked over the stove's heat. She heard Mateo come into the house. She knew it was him. Raven had told her he was on his way back. How the woman knew that was beyond her, but how they communicated wasn't her concern, although it was curious. Cell phones only worked in certain areas because of the sparsity of towers in the area.

She glanced over her shoulder to see Mateo

leaning against the doorway, arms crossed, watching them.

"Here." She reached over and tossed him a bag of cornmeal. "You can help. Do you remember how to make arepas?"

Mateo didn't answer. Instead, he stepped into the cramped space and pulled down a bowl from the shelf. "How many are eating?" he asked as he opened the cornmeal.

"Mom is at Tia Louisa's today. She's not feeling well, so she is making food and cleaning. Uncle Ruben will bring her back when he comes for the milk tonight. So, just the four of us."

"Three. Raven is on an errand."

Eira glanced over at him. "What kind of errand?"

Mateo shrugged. "We need some pictures."

"As in drawings?" she asked as she grabbed a spoon to stir the beans she was cooking.

"As in photos," Mateo said. He sprinkled some of the cornmeal into the small bowl Teo was playing with. Teo smiled up at his father. Eira's heart almost stopped. The boy didn't even question Mateo's presence. He was eighteen months old, and while he could say a few words, he was still mostly pointing and grunting or laughing.

They worked together in the kitchen the way

they had years ago. Falling into a rhythm formed over countless nights cooking their dinners together.

When he finished, the arepas were a little too thick, and a couple were too well cooked. She hid a smile and corrected herself, no, they were burned, but plenty weren't and looked good. Teo sat on her lap while they ate. She tore apart an arepa and blew on the inside to cool it before she stuffed it with a small amount of cheese and beans. Teo took it from her and started to eat it.

"I thought he would still be on a bottle?" Mateo said as he watched Teo eat the food. Mateo reached out with stunning speed, catching a large portion of Teo's arepa that fell. The little boy took the food from Mateo's hand and shoved it into his mouth.

She chuckled at the drop and food smash. "He takes a bottle only when he's inconsolable. It's more comfort for him now than necessity. He'll be completely weaned soon."

Mateo stopped with his food halfway to his mouth. "Is that good for him? Does he need formula or something? I can get some."

She smiled and shook her head. "No. He's eating foods like this. Everything has to be cut small so he doesn't choke. But he's fine."

Mateo nodded and ate his food with the gusto she remembered. The man could consume a mountain of food. They ate while also giving Teo bites of everything. "Could you hold him so I can get him some milk?" She stood up and held Teo out.

"I can get it," Mateo said. A look of complete terror crossed his face.

"He won't bite you, Mateo." She dropped her son into his father's lap, got a glass, and poured some fresh, raw milk into the cup. She glanced over her shoulder and smiled as Mateo's hands guarded his son but didn't touch him. She chuckled. "He won't break."

"Are you sure?" Mateo asked. "He's so small."

Eira turned to him and smiled, saying, "He's a big boy."

Teo looked up at Mateo and parroted, "Beeg boy."

Mateo blinked, and then a wide smile formed across his face. "He talks?"

"Sure. He can't talk in full sentences, but he knows words and can parrot. So, no curse words," she warned as she set the glass in front of Teo.

The boy reached with both hands and brought it to his mouth. He slurped and sloshed the milk but drank his fill without Mateo wearing the rest of it before offering it to Mateo. Taking the cup from him, Mateo set it on the table, then wiped off the milk mustache with his finger. "I missed so much."

"You have." Eira wasn't going to let him off the hook. But she wasn't going to beat a dead horse, either. It was a fact. He'd missed so many milestones.

Mateo was quiet for a long moment. "How long has the farm to the west been abandoned?"

Eira blinked at the question. "Over a year. They loaded up their truck and left. I don't know where they went. Why?"

"Simón wants to meet me," Mateo said as Teo turned and slithered down his legs to the floor.

He lifted his arms while walking to her. "Momma, up."

She lifted him up, and he tucked his head under her chin. "Yeah, it's almost nap time, isn't it?" Eira rubbed the baby's back and glanced at Mateo. "I'll be back."

"Can I help?" he said and stood up, picking up the plates off the table.

"Put him down?" She frowned.

"Yes. I should know how to do that, shouldn't I?" Mateo looked at her. The sincerity in his eyes almost floored her.

"If you'd like, sure." She went into the bedroom. Mateo took the cloth diaper from her and changed

Teo before picking him back up. He sat in the chair with his son. "What do you do now?"

"Sing him a song."

Mateo chuckled and began singing a lullaby she suspected was American. He hummed some of the words that he probably couldn't recall. When he was done, she took Teo from him and laid him down in his crib. He fussed for a moment but quickly lost the battle to stay awake.

She kissed his soft hair, and Mateo did the same. They left the small room and she closed the door behind her. She leaned against the door and watched him walk back into the kitchen. It took her a few moments to swallow the emotion that had built in her chest as she'd silently watched father and son. *Please, don't hurt us.* She drew several deep breaths and pushed her shoulders back before she walked into the kitchen.

Mateo was cleaning the dishes when she walked back into the kitchen. "Why would Simón want to meet with you?"

Mateo shrugged. "I don't know. He's the only person who detests Ortega as much as I do. Did you know he has a woman?"

"Yeah. Adriana. She lives in town. Her husband died in the wars. Simón has paid for her house and has food for her delivered from Ortega's convoys. She's ostracized because of it. A kept woman. I talk to her because we're both tainted. She really is a nice lady."

Mateo stilled, and he slowly turned his head toward her. "Say what?"

Eira blinked and looked at him. "A baby out of wedlock. The people here don't say it as openly as they do about Adriana, but the religious implications are the same."

He straightened, and she could sense an anger rising in him. "Has anyone treated you badly?"

"Badly? No. My family knew what you were, although they didn't tell me until later after you'd left." She took a dish towel and wiped the dishes he'd washed, setting them back in the stack on the shelf. "Your reputation kept things to cold shoulders, whispers as I pass, things like that." She shrugged. "As you'd expect."

"I wouldn't expect that at all." Mateo handed her the last bowl, and she wiped it and placed it in the small cupboard. "We can marry immediately."

Eira snorted. "Not likely."

"Why not?" Mateo frowned.

"Oh, I don't know." Eira crossed her arms and looked at him. "Why don't you take a guess?"

"Listen, this wouldn't be for me. It wouldn't be a way to edge myself back into your life. I would give you my name in a heartbeat." Facing her, he put his hands on her hips before quickly removing them as if he'd forgotten he didn't have that privilege anymore. "No one should look down at you. Especially because of me."

"Too late." She shrugged. "I need to go collect the eggs while Teo is sleeping."

"Do you need help?"

She stopped and looked back at him. "Do you know how to gather eggs?"

Mateo frowned. "I can be taught. Will he be okay alone?"

She nodded. "He's going to be out for at least an hour and a half. Gathering and sorting the eggs will take twenty or thirty minutes, and I can hear him if he cries. The window is open a crack."

"Sort?" Mateo asked as he fell into step with her.

"Some I keep for hatching. Most go to Ortega's men. What I can keep, we use, and I give to family."

"How does Ortega get the eggs?" Mateo asked as he walked through the chickens, pecking at the gravel. The flock knew it was time to be fed, and they followed or darted between their feet as they walked. She laughed at the way Mateo almost tiptoed through the hens.

"They'll get out of your way," she said as he almost tripped, trying to step around one of her chickens. "He gets a supply convoy every other day or so. They stop by, bring me empty cartons, and take the ones I have for them. I don't talk to them, and they don't talk to me."

He grunted something, and she picked up a bucket, then went over to a sealed garbage barrel and scooped out some feed. She filled the feeder and asked Mateo to get them some water from the rain barrel. When they were done, she opened the coop's door, and they walked in. She handed him a basket.

"They might peck you if they're laying on the eggs, but they won't hurt."

"Good to know," Mateo said as they moved through the nesting area. It was a good yield. It normally was. The days were long, and there was plenty of sun to keep the hens laying eggs. She put most of the eggs into the old cartons on a small table. A huge tree shaded the small work area and was pleasant, even in the midday heat.

"You've done well here," he said as they filled the cartons.

She glanced around. "I'd leave it." And she would if she had a way to support her family.

Mateo stopped placing eggs and looked up at her. "Then let me take you away."

She nodded. "When it's time, we'll go. But not until then." She looked up at him. "You said you'd give me time."

Mateo reached out and tucked a piece of hair that had escaped her braid behind her ear. "We've got the rest of our lives. I won't rush you. I told you that, and yes, while it's still relatively safe here, I'll honor my word."

"And I'll honor mine. When you or Raven tells me it's time to leave, we will."

Mateo smiled and leaned down, pressing a kiss against her lips. She shouldn't let him continue doing that, but it was the most warmth she'd felt in years. This was the man she remembered. The gentle giant who'd always treated her like she was a treasure. This was the Mateo she loved. Her eyes popped open at the thought.

He cocked his head and frowned. "What?"

She frowned and shook her head. "Nothing. Nothing ... did I hear Teo?" She turned and headed to the house. "I'll be back in a minute."

She was acting like a chicken, but the emotion

coursing through her needed to be processed alone, not in front of Mateo. She hadn't stopped loving the man. She couldn't deny that, no matter the circumstances of his return. She closed the screen door behind her and dropped onto the old, worn couch. "Why couldn't you be a farmer?" She huffed out a bitter laugh. If he were a farmer, he'd be dead. No, the man he was was the man he needed to be for him to survive while doing his job. And because he was who he was, she was alive, prospering, and out of Ortega's reach.

She stared up at the ceiling. "Wow," she whispered and then closed her eyes. He was who he needed to be. He was the Mateo she knew and, more, the Mateo he needed to be to protect them. The reality of that thought settled against her heart.

Could she forgive him? No, because there was nothing to forgive. He did what he'd thought was best. His reasons, his actions, and his absence were all orchestrated to protect her. And he had. He always had.

CHAPTER 15

Jinx stood hidden in the shadows of a weathered outbuilding as the sun dipped low over the Venezuelan horizon, staining the sky in rich shades of orange and violet. The humid air clung to his skin, heavy with the scents of dust, hay, and distant smoke. The meeting time wasn't for some time, but he'd arrived early on purpose. Trust wasn't a luxury he could afford, not when Simón was involved.

Jinx leaned against the rough lumber as he thought of the last two days with Eira and Teo. There had been a subtle shift in her attitude toward him. He prayed that she remembered his love for her and perhaps was letting down her guard. If she would give him a chance, he'd prove he was worthy of her love.

Raven's voice crackled over the comms. "I told you, the perimeter's clear. No one's followed him," she reported, the casual confidence in her tone starkly contrasting the tension twisting Jinx's gut.

Brando chimed in, his voice slightly distorted. "She's right. Satellite only shows you and Raven within a half-mile radius of the ranch."

"Where do we stand on identification of the personnel in the military unit?" Raven asked.

Brando groaned. "It's not easy working with a third-world country's identification system."

"You mean they *have* identification systems?" Raven teased dryly.

Brando chuckled. "They have what I would call a … collection of photographs. As far as actual technology goes? That's debatable. Their passport system is modern enough, though. I've been cross-referencing through that. Had to use AI to fill out faces and guess characteristics based on the photos you sent."

Raven huffed. "Hey now, I'm a damn good photographer. It's the subjects who're lacking."

"Yeah, okay, we'll go with that." Brando laughed again before quickly sobering to ask, "Jinx, what do you want me to do about transport for Eira and her family?"

Leaning back against the rough wooden wall of the shack at the edge of the farm, Jinx glanced upward. Stars were beginning to prick through the bruised colors of twilight, scattering across the sky like tiny silver promises he didn't deserve. He exhaled slowly.

"She'll leave," he said quietly, "but not until I can tell her for sure that things are about to get bad. I believe she wants to prepare the family to take over the business."

"Is she going to tell the family what's going on?" Raven asked. "Because that's gonna leave a lot of questions, and if it leaks back to Ortega's cartel, it could turn real ugly."

Jinx shook his head, even though she couldn't see him. "No. From what she told me today, she's just working on a list of chores. Things they need to do to care for the animals on the farm."

"Yeah, that sounds like something you'd do, too," Raven teased. "I'm honestly surprised you haven't adopted the whole damn herd of milk cows."

Jinx chuckled low in his throat. "If they were being mistreated, I'd find a way to get them back to my ranch."

Brando laughed. "Yeah, Fury would have *so* much fun with that."

Raven giggled, but the lighthearted moment snapped away when Brando's voice cut in sharply.

"You've got a truck incoming."

Instantly alert, Jinx slipped deeper into the shadows, pressing against the cool side of the shack. The comms went dead silent. He watched as the vehicle, a black SUV, the kind Ortega's men favored, rumbled into the front clearing of the small ranch house. Dust curled up around the tires before settling back to the parched earth.

The headlights blinked off, plunging the yard into twilight gloom. A single figure stepped out and moved to the front of the vehicle, standing still.

"He's the only heat signature I see," Raven said quietly over the comms. She'd obviously switched to infrared.

Jinx let the silence stretch for a heartbeat longer before moving. His steps were silent on the dirt, his presence a whisper in the thick night air. He closed the distance until he was barely four feet away before Simón finally heard him and spun around, eyes wide.

"Jesus, man, you're like a fucking ghost!" Simón

gasped, hand twitching toward his side before he realized Jinx hadn't drawn a weapon.

Jinx merely lifted his arms in a loose shrug. "Benefits of the trade, I guess."

Simón swallowed and shifted uneasily.

"Why did you want this meeting?" Jinx asked, his voice low and sharp.

Simón ran a hand through his sweat-dampened hair, his posture edgy under the oppressive heat. "Several reasons," Simón began. "When I told Ortega you were back, he—" Simón placed his hands on his hips, searching for words. "Well, I don't know how to explain it. The man's paranoid. Like ... he thinks the boogeyman's hiding under his bed."

Simón chuckled nervously, but Jinx didn't crack a smile.

"But his paranoia's not unfounded," Simón continued, lowering his voice. "After he kicked me out for telling him I hadn't brought Eira back, and that you were the reason why I was empty handed, I gave him some time, I went back later, hoping he'd cooled off. I caught him on the phone. The speaker was on." Simón shook his head in disgust. "The man's a moron. Broadcasting shit like that."

Jinx silently agreed. Ortega's recklessness had always been one of his greatest weaknesses, and a dangerous liability now. Jinx studied Simón carefully, watching the man cross his arms and spit into the dusty ground.

"I don't know who he was talking to," Simón said, his mouth twisting in disgust. "But whoever it was, that person was inside the military unit. The way they talked ... it was like Ortega has a man embedded. They discussed your connections, or possible connections, and how you might be useful."

Simón paused, his gaze cutting to Jinx with a rare flash of seriousness. "The guy in the military said he needed to make some calls. He wanted information on your whereabouts for the time you were not here. About your connections ... and whether you could help him with *his* ultimate goal." Simón stopped, shifting on his boots, dust swirling around his ankles. "Not Ortega's goal," he added meaningfully.

Jinx stiffened. That small clarification changed everything.

"I left as soon as Ortega hung up," Simón continued. "But about twenty minutes later, he called me back to his office. He told me it would be a couple of weeks before he approached you...one way or the other. He wants to see if you're back in Venezuela for profit or family."

Jinx rubbed the back of his neck, feeling the

sticky heat of the night pressing down. Two or three weeks. He could work with that. It wasn't ideal, but it bought him time.

The bigger problem was Ortega having an inside man in the military. Whether he controlled or worked alongside that man would complicate everything. Jinx made a mental note to put extra pressure on Brando to identify the unknown players.

"You said there were *reasons* you wanted this meeting," Jinx prompted, eyeing Simón with renewed suspicion.

Simón hesitated, then said, "I know you killed Montoya."

Jinx was a master at not reacting to dangerous statements. He kept his face utterly still, breathing slow and measured.

Simón chuckled dryly. "Really. And I know because I was with Montoya's mistress the night he died. She told me she didn't think he'd be living much longer."

Jinx's brow furrowed slightly. That *was* unexpected.

"Why's that?" he asked, voice low.

"Because she said she told *you* that Montoya was alone that week. And then, suddenly, your shift was swapped. Which it was. I took it. And that night,

Montoya was killed." Simón's grin was humorless. "I'm glad she warned me. Saved my ass from the bloodbath that happened after the news broke. As soon as people found out he was assassinated, the fighting started. Everyone scrambling for power."

He kicked the dirt again, uneasy. The sound of insects buzzing filled the thick, humid night.

"I knew when my shift ended, I needed to disappear. I'm not too proud to admit it. I went to my mistress's house and stayed low until most of the bloodshed was over. I threw in my loyalty card when I saw who was winning."

Simón shook his head with a bitter laugh. "Unfortunately, it was that fucker Ortega being propped up. Had access to arms, money, and men. Suppose he had a man in the military. That explains how he pulled it off. He had the muscle, information, and firepower to take control from guys who were way stronger than him."

Simón rubbed the back of his neck, looking away for a moment. "I'm willing to make a deal with you, Mateo," he said, his voice dropping into something almost pleading. "I'll keep you informed … leave notes in the old mailbox here at this ranch. No one uses this place anymore, and it's on my way to see my woman. No one will think it's strange I'm driving this way."

Jinx narrowed his eyes. "Why would you do that?"

Simón scuffed his boot against the dry earth. "Before you take out Ortega, give me one day's notice. Just one. My woman and I can disappear. I've got some money saved. We can be gone if you just give me the time." He hesitated, then added, "And I can keep Ortega's people away from Eira's place, too. I can let you know if Ortega starts moaning about wanting her at the compound again. If you want to get her out, you'll have a warning."

Jinx stared at the man for a long, silent moment. The heavy Venezuelan night wrapped around them, thick with the scent of rain brewing somewhere beyond the jungle.

Simón shifted nervously under the weight of Jinx's gaze. "Dude, I've told you everything I know. I've laid it all out on the line for you. You could go to Ortega tomorrow and sell me out, and I'd be dead. I'm trusting you here."

Jinx understood just how precarious a position Simón had put himself in. Finally, he extended his hand. Simón grasped it quickly, the handshake firm and sweaty under the oppressive heat.

"You have my word," Jinx said.

Simón nodded, and Jinx could almost see the tension drain from his body.

"Good," Simón exhaled, relief raw in his voice. "That's good."

He stepped back, glancing once more at Jinx. "I know there's no honor among thieves," Simón said, "but there *is* honor among men who must fight to live. I'm trusting your honor, Mateo."

With that, Simón turned and walked back to his truck. By the time he climbed inside, Jinx had already disappeared into the shadows, swallowed by the night.

The engine rumbled to life. The truck's headlights cut through the gloom as Simón pulled a tight U-turn and headed left, back toward the small town, and to his mistress.

Raven's voice crackled over the comms. "He said you were going to kill Ortega. Why would he think that?"

Jinx smirked faintly, even though no one could see it.

"Because he knows I'd be a better leader," Jinx said. "And he knows I'd get Eira out of here before the war starts. I'd make sure she's safe." He toggled his comm. "Brando, get me an ID on those photos. Stat."

“Roger that. I’m calling in the big guns. We’ll get them to you ASAP," Brando confirmed.

Jinx turned and began making his way back across the fields, the ground soft under his boots. The night air smelled of damp earth and growing things, a reminder of the jungle pressing in just beyond the cleared farmland.

Raven fell into step beside him, her movements silent and catlike. "I’m going back to the small house," she said. "Eira’s mom still isn’t home. From what I understand, the aunt’s not doing well."

Jinx grunted in acknowledgment. Eira had told him as much earlier, and worry had clouded her beautiful eyes. They’d sent for a doctor, but the man still hadn’t arrived.

"Be safe," Jinx said, his voice rougher than intended.

"Always," Raven replied with a small smirk, veering off toward the Land Cruiser she’d parked in a hidden spot nearby. Moments later, the comms went silent.

CHAPTER 16

Three days later, Jinx sat down on the worn wooden bench outside the small house, the thick night air curling around him, rich with the scent of damp earth and blooming night jasmine. He could hear Eira's soft voice floating through the open window, talking to Teo, and a small smile tugged at the corner of his mouth.

She was such a good mother to his son.

The work on the little ranch was hard. Damn hard. They were up before the sun to bring in and feed the cows as they hand-milked the small herd. Eira's cousin was now fetching the milk while her uncle was with his wife and Eira's mother. The woman had continued to decline. After they milked and turned out the cows, they moved to the chickens. Gathering the eggs was a full-time gig. Having Teo help them with the chore made it all the more enjoyable. He had a chicken that would come and sit on his lap, and he'd feed them by throwing small handfuls of grain about six inches from his feet. He'd giggle as they pecked around him. The joy on the boy's face was mirrored in Eira's. It was a memory he wanted to store forever.

He wanted so badly to take Eira away, to wipe out the years of backbreaking work she'd poured into this small farm. Not her accomplishments. Those were hers and should be honored, but the ceaseless grind that had worn her down. She was milking cows in the battered barn if she wasn't feeding chickens or gathering eggs, cleaning, washing, or cooking simple, honest meals, always moving, always working.

Earlier, he'd watched her uncle's old transport truck rumble down the dusty road. The uncle avoided him, but the younger family members didn't seem to care about his reputation. That was either exponentially stupid, or they'd been told he was caring for Eira, her mom, and Teo. He hoped it was the latter. People survived by having suspicions and keeping dangerous people at a wide berth. He waved at her cousin as the truck disappeared into the night.

Eira's mother had made it clear she wouldn't return until her sister was better.

So, it would be Eira and Teo alone here for the foreseeable future if Ortega made his move.

Alone? No. Raven would stay nearby, keeping watch during the times Jinx couldn't. She spent nights at the small house, to give Jinx space.

He knew exactly what that meant, but he didn't fool himself. He didn't expect anything between him and Eira to turn physical. Not yet. Maybe not ever.

He'd shattered her trust. He was doing everything he could to rebuild it, brick by painful brick. But trust wasn't built overnight. And no matter how good his intentions had been, the truth was brutal: By thinking he was protecting her, he'd robbed himself of this time of his son's life, and with the woman he loved.

The creak of the door pulled him from his thoughts.

Eira stepped out onto the porch, holding Teo's small hand as he toddled beside her. Jinx's heart twisted painfully at the sight.

When Teo saw him, the boy's face lit up. He toddled straight toward Jinx, patted his knees insistently, and said, "Up!"...or something close to it.

Jinx carefully reached down and scooped the

little boy into his arms. He was heavier than Jinx expected for such a small kid, but Teo settled easily into his lap, spinning once like a puppy before curling up against Jinx's chest with a contented sigh, thumb finding its way into his mouth.

The first time that had happened, Jinx had frozen, gone completely still, unsure of what to do next. Now, he easily draped his arm around the little boy and held him securely. Teo let out a deep, sleepy sigh, opened his eyes briefly, giggled at absolutely nothing, then closed them again.

Eira chuckled softly and sat down beside Jinx on the bench, close enough he could feel the brush of her warmth.

"The stars are always so brilliant here," Jinx said, tipping his head back to stare at the sky. Above them, a million pinpoints of light scattered across the velvet dark, clear and untainted by city glare. "Nothing like this in the cities in America. Too much light pollution."

"They're not as bright in the city. Only the brightest peek through," Eira agreed. She tucked her legs up onto the bench, leaning sideways until her feet brushed his thigh. Without thinking, Jinx reached down, grasped her ankle, and gently pulled her legs across his lap, lifting Teo out of the way to do it.

She smiled softly, letting him arrange her legs as she crossed them at the ankle. Teo patted his mother's foot and mumbled something around his thumb.

Jinx glanced at Eira, raising a brow. "What did he say?"

She laughed lightly, the sound wrapping around him like a balm. "I have no idea. Sometimes, I think he just talks in ... baby."

Jinx chuckled quietly, soothingly running his hand along her calf, savoring the closeness.

"How hard was it for you without me here?" he asked, voice low.

Eira sighed and propped her head against her hand, her elbow resting on the back of the bench. Her silhouette was bathed in soft silver light from the rising moon.

"My mother, aunt, and uncle took care of me," she said simply. "It would've been easier with you here, yes. But I managed."

Jinx nodded silently, his hand still stroking her leg with slow, reverent movements. His heart ached at her quiet resilience.

"And how hard was it for you?" Eira asked gently, her voice barely above a whisper.

Jinx shifted slightly, moving his arm as Teo slid deeper into the crook of it, sleeping heavily now. He stared at the boy's innocent face, his heart squeezing tight.

"You're the love of my life," Jinx said quietly, lifting his gaze to meet hers. "I never stopped loving you."

Eira's eyes shimmered, misting over with unshed tears. She blinked quickly, but a few escaped, trailing down her cheeks.

"And I never stopped loving you," she whispered back.

Jinx realized the magnitude of the point they'd just reached, and it damn near choked him. He tried to speak, cleared his throat, and then whispered. "So, what do you want the next step to be?" Jinx asked, his voice low, steady.

Eira shook her head slowly. "I'm not sure … Going to America sounds scary. Do you think my mom and I would even be welcome there?"

Jinx nodded without hesitation. "My company will ensure you have all the paperwork you need to stay legally. And I'll make sure you have everything you've ever wanted."

He smiled, the moonlight catching the softer lines of her face as she looked at him. "I have a small ranch in South Dakota. It's just a little north of Belle Fourche, a small country town."

"Like this one?" Eira asked, tilting her head.

Jinx chuckled, the sound low and warm. "No, Belle Fourche would feel more like Maracay. A little town much farther north, Hollister, reminds me of your village. The land in South Dakota is wild. Wide open spaces, fewer people. In South Dakota, you can see forever. The stars are just as brilliant as they are here. The only real difference is the cold winters and the snow."

"Snow?" Eira's face lit up, a bright laugh escaping her. "I would *love* to have a Christmas in the snow!" She paused, then giggled. "Although I don't have the clothes for cold weather."

"You wouldn't want for anything," Jinx promised, his voice deep with certainty. "The ranch has about a dozen horses and a growing menagerie of dogs and cats. A couple of mules, too. They were abandoned, left to fend for themselves in a pasture. Skin and bones by the time someone rescued them."

Eira smiled tenderly at him. "So, you took care of them."

He shrugged modestly. "I did."

"How large is your farm?" she asked curiously.

"Ranch," he corrected gently, his mouth curving

into a small smile. "In America, when you raise animals, it's called a ranch. Farms are more for crops."

She nodded, listening intently.

"I've got about four hundred acres," Jinx continued. "I'll need to build a better house for us. A bigger one, so your mom can have her own space, too. But we'll make it work until then."

"We *can*?" Eira asked softly, uncertainty flickering across her face.

Jinx's head snapped toward her, heart thudding. "I'm sorry," he said quickly. "I didn't even ask. Would you *want* to come to America? Would you live with me? Marry me and raise our son?"

Eira stood, carefully lifting Teo from Jinx's arms and cradling the boy against her shoulder, soothing him back into sleep. "I'll be right back," she whispered.

Jinx watched her disappear inside, the door closing gently behind her. He sat there in the dark, staring into the night, cursing himself for being too forward, too assuming. But when he was near her, everything else fell away. She made him feel whole. And the addition of Teo only deepened that feeling, anchored it even more fiercely to his soul.

Eira returned about five minutes later, the faint glow of the porch light illuminating her.

"Where's your friend? Raven?" she asked, glancing around.

"She's sleeping elsewhere," Jinx answered. "There's a small house tucked back near the woods just past the village. I used it to stash supplies while still with the cartel. She's staying there."

Eira leaned against the porch post, crossing her arms as she stared into the darkness. Though he could barely see her expression, Jinx could *feel* the intensity of her gaze.

"Mateo," she said, trembling slightly, "I love you."

The words struck him like a blow to the chest.

"I realized," she continued, "that you became the man you needed to be. You did what you thought was right. I never want to lose you again. If you want to take us to America, we will go with you, *but* you still have so much work to do. Love isn't enough sometimes. I need to be able to trust you won't leave us again. That you will stay beside us. It is a fear that may take years for me to get over, if I ever do."

Her voice broke, but she pushed through.

"My uncle and cousins can take over operations here. When Raven says it's time to go, you don't have to worry about us. We'll go with her. We'll leave, so you can do what you need to do … and then you can come back to us and prove your words."

"I will spend the rest of my life proving my words. They are true. My love is true. You'll see. I will *make* you see." He swallowed hard. "We'll be a family. Maybe someday we'll have a girl as beautiful as you."

Without hesitation, she crossed the porch and sank to her knees before him. "No. That can't happen. There's something else you need to know," she said, her voice barely a whisper. "I can't have any more children."

Jinx stiffened, the words hitting hard.

"Things went wrong after Teo was born," Eira continued. "My mother had to drive me into Maracay. I was hospitalized for three weeks after they did the surgery."

Jinx leaned forward, cupping her cheek with infinite gentleness, feeling the fine tremble in her body.

"Dear God," he breathed. "I'm so sorry." He felt as if someone had stabbed him in the gut and twisted the knife. What this woman had been through. The pain, the suffering. No wonder she didn't trust him to stay beside her. But he would gain her trust. He would prove he was more than an enforcer and an assassin. He was hers. Body and soul.

She leaned into his touch, her eyes swimming with pain. "Will it make any difference? In how you feel about me?"

For a moment, he was too stunned to speak. His mouth opened, then closed again. Finally, he found his voice. "Good God, no," he said fiercely. "The fact that you gave me Teo ... that you gave me *him*...it's a blessing beyond anything I ever deserved. I love you, Eira. Nothing will ever change that."

He leaned down, brushing a soft, reverent kiss across her lips. He wanted to crush her to him, to swear she would never hurt again. But he didn't have that right, not yet.

When he pulled back, she looked up at him with tears streaking her face.

"Mateo ... I'm afraid," she admitted, her voice raw. "I'm afraid you'll hurt me again. But I'm willing to try. Take me inside." She grasped his arms, nails biting into his skin, anchoring herself to him. "Take me inside and show me how much you love me."

Jinx rose to his feet, pulling her up with him. He framed her face with his hands, gazing down at her as if she were the most precious thing in the world. "You don't have to do this," he said roughly. "Not now. Not until you're ready."

Her fingers dug deeper into his arms. "Mateo,

you're here. You're alive. I've never stopped loving you. Yes, I'm afraid. Yes, I'm confused. But I *know* I love you more than life itself. Take me inside. Make me feel the way we used to feel. Make me feel the love you still have for me."

Jinx lifted her gently into his arms, cradling her against his chest as if she might shatter. Eira clutched the front of his shirt, holding onto him like he was her anchor in a world that had spun too fast, too violently.

Neither spoke as he carried her inside the small house. The door creaked open on its old hinges. He kicked the door shut behind him with a soft thud, sealing them off from the world.

He could see the sheen of tears still clinging to her lashes in the dim light from a single lamp near the couch. She was so beautiful it wrecked him. He set her down carefully, but when he tried to pull away, her fingers fisted in his shirt, keeping him close. Her gaze was wide open, vulnerable, trusting, and filled with a fierce love that hit him savagely.

Jinx cupped her face, brushing his thumb across her cheekbone. "We go as slow as you want," he murmured. "You tell me what you need, Eira."

Her answer was a whispered plea against his mouth. "Just love me."

Jinx bent his head and captured her lips in a kiss that was both reverent and desperate, a clash of the time lost between them. Eira melted into him, her hands threading up into his hair, anchoring him to her.

His mouth moved against hers slowly, savoring the taste of her and the soft whimper she made when he deepened the kiss. He framed her face with his hands, brushing his thumbs over her heated cheeks, pouring everything he *couldn't* say into how he touched her.

Eira tugged at his shirt, her fingers eager. Jinx pulled back just enough to help her, stripping the shirt over his head before tossing it aside. As she stared at him, her breath caught. She traced a finger across every scar on his chest. Each line had been etched by the life he'd led.

He caught her hands in his and kissed the tips of her fingers. "I'm here," he whispered. "I'm not going anywhere."

Her answering smile trembled, but her hands moved to the hem of her shirt, and he helped her, peeling the garment over her head. His breath hitched at her. Below him, she was bare, vulnerable, and unbelievably stunning.

Slowly, reverently, he bent his head to press

kisses along her collarbone, down the slope of her breast. Eira arched into him, her body trusting him even if her heart was still stitching itself back together. He lifted her into his arms again and carried her to the worn bed tucked into the corner of the room.

Lying her down, Jinx followed her, bracing his weight so he wouldn't crush her. Their bodies aligned naturally, lovers and soulmates finding each other again.

For Jinx, every kiss and touch was an apology. A vow. A promise. Eira gasped his name, and he soothed her with soft words in Spanish, the language slipping out like a prayer.

"Eres mi corazón." *You are my heart.*

When he finally entered her, it was slow and deep. The moment claimed their past and each other's souls as much as their physical bodies. Eira clutched him to her, tears slipping from the corners of her eyes.

Jinx kissed them away, whispering her name over and over. They moved together, a rhythm built on old trust and new promises, neither rushing nor holding back. The past, pain, and loneliness disappeared until nothing was left but their love.

When they fell over the edge together, it wasn't

frantic or desperate. It was complete. That was the healing his body and mind had needed. He prayed it was the same for her.

Jinx collapsed beside her, gathering her against his chest, his heart thundering under her ear. She curled into him, sighing in contentment.

"I love you," she whispered.

He kissed her hair, holding her tighter.

"I love you more than life, mi alma." *My soul.*

And for the first time in what felt like forever, Jinx believed he might actually deserve the future shining just beyond the horizon. A future with this woman. His woman.

The night wrapped around them like a cocoon, the world outside fading into nothingness.

Eira laid curled against Jinx, her head resting over his heart, her fingers tracing slow, lazy patterns across his chest. His arm was wrapped firmly around her, anchoring her to him like he couldn't bear to let go even for a second.

Jinx closed his eyes, breathing in her scent, her soap, warm skin, a hint of the earth, and sunshine that always seemed to cling to her.

His fingers moved slowly up and down her spine, feeling the small shivers that danced along her skin. It wasn't cold because Venezuela's night was thick and warm, but she pressed even closer to him, sighing contentedly.

For the first time in years, he felt still. Settled. Whole.

"You okay?" he murmured against her hair, his voice a low rumble.

Eira shifted just enough to tilt her head up and look at him. Her eyes were soft and heavy-lidded but filled with a peace he hadn't seen in them for so long.

"I'm better than okay," she whispered. "I feel safe. I haven't felt that in a long time."

His chest tightened painfully, and he bent his head and kissed her forehead, lingering there.

"You'll always be safe with me, corazón," he said, the words a fierce promise.

They laid there in silence for a while. The only sounds were the faint rustling of leaves outside the open window and Teo's occasional sigh in the other room.

Jinx stared up at the rough wooden beams of the ceiling, feeling a slow, cautious hope uncurling in his chest. For so long, he'd believed he didn't deserve happiness, that his hands were too stained and his soul too battered.

But Eira ... Eira was showing him that maybe

redemption wasn't something you earned. Maybe it was something you were given.

He tightened his hold on her, feeling her heartbeat thrum against his skin.

"I'm going to build us a life," he said quietly, almost to himself. "We will no longer just survive. I want to give you everything you've ever dreamed of. A real home. A future."

Eira smiled sleepily against his chest.

"We already have everything we need," she murmured. "We have each other."

Jinx swallowed hard, emotion thick in his throat. He kissed her again, softer that time, reverent.

Outside, the stars blazed like scattered diamonds across the sky. Jinx dared to let himself dream of tomorrow for the first time in what felt like a lifetime.

Sunlight spilled through the old wooden shutters, slanting in warm golden beams across the bed. The air was cooler in the early morning, fresh with the scent of damp earth and blooming bougainvillea outside the window.

Jinx woke slowly, blinking against the light, feeling the weight of Eira still nestled against him. She was sprawled across his chest, one leg tangled with his, her soft breath fanning his skin in slow, steady puffs.

For a long moment, he didn't move. He should get up and tend to the cows, but moving might shatter the sensation he was feeling. He just laid there, memorizing the feel of her in his arms. The steady beat of her heart. The faint rise and fall of her chest. The way her fingers still curled lightly against his side, even in sleep.

It was everything he'd dreamed of and once believed he could never have.

When a soft giggle drifted from the doorway, Jinx turned his head just in time to see Teo standing there in his tiny pajamas, one thumb in his mouth, the other hand clutching a battered stuffed donkey by the ear.

The little boy's eyes were wide, curious, and bright with mischief. Eira stirred against him, her lashes fluttering before she blinked herself awake. She lifted her head, following Jinx's gaze, and smiled.

"Good morning, mi amor," she said softly to Teo.

Teo beamed, waddling toward the bed with the determined energy only toddlers possessed. Jinx sat up and reached for him, lifting him easily onto the mattress. Teo immediately flopped against Jinx's chest with a contented sigh as if that were exactly where he belonged.

Eira laughed quietly, brushing Teo's messy curls out of his eyes.

"I think someone likes you," she teased, glancing at Jinx with a smile that melted him from the inside out.

"I ... I love him," Jinx said gruffly, pressing a kiss to Teo's head.

The three of them sat there in the soft morning light, tangled together, the world outside forgotten for a little while. Jinx let his eyes close briefly, feeling the boy's tiny heartbeat against his chest, the familiar weight of Eira beside him.

He could have stayed like that forever.

But reality had a way of creeping in. The now rather urgent moos of the cattle carried through the window.

"I'll go take care of them," Jinx said as he stood and dressed.

"Breakfast will be ready when you come back," she said softly, a knowing look in her eyes.

He smiled faintly and nodded.

Together, Eira and Teo climbed out of bed. Eira padded into the kitchen, barefoot and beautiful in the oversized shirt she'd thrown on, with Teo bouncing happily in her arms as Jinx followed but veered out the front door to do the morning chores.

When he returned, she'd dressed, and Teo wore fresh shorts and a T-shirt. He was playing on the floor when Eira handed Jinx a battered mug, their fingers brushing, and for a moment, their eyes met, and a smile passing between them.

No matter what came next, they were in it together.

Teo giggled, climbing onto one of the chairs and banging his fists on the table in excitement. Eira laughed and set out his breakfast, a few eggs, and some bread. It was simple, rustic, and absolutely perfect.

Jinx took a long sip of coffee, watching her move around the kitchen, Teo babbling happily. He'd fought wars. Walked through hell itself. And yet this … this messy, imperfect, *beautiful* morning was the hardest and most important battle he'd ever won.

Family.

Home.

It was reality. Yes, there was a storm in their future. One that he would win because, for the first time, he wasn't just fighting for his company or the good of humanity. Now, he was fighting to return to his family.

CHAPTER 17

Jinx took a stroll across the stretch of pastureland that connected Eira's ranch to the abandoned property behind her. The warm night air clung to his skin, carrying the scents of dust, dry grass, and distant woodsmoke. The stars hung low, heavy against the ink-black sky.

It had become his habit. When Eira tucked Teo into bed, he'd slip out and check the old mailbox where Simón sometimes left messages. It was also the hour when he, Brando, and Raven touched base.

As soon as he was out of earshot, Jinx tapped his comms.

"Where are we with the identification of the photos?" he asked, voice low.

Brando's chuckle rumbled through the line. "Well, hello to you, too."

Raven's voice immediately broke in, dry as the cracked earth under Jinx's boots.

"You know, he's really not all that friendly. Kind of a loner. Not at all like me. How you doing, Brando?" Raven continued with a mischievous lilt. "By the way, could you tell your cousin to stop contacting me? I mean, I'd appreciate it."

"He's a grown man," Brando replied with a careless shrug in his tone. "What do you want me to do?"

"Oh, I can think of lots of things I want you to do to him. I have a zombie doll being made in the village. Until I get some pins to shove into it, shoving a sock in his mouth would be a start," Raven muttered.

Jinx shook his head, a ghost of a smile curving his lips. Their banter was a constant background noise and it was sharp and familiar. But tonight, he wasn't in the mood to play.

"Could we get back to business?" he asked, scanning the tree line ahead.

"Absolutely," Brando said. "Found out something today that's very, very interesting."

"I love interesting shit," Raven said brightly, right before the sound of her small puppy barking in the background made her curse under her breath.

Jinx muttered, "One minute out." The dusty road ahead looked clear, but he needed confirmation.

The comms crackled. "Copy," Brando said, his voice dropping low. "The area is clear. You're the only heat signature. We just got some intel on your boy Ortega."

Jinx ducked beneath the heavy sweep of a tree branch, the rough bark scraping the top of his shoulder. Even alone, every muscle in his body stayed coiled, ready.

"Go ahead," Jinx said quietly.

A beat of silence. Then Brando's voice, cold and steady. "Tomás Ortega has a brother."

"Right. Esteban," Raven said. "Rumored to be dead."

"I wish," Brando growled. "Listen to this, Esteban Ortega isn't just another thug, Jinx. He started young. Bodies on him before he hit twenty. But they never stuck a real label on him. No cartel ties. No loyalties. Just pure predator."

Jinx stayed crouched low, his eyes sweeping the dark, empty field. Across the cracked dirt road, the battered old mailbox stood alone, half leaning off its post.

"And?" he whispered.

"Check your phone when you can," Brando instructed.

"You sure I'm clear?" Jinx asked again, still feeling the prickling weight of being watched.

"Positive," Brando said after a pause. "The cows back at Eira's place are the closest heat signature to you."

Jinx drew his phone, shielding the screen with his hand to block the glow. A grainy photo loaded of a younger man stared back at him, dark-eyed and smirking like he owned the world. He resembled Tomás, but where Tomás looked brittle, the man's demeanor was carved from stone. The glint in his gaze held coldness and absolute confidence.

"Meet Esteban Ortega," Brando said. "Born on a farm not far from Eira's place. Started killing before he could legally drink."

Jinx scrolled through the file, gaze sharpening. "Serial?"

"Yeah," Brando confirmed. "Started small once he hit Maracay. Gang initiations, some contract work. But by the time he was twenty-two, he was hunting for fun. Patterns suggest he preferred isolated victims like street kids, women no one would miss. Real psychopath. He was finally nailed for a triple homicide, but the evidence barely stuck. They dumped him in Tocorón Prison."

Brando paused, letting the weight of the name settle in the dark air. "That's where things got worse," he said quietly. "Way worse."

Raven's voice sharpened, all business now. "Tocorón. That's where Tren de Aragua was born."

"Exactly," Brando said grimly. "Tocorón wasn't a prison. It was a kingdom. Inmates ran it like a cartel hub. Tren de Aragua controlled everything , drugs, weapons, trafficking networks. You name it."

Jinx tapped through the files quickly, crouched low against the soft wind that whispered through the brittle grass.

"Ortega didn't just survive in there," Brando continued. "He thrived. Most guys would've been fresh meat. But Ortega already had the instincts. Violence. Ruthlessness. He caught the eye of the higher-ups fast."

Jinx shut off his phone, letting his eyes readjust to the dark. "They groomed him," he muttered.

"Yeah," Brando agreed grimly. "First as an enforcer. Then as a strategist. Taught him how to build networks and how to move product and people without getting caught. Gave him access to outside contacts, cartel liaisons, corrupt military, even international smugglers."

"How did you get this information?" Raven asked.

"An inmate from Tocorón wanted to migrate to the United States," Brando said. "He wanted political asylum. In order to get it, he sold out everyone and everything. He was a mid-tier gangster, but everyone inside Tocorón knew what was happening. As soon as I saw the prison mentioned on Ortega's rap sheet, I pulled everything I could. This guy spilled on damn near every fucking inmate in the facility."

Jinx took one more careful look up and down the deserted road before crossing to the battered mailbox. The dry wind lifted the dust around his boots, and the distant murmur of crickets filled the humid Venezuelan night. His voice was low, almost a growl. "They turned a predator into a professional."

Raven made a small, frustrated noise through the comms. "What happened after Tocorón?"

Brando exhaled heavily, his tone grim. "Details are sketchy, but when the government started pressuring Tren de Aragua leadership, a lot of high-value inmates 'escaped.' Actually, they evaporated. Ortega disappeared into the wind. Since then, we've tracked whispers of an operator moving between Venezuela,

Colombia, and Mexico. Smuggling routes. Targeted hits. Cleaning up problems for cartel elites."

Jinx's jaw tightened, a muscle ticking along his cheekbone. "Ortega is the Ghost."

"You're damn right he is," Brando said, his voice cutting through the line. "Man, I *know* he is. He's the right profile. And if I'm right, he's more dangerous now than he ever was behind bars. He's not freelancing," Brando added, voice dropping even lower. "He's building something. Networks. Routes. Alliances. His reach is global now, and he's using Tren de Aragua's old playbook to do it. Only this time, there's no leash. No rules."

Raven snarled softly, anger vibrating through the comms. "He's playing servant to that big-nosed bastard Guardian thought was the Ghost. Always standing near. Always in on conversations. Why didn't we see it when we were observing the camp? This guy is innocuous and almost... mousey."

Jinx reached into the rusted mailbox, fingers brushing the rough, cool metal.

"Which is his intent, and we didn't see it because he wasn't our focus," he said, voice clipped. A thin piece of paper rested inside the mailbox. It hadn't been there the night before.

"Dude, the guy in the military camp isn't a plant

for Tomás to get information," Raven said, her voice sharp with realization. "Tomás is a plant for Esteban. Esteban is the reason Tomás rose to power."

"Which means Esteban is holding all the cards, and Tomás is his puppet," Jinx muttered, pulling the paper free and folding it quickly. He tucked it into his jacket and jogged back across the cracked road, ducking under the tangled brush at the edge of the field.

He crouched low, shielding the light from his phone as he opened Simón's message.

The words were scrawled quickly, but they hit like a bullet. "The note says Ortega will be asking for your allegiance soon." Jinx's blood went cold.

Raven's voice was immediate. "Eira, Teo, and I will need to activate our exit strategy." There was a pause, filled only by the rustle of dry leaves in the night wind. Raven's voice softened slightly. "Her mom won't leave the aunt. Her sister is sick. The doctor said she might not get better right away."

"I can get the plane to you by noon," Brando replied without hesitation.

"Do it," Jinx said, already moving, his body on autopilot as he cut back across the field toward Eira's ranch. "Shit's about to get real."

The stars above seemed to sharpen, burning

colder as Jinx picked up speed, the weight of what was coming pressing hard against his chest.

The house glowed soft and golden against the heavy dark of the Venezuelan night.

The fields stretched quietly around it, the dry grass whispering under the slow press of the wind. The cattle moved slowly, a soft call reached him every now and then.

Jinx crossed the pasture while his heart screamed to stay there, just a little longer. That wouldn't happen. Not when his family's safety depended on action. Through the kitchen door, he saw Eira.

She was standing at the counter, humming under her breath as she wiped it clean, barefoot and comfortable in one of his old shirts. Her hair was twisted up in a messy knot, a few loose strands falling around her face. She looked soft, peaceful.

Happy.

The sight of her like that, relaxed, trusting, *safe,* hit him like a knife to the gut.

She didn't know that in a few minutes, he was going to shatter her world. Again.

Jinx moved up the porch steps quietly, every creak of the old wood feeling like a sin.

He hesitated at the door, his hand on the handle,

his knuckles white. He could not mention it. Give her one more night of peace.

But peace was a lie, and he couldn't lie to her. Not anymore.

He pushed the door open. Eira turned at the sound, her face lighting up when she saw him.

"Hey, you," she said, smiling, the kind of smile that made the whole damn world fall away.

God. She was so damn beautiful it hurt to look at her. "Hey," Jinx said, voice rougher than he wanted it to be.

She crossed the kitchen to him without hesitation, sliding her arms around his waist and pressing her face against his chest.

He held her close, breathing her in, memorizing the feel of her. Every curve, every breath, because he knew what was coming.

"You're tense," she murmured against his shirt, her fingers tracing slow, lazy patterns across his back. "Everything okay?"

"I have something I need to talk to you about," he said, closing his eyes.

For one heartbeat, he let himself just hold her. Pretend everything was normal. Pretend he wasn't about to shatter her all over again.

Eira leaned back to look up at him, her eyes warm, teasing.

"Sure. Teo's already out. I made coffee. Was thinking we could sit out back for a while." Grinning, she tugged him toward the porch, and it was *so easy* to imagine slipping into that life. A life where she smiled at him like that every night, where Teo called him *Dad* without even thinking about it, where the world couldn't touch them.

But that wasn't their reality. And tonight, reality was there to collect. He caught her hand, stopping her gently. She frowned up at him, confused at first, then worried when she saw his face.

"Eira," he said softly.

She went still, the air between them thickening.

"I have to move you and Teo out," Jinx said, voice raw. "Tomorrow morning." She just stared at him for a second, like she hadn't heard right. Like she was still waiting for him to smile and tell her it was a joke.

But no smile came.

Her mouth parted, a small, broken sound escaping. Her fingers tightened around his.

"It's happening?" she whispered.

He nodded once, feeling like he was cutting his

heart out with the motion. "I'm sorry, baby," he rasped. "Ortega's moving. It's not safe anymore."

She blinked fast, swallowing hard, her free hand curling against his chest like she could anchor herself there. He covered her hand with his, holding her to him. "You'll be safe with Raven," he promised. "We will have a future together, with Teo."

Tears welled in her eyes, but she shook her head fiercely, dragging in a breath like she was preparing for war. "I'm not scared for me," she said, voice trembling. "I'm scared for you."

"I know," he said, brushing a hand down her cheek. "But you have to go. You and Teo."

Her face crumpled for a second, just a second, then she squared her shoulders and nodded once.

"I'll be ready," she said, fierce and quiet. "But we have tonight, right?" And that, more than anything, nearly broke him.

He leaned down, pressing his forehead to hers, breathing her in deeply. "Yes. We have tonight. I love you," he said hoarsely, the words a vow and a prayer all at once. Her fingers fisted in his shirt.

"I love you, too," she whispered.

Jinx kissed her hard and deep, wishing he could carve the memory of her into his bones.

CHAPTER 18

She couldn't breathe. Mateo finally lifted away from the kiss. No, she couldn't breathe, and it was because of this man. Because of the way his eyes fixed on her. Like the only thing anchoring him to the earth was his connection to her. Her fingers dug into his chest, feeling the wild thrum of his heart against her palms. He was trembling. She was, too. Two broken pieces, rattling apart, desperate to be whole.

"You should hate me," he choked out, voice wrecked. "After everything—"

"Don't," she cut him off, her throat burning with the pain of unshed tears. "Don't say it. Don't put that between us."

His eyes shuttered, pain flashing through them

sharp and intense. His hands fisted at her sides as if touching her was shattering the last of his control.

But she was already shattered.

And then suddenly, she wasn't looking at him anymore. She was *clawing* at him, pulling on his shirt, hauling him down to her mouth. Kissing him like she could tear the hurt out of them with a simple kiss.

He kissed her back just as violently, his hands tangling in her hair, dragging her head back to devour her mouth. His body shook against hers as if he were barely holding himself together.

"I never stopped loving you," he growled against her lips. "Never. Not once. I'd die before I let you go again."

"Prove it," she gasped, her nails digging into his bare skin, leaving angry red streaks. "Prove you're still mine."

A savage sound ripped from his throat. Was it a growl, perhaps a prayer, or maybe a curse? They were pulling at their clothes, frantic and wild and clumsy. His shirt slipped over his head. Hers hit the floor in a tangled mess. His hands roamed her body like he couldn't believe she was real, rough, and tender in turns. His mouth chased hers, then moved down her neck, over the pulse hammering just beneath her skin. Her body trembled uncontrollably. Mateo bit her neck, and her core heated in a tight grip of lust and need.

"You're mine," he breathed against her throat. "Mine, Eira. Always."

She arched against him, desperate to feel every inch of him, desperate to banish the fear clawing at the edges of her heart.

"Yours," she whispered, fierce and broken. "Always yours."

He lifted her and carried her toward the bed with a force that stole her breath. But when he laid her down, he wasn't rough anymore. His hands and lips transformed into something like a prayer. Soft, honest, a voiceless conversation of his hope, and their future.

She realized this, tonight, was everything he couldn't say in words. This night was all the love, guilt, need, and promises crashing into her as he covered her body with his own.

She spread her legs open for him, inviting him closer, needing him inside her. As close as two humans could become. Their mouths found each other again, slower now, the fury fading into something deeper, more powerful in its tenderness.

When he finally moved inside her, it wasn't just

their bodies that spoke. It was as if their past, present, and future formed anew in that moment. The past, their loneliness, and the pain of separation were gone. The fear of tomorrow and the days they'd be separated was forgotten. Their future as a family was a dream yet realized. There was only them. There was only this moment. She shattered under him. Her core clenching so tight she ached. The spasms continued as he peaked inside her. She gasped as she shattered again.

When she managed to sense something besides the orgasm, she smiled. The room smelled like him. Warm skin, sweat, something wild and fierce she couldn't name. Eira buried her face against his chest, breathing him in, trying to memorize everything, like the way his heartbeat thudded strong and steady under her palm, the rough scratch of his beard against her body, or the way his fingers traced lazy, absent-minded circles against her spine.

She never wanted to leave this moment.

Mateo shifted slightly beneath her, pulling the blanket higher over their tangled bodies. His other hand slid up her back, threading into her hair and cradling her head like he couldn't bear to let her go.

"You're not sleeping," he whispered.

"Neither are you," she hummed back.

He grunted, low in his chest. "I can't waste a moment."

The words were so rough, so broken, she felt them crack something inside her.

She tilted her head up, and he was watching her in the dark, his eyes softer than she'd ever seen them. The enforcer he portrayed was gone. All that was left was Mateo. The man she knew before.

"I have to leave in the morning," she said quietly, the words like knives against her tongue.

His hand tightened slightly in her hair. Not enough to hurt. Just enough to say he hated it, too.

"Yes," he murmured.

"You …" She swallowed, her throat thick. "You're going to kill Tomás and the other one you're looking for." It wasn't a question.

His jaw flexed, the muscle ticking hard enough she could feel it under her palm. "I have a job to do. I have to finish it, " he said, voice low and grim.

She blinked fast, trying to chase the tears back. She didn't want him to see her fall apart. Not now. Not when there was so little time left.

"You'll come to us," she whispered fiercely as if, through sheer willpower, she could make it true. "You'll be careful?"

He cupped her face, brushing his thumb under her eye.

"I swear to you, baby. I'll come to you." He leaned in and kissed her forehead, her cheeks, the corners of her mouth, like sealing the words on her skin. It was reverent and intentional. He whispered between kisses, "Nothing's keeping me from you again. Nothing."

A tiny sob slipped free, but he stopped it with his kisses, absorbing her pain with a slow, tender, heart-breaking connection.

They didn't speak again. Words would only make it harder. Instead, he shifted them, tucking her fully against his side, his arm heavy around her waist, his hand splayed protectively over her hip. She curled into him, resting her ear over his heart, listening to the steady, grounding beat.

Mateo murmured something against her hair. It was something low and Spanish and too soft to understand. She let it wrap around her like his protection, warm and unending.

Tomorrow, she would take Teo and run.

Tomorrow, he would become the man everyone said he was, and he would start his hunt.

* * *

The sun was barely skimming the horizon when they left the farm, mist curling low over the fields like ghostly fingers trying to pull them back. She held Mateo while he held Teo. The little boy was still asleep in his father's arms. The plane scheduled to retrieve them was going to be earlier than expected, and Raven had arrived with the information, waking them and sending her into a rushed packing of Teo and her essentials.

"My mom can come to us after my aunt gets better." She looked up at Mateo, silently begging him to let her mother come.

"Absolutely. We'll make sure," Raven said as she grabbed the small bundle Eira had made with their things. Both dogs were already in the Land Cruiser, and Raven was getting everything else settled.

Mateo looked down at her. "Your mom belongs with us. With Teo."

"Yeah, that's what I said. Give me the baby. I'll get him settled in the truck." Raven took Teo easily, proving she was more capable with children than she'd alluded to.

Eira turned back to Mateo. "I love you," she whispered. The words were for his ears only.

He bent down. "Remember what I said last night. Believe in me, mi amore."

Her heart felt like a fist was squeezing the life out of her, but she whispered the truth, "I do."

Mateo kissed her. Soft, reverent, and promising. She slipped out of his arms and walked to the truck hand in hand with him. He opened the door for her and shut it afterward. "Take care of my family, Raven."

"With my life, dude, you know I will," she said before she put the vehicle into gear and drove away.

Raven drove with one hand light on the wheel, the other resting casually on the gearshift, but Eira could feel the readiness and tension in her every movement and look. Each move of the woman's body was deliberate. Each glance in the rearview mirror was sharp and assessing. Eira felt the situation's intensity, and it was more than she'd believed it would be. Would Tomás send someone to take her and Teo? Would he bring the wrath of Mateo down on himself? Well, Tomás had accomplished more than Eira had thought the man could do. He was the head of the cartel in the area, and that … well, she just couldn't understand it. Tomás was many things, but he wasn't a leader.

The road twisted through patches of tired farmland and dense jungle scrub. Trees grew in close, casting shadows across the cracked asphalt. Along the edges, makeshift homes made of crumbling cinderblock with rusted roofs clung to the landscape. They lined the drive like battered survivors in a country on the brink of imploding.

They passed a few others on the road. Battered motorcycles overloaded with cargo, farmers herding skinny cattle, and the occasional truck coughing up dust in their wake. Most people kept their heads down and eyes low. Everyone knew how dangerous it was to be noticed these days.

As they neared the highway, the environment changed. Traffic thickened with military transports and beat-up government trucks, not with families or traders. Soldiers manned temporary roadblocks, standing beneath sun-bleached flags with rifles slung low and suspicious glares cutting through the windshields.

Raven relaxed. She was a study in careless caution. Her shoulders loose, and her fingers drumming lightly on the steering wheel. She wore a field worker's rough, practical clothing: sun-faded jeans, a dusty button-down, hair pulled back in a no-nonsense braid. Just another local woman ferrying supplies, nothing more. The dogs must have sensed the stress in the cab. They lay on the floorboards and didn't move. It was eerie how they tried to disappear as much as the humans going through the checkpoints did.

Eira could tell that underneath that easy, almost careless mask, Raven calculated every threat and angle. At each checkpoint, they rolled to a stop. Young soldiers, barely out of boyhood, scanned the truck with wary eyes. Some looked at Raven longer than necessary. Their stares lingered. Women traveling alone with a child always drew attention.

Raven played it perfectly. A slow smile. A bored, almost impatient look. A few sharp, clipped words in regional Spanish, which Raven mimicked perfectly. Eira listened as Raven talked about government permits, food deliveries, delays, and heat exhaustion. She made herself seem harmless, even weary. This wasn't the woman who drove her away from Mateo that morning. She'd morphed into someone else, a person who could've grown up next door to Eira. But she wasn't. She was an American, although you couldn't tell it now.

Most of the soldiers waved them through. Some took longer, asking questions, lingering, as if debating whether to pull them out and search the truck. Each time, Raven remained unbothered, tilting her chin slightly, giving just the right amount of eye contact. She was confident but not challenging. The guards relented and let them pass.

Eira kept Teo low in the back seat, mostly hidden beneath a battered blanket, murmuring soft, steady nonsense in his ear. Her heart hammered against her ribs, but outwardly, she stayed still and tried to become invisible.

The farther they drove, the more the world seemed to fall apart around them. Potholes cracked the road to pieces. The jungle crept closer to the crumbling shoulder. Shacks gave way to open fields and abandoned stretches of land where even the scavengers seemed too afraid to settle.

When Raven finally turned off onto a narrower dirt track, Eira let herself exhale a brittle breath. The path ahead was nothing more than a jagged scar through the field. Tall grass skirted the edges, and the brush pressed tight on either side, making walls of tangled green vines.

"We're close," Raven said, her voice low, steady.

Eira nodded, tightening her hold around Teo. Mateo had told her that morning that the landing strip would be little more than a hacked-out strip of dirt, hidden from casual eyes. No radios. No runways. Just a small twin-engine plane waiting to take them away from everything.

The truck bounced over ruts and stones, dust kicking up in thick clouds behind them.

At one checkpoint, a soldier stepped forward. He was older, sharper-eyed. He didn't wave them through like the others.

He motioned for Raven to roll down the window.

She did, slow and steady, flashing a practiced, annoyed smile.

"Perdón, oficial," she said, voice light, almost bored. "Running late. Supplies for the base at Puerto Santo."

The soldier didn't move to wave them through. He leaned down, peering inside the truck. His gaze lingered too long on Eira, on the barely concealed bundle of Teo beneath the blanket.

Raven arched an eyebrow, tapping the fake permit clipped to the dash with two fingers.

The soldier grunted, unimpressed. His hand shifted casually toward the rifle slung across his chest.

Eira's breath froze. Raven's smile sharpened just a little. She shifted her weight, subtly angling her sidearm just out of sight near the doorframe.

For a moment, the world hung suspended.

Then another soldier, who was younger and impatient, shouted something from the back of the checkpoint, waving them forward. The man hesitated, then stepped back with a grunt, smacking the side of the truck twice.

"Move." He said with a clipped voice.

Raven didn't hesitate. She rolled up the window, shifted gears, and drove on, the truck chugging and choking forward like it had been holding its breath, too. Eira didn't exhale until the checkpoint was just a smudge in the dusty rearview mirror.

And then, at last, the landing strip came into view. It was rough and ragged, but it was also the most beautiful thing she'd seen all day.

A man stood by the plane, his silhouette framed by the rising sun, arms crossed, watching the horizon for trouble. Raven didn't slow down. She pushed the truck harder, getting them to safety before anyone could change their minds.

When she pulled up, the pilot walked over to the vehicle and took the small bundle of possessions from Eira. Raven walked around the vehicle and smiled at another man who appeared from the brush. "Z. Glad you're here. Do you have the intel?"

The man nodded. "Got it. I've got his back, Raven." When the man looked at Eira and Teo, a slow smile crossed his face. "Now I see the urgency." He extended his hand to her. "I'm Z." Eira shook it as she let Teo toddle a bit before he had to sit down again.

"Eira. Do you work with Raven and Mateo?"

"I do. I'm here to make sure Mateo comes home to you."

Eira smiled, her eyes misted with tears almost instantly. "Thank you."

Raven handed the keys to the Land Cruiser to him. "Papers to get through the roadblocks are on the clipboard. New plates are under the driver's side seat. Change them before you take off."

"Got it. Safe travels," Z said and gave them a two-finger salute.

"Ladies, we need to go. Now," the pilot said as he opened the door to the small aircraft. The dogs went in first and settled into the very back space of the small cabin. Raven swooped up Teo, making him laugh. "Brando, we're getting on the plane, and Z is on scene."

Eira glanced at the pilot, who seemed to ignore Raven's comments. She shook it off. Perhaps her statement didn't need an acknowledgment, but it wasn't polite. She got into the plane, and Raven handed her Teo. She strapped in and held her son tightly. The pilot handed all of them earphones. Teo laughed and patted hers before doing the same to his. She smiled at him as the aircraft roared to life. Raven strapped in next to the pilot, and the small aircraft moved. It bounced rapidly down the runway before it took off. Eira's stomach lurched, and she closed her eyes and hugged Teo tightly. There was no turning back now.

CHAPTER 19

The low growl of engines pulled Jinx from his thoughts. He stood at the edge of the porch, arms loose at his sides, watching as two blacked-out SUVs rolled down the dirt track leading to Eira's farm. Dust plumed in the heavy Venezuelan air, wrapping the vehicles in a cloud until they came to a halt in front of the house.

The passenger door to the first SUV opened, and Simón stepped out. As expected, he wore the uniform of all enforcers. Crisp khaki pants and a button-down shirt, with the sleeves rolled back. Of course, mirrored aviators completed the look. Everything about him said "casual," but Jinx knew better. That was what Simón had warned him about. This was his so-called invitation back into the cartel.

Behind Simón, four others fanned out, weapons holstered but hands loose at their sides. Jinx knew they weren't there to intimidate him, at least, not immediately. They were sent as a reminder that if he didn't comply, he'd be dead.

Jinx stepped down from the porch.

"Mateo," Simón called, voice easy. Friendly, even. So much different than the honest concern the man had spoken to him with at the abandoned ranch. This was Simón's persona, a cloak he wore to prevent anyone from seeing the man underneath the pretense. Jinx knew all about that protective barrier. He'd perfected it.

"Simón," Jinx answered flatly, standing his ground.

Simón flashed a smile that didn't reach his eyes. "Nice place you got here. Quiet."

With that one comment, Simón had told him that Simón hoped Eira and Teo weren't around. "Eira and Teo are visiting family."

"Ah." Simón's smile sharpened. "Then you've got a minute, hermano."

The "brother" was almost convincing. Almost. Jinx glanced toward the barn where one of Eira's cousins was filling the tank with the morning's milking. His jaw ticked once before he nodded. "Walk with me."

They moved toward the tree line, far enough for privacy but close enough that the tension stretched between the guards and Jinx like a live wire.

Simón waited until they were out of earshot, then spoke low. "She's safe?"

"Yes," Jinx confirmed.

Louder so the men behind them could hear, Simón said, "Boss is excited. You made an impression." He paused. "Two impressions, actually."

The men he'd killed at the cantina. Jinx shrugged. "If they don't know how to treat an animal or a man, they shouldn't be breathing."

Simón chuckled under his breath. "They're not crying about it, trust me. Still …"

He turned slightly, facing Jinx squarely. "We need the formality, Mateo. You understand."

Jinx's mouth curled into a humorless smile. "Blood in, blood out."

Simón nodded. "Exactly."

He hooked a thumb back toward the SUVs. "We got a place set up. It shouldn't take long. After that there will be no questions. No doubts."

Jinx lifted an eyebrow. "And if I say no?"

Simón spread his hands. "Come on, hermano. You won't."

Jinx stared at him for a long moment, then jerked his chin toward the vehicles. "Let's get it over with."

Simón's smile widened. "Knew you were smart."

Jinx let Simón walk ahead. Instinctively, his mind had already sliced the current situation apart. He'd counted guards and knew how to use the pistol tucked against his back. They hadn't searched him. He'd be a fool if he weren't carrying at least one weapon. All the men watching him return to the SUVs knew he was armed.

However, for now, survival meant playing the part of being loyal. And Mateo was nothing if not loyal. Only his loyalty was to Guardian Security and his family. The cartel wouldn't know that until it was too late. Any test they put in front of him, he would pass. With the connection between the two brothers now known, going with the cartel's offer was the only way to get to Tomás's brother. Tomás would die first. Then Esteban.

The ride was silent.

Simón sat in the back seat with Jinx, pretending to have casual ease, but Jinx could feel the tension vibrating through him. The other SUV followed close, in case Jinx decided to kill the occupants of the SUV he was in. He'd seen it happen when he was an enforcer. The damn fool was drilled full of holes for his trouble. Whether it was stupidity or nerves, the guy never stood a chance.

Thick country blurred past the windows, the road narrowing the farther they traveled.

After twenty minutes, they turned off onto a whisper of what was once a gravel road. Jinx's hand rested lightly on his thigh. His back was angled toward the door, giving him access to his weapon should he need it, but he made no move for it. Mateo Rivas was back. The mentality and personality slipped over him like a well-worn garment. Since Eira and Teo had left that morning, he'd shaken off the last vestige of civil humanity and become that stone-cold killer again. Killing didn't bother him. The people who were at that level of the cartel were not innocents.

The SUV rolled to a stop in front of a crumbling hacienda. He could see that it had once been a grand estate. White stucco walls, tiled roof, and wide archways were covered in dirt and weeds. It was a ruin, which was perfect for blood and secrets.

Jinx stepped out of the SUV first, scanning the edges of the property. There were three guards at the gate they'd just entered. Two more were near the entrance of the dying hacienda, and there were probably more inside.

Simón walked around the SUV and stood beside him. "After you," Simón said as if they were entering a bar for a drink. Jinx saw everything. The guards tightened as he walked past and went through the door. Inside, it was darker, and he slowed his walk a bit to allow his eyes to adjust. The air was thick with mildew and old wood smoke. Graffiti smeared the walls. Bullet holes peppered the far arch. As they passed through the entryway, an open courtyard expanded in front of him. A single chair sat in the center of the tall grass and weeds that had overrun the area.

Tied to the chair was a bruised, bloody man. He recognized him from years ago. He'd worked with him. Drank with him. The man was a bastard of the highest order. He was a rapist, a murderer, and a greedy son of a bitch who would do anything to make a buck.

Jinx's expression didn't flicker.

"Luis has gotten greedy," Simón said. "He was selling information to people who want to dismantle our grip on the area."

Jinx knew the drill. Because Mateo knew this man, because they thought they had a relationship, Luis was here and offered up for a test of loyalty.

Simón strolled forward, pulling a pistol from his

waistband and flipping it in his hand grip-first toward Jinx.

"Your old friend," Simón said conversationally. "Caught selling intel to the wrong people."

Jinx took the weapon. The weight was familiar. It was loaded. He could tell by the way it felt in his hand. Jinx looked at Luis, who lifted his head. One eye was swollen shut. His face was a roadmap of bruises, and his lips were cracked and bleeding.

"Mateo," he croaked. "Good." He nodded. "Good."

No plea. No apology. Just recognition of what was to happen. Jinx approached slowly, every step echoing against the broken stones. Simón and the others formed a loose half-circle, giving him space and also ensuring he'd be killed if he didn't do what was intended.

Jinx stood over Luis, pistol loose in his hand. "You disappoint me," he said quietly.

Luis's jaw trembled, and a tear leaked from his good eye. Jinx raised the gun. Any hesitation would be his death. Mateo wouldn't hesitate. It was what Luis needed, too. Immediate. No more torture. He pulled the trigger. The shot cracked like a whip, echoing in the confines of the small courtyard.

Luis's head snapped back before his body sagged against the ropes. Silence swallowed the courtyard.

Jinx lowered the pistol and turned back to Simón, handing it over with a clean, steady grip.

Simón grinned, sharp and approving. “Bien hecho,” he said. "Well done."

The others murmured agreement, some nodding. Jinx met Simón’s eyes and smiled.

A cold, feral thing. Simón clapped him on the back. “Welcome home, hermano.”

The others closed in now, looser, friendlier. They were no longer guards but his comrades, his family. Jinx let them believe that, at least for now.

Back at the SUVs, Simón offered a cigarette. Jinx declined. “You’re in, Mateo. No more questions.” Simón leaned in slightly. “The bosses are going to want to meet soon. Big things are coming.”

Jinx just nodded as he calculated Tomás’s next moves. Esteban was the wild card. He needed intel on the man, and he knew how to get it. He’d establish his old connections and give Tomás every reason to trust him. He needed access. He needed to dismantle the organization, both organizations, from the inside. All he had to do was be Mateo for just a little longer.

Simón opened the door for him like an old friend, and Jinx slid in without a word. The convoy rolled out, engines growling, leaving behind the body, the blood, and the hollow shell of a forgotten estate.

He was deposited back at the farm, and the SUVs departed in the same fashion they'd arrived. In a cloud of dust. He spoke into the air. "Is the farm clear?"

"Yeah, mate. The one guy who was here left in that truck."

Berserker's words put a smile on his face. "Z, glad you're here."

"Do what you need. I have eyes on the place," Z said. "I take it you passed whatever test they had for you."

"Always." Z knew exactly what he'd just done. Z had been in the position once or twice, too.

"Need anything?"

"I have to make a call. Come up to the house after dark."

"You know it. Hope you can cook. My stomach thinks my damn throat has been cut."

"Simple food, but it'll fill you up."

"That'll work," Z said. "See you then."

"Brando, does Dr. Wheeler have access to Esteban's file?"

"I can make it happen."

"Do it and tell him I need a call as soon as he's digested it."

"Roger that."

JINX WAS outside sorting the eggs he'd collected. Eira's family would depend on any payments they could get before the cartel exploded. He wouldn't disappoint them by not doing the chores Eira had done daily.

"I have Dr. Wheeler on comms for you."

Jinx tapped his ear. "Go."

"Dr. Wheeler, Jinx is on the line. I'm clear," Brando said. Jinx turned around and leaned against the table he'd been working at.

"Jinx, do you have five minutes?"

"Yes, sir. And if I didn't, I'd make the time." Esteban was too much of a question mark not to get as much information about the man as possible.

"I just finished your psychological briefing on Esteban Ortega. I can send the file through when we get done."

"Thank you." Jinx crossed his arms and stared out over the pasture where Eira's milk cows were lying down and chewing their cud. "Tell me about him."

"All right, here's the rundown. Esteban Ortega grew up hurting animals. Then killing them. He has no empathy. No remorse. By sixteen, he'd already killed at least two people. All of this was documented while he was in a local prison before he was transferred to Torcorón and became involved with Tren de Aragua. Once the police transferred him to that hellhole, he flourished. Most people would have been crushed, but he learned the system. He used it. Built contacts and learned the mechanics of fear. I'm reading several different files to glean that information. The people who remained at the prison after the Venezuelan government retook it were thoroughly debriefed. Everyone knew of Esteban. He was mentioned in at least twenty different files. This guy didn't survive hell; he flourished in it." Dr. Wheeler sighed.

Jinx grunted. "Sounds charming."

"I speculate he's worse now. If what Brando briefed me is correct, and I have no reason to assume it isn't, you believe he's El Fantasma, the Ghost. I've done several workups on what we know about him and his work. If I meld what I know about Esteban into those workups, we have a pretty full picture of what this man is. He's moving between Venezuelan cartels as an assassin, and in his capacity with the organization he's building, he's brokered deals across Mexico and Central America. What we've learned is he has the logistics, drugs, arms, and trafficking tools in place. He doesn't have connections to the organizations in Europe."

"That's where I come in," Jinx said.

"Your cover has those connections?" Dr. Wheeler asked.

"Yes, and then some."

"Be careful. This guy is a primary psychopath. High functioning. No conscience. No loyalty and absolutely no fear. He doesn't react emotionally. Threats bounce off him. Fear makes him sharper and more interested. If you try to talk him down, he'll eat you alive. No speeches, no hesitation with this one, Jinx. Fast and final. I cannot stress that enough. So, the quick version of all of this. His murders are never random. Everybody he drops is a step up. He has no loyalty. None. Family, friends, blood ties, none of that matters. If they're useful, they live. If not, you're disposable. The only thing a man like this would respect is raw power. Period. Esteban doesn't get handled."

"No, he gets ended," Jinx said casually.

"Exactly, and if he even sniffs you're onto him,

he'll hit first. He'll use anyone, innocents included, to do what he thinks he needs to do."

"Noted."

"Be careful, Jinx. Don't let this mission make you forget where the edges are."

"I know where they are, Doc. I have a firm grip on them."

"Good," Dr. Wheeler said, and Jinx could hear the relief in his voice.

"Hey, Doc, one more thing. Tomás Ortega is Esteban's little brother. He's using Tomás to control the cartel here. What is the dynamics between the two of them?"

"Ah. Family dynamics. Esteban would treat Tomás like an asset. Not a brother. He'd think of Tomás as a disposable chess piece. He's useful if he's obedient but expendable if he's weak."

"He is weak. Very weak. Why is Esteban keeping him around?"

"Two reasons I can think of. First, blood is useful. It makes the cartel look like a family business when Esteban finally makes those contacts he's looking for in Europe, a consolidation of power. He'll look stronger. The second is loyalty. Not his, but Tomás's. The kid grew up under Esteban's shadow. He's been conditioned by the past trauma of growing up around Esteban already. Tomás obeys because he knows if he doesn't, Esteban will eliminate him."

Jinx narrowed his eyes and stared at the toe of his boot as he asked, "So, how tight of a leash do you think Esteban has on Tomás?"

"Well ..." Dr. Wheeler hesitated. "Speculating here, but I'd say not as tight as Esteban thinks. Tomás has to know he's being used. I'd say Tomás would resent the hell out of Esteban, telling him what to do and when to do it. Why?"

"I want to work Tomás against Esteban. The idea started before I knew Esteban was controlling Tomás. Would it still work?"

Dr. Wheeler made a sound deep in his throat. "You'd need to give him what Esteban never will, your respect. Feed the man's resentment. But don't push it. Make him think any loyalty to his brother is suicide. Make him think loyalty to you is the way to survival. Tomás is weak. He won't move away from his brother unless there's a safe exit. My gut is telling me if you build that bridge, he'll run like hell to get away from his brother."

"How would I do that?" Jinx wanted as much information as the doc could give him.

"Speak to Tomás like an equal. Ask his opinion, even if you already know the answer. Casually mention how people are replaceable to someone like Esteban."

"He doesn't know I know Esteban is controlling him."

"Then make up a story, some type of string to pull him along, where he could easily swap his brother for the person in your story."

"Got it."

"Suggest a better future if things were different, but this is important. Tomás needs to think all this is his idea. If he thinks he's being played, you've lost. Throw the board and pieces away and punt because he'll run to Esteban with what he suspects."

"Well, thanks for the tightrope act," Jinx said with a humorless laugh.

"I'll send my report, and Brando can load it. Be careful, Jinx. I've dealt with someone like Esteban before. Don't hesitate, and I say that from experience."

"You'll have to tell me about that sometime," Jinx said. "Thanks, Doc. I'll talk to you when I'm on the other side of this."

"I look forward to it. Wheeler out."

Jinx turned back to his work. He hit the tone to

summon his operator. As soon as the line connected, Jinx snapped, “Brando, put Z back online.”

“Copy,” Brando said immediately.

“What’s up?” Z asked.

“Did Raven give you the directions to the safe house?” He finished placing the eggs into the cartons as he spoke.

“Yep, and the stash location,” Z acknowledged.

“I think Tomás will move me in sooner rather than later. As in tonight, tomorrow morning at the latest. There are food and weapons there. Brando can give you my location based on the comms. From my conversation with Dr. Wheeler, it could take weeks before I’m positioned for action.”

“I copy,” Z said. “Anything you need me to do while you’re gone?”

“Eira’s mother.”

“Raven left me a long two-page letter in freaking Italian. I’ve spent most of the day translating the damn thing. I know where she is and about the aunt. I’ll take care of them until you need me.”

Jinx could hear Z’s eyes rolling from where he was standing. “I’m not sure how this will play out. You could be here for no reason. And she did that so no one else could read the letter.”

"Whatever. It was a dick thing to do. She could have written it in English and put it in the stash."

"That's true, but do you expect that from her?" Brando said.

"No," Z admitted reluctantly. "I'll get Eira's mom out of the country when she's willing to leave. Brando, I'll need an escort for her. I'm not leaving Jinx alone."

"Raven," Jinx said. "She knows Raven."

"Done," Brando said. "By the way, they're out of Venezuela's airspace and heading home."

"To my ranch, right?"

"Yes," Brando acknowledged. "I hope you don't mind. I called your ranch manager and told him they'd be arriving. He said he'd get supplies and make sure they got settled. His wife is going to get diapers and all things baby."

Corey and Helen Macy were amazing with the animals, and he had no doubt they would be wonderful to his little family. Their son was a large animal vet who practiced north of his small spread in Hollister. Having Eira and Teo safely home with them sent a surge of relief through him. Jinx felt the lingering worry lift from his shoulders. "Thank you."

"You know we've got your back," Brando replied. "Whatever it takes."

"As long as it takes," Jinx and Z answered at the same time. Jinx tapped to mute his comms, and then he closed his eyes and let the last connection to the world outside of Mateo Rivas slip away.

CHAPTER 20

The farm was dead quiet. Jinx stood at the edge of the porch, hands loose at his sides, watching the horizon bleed into a washed-out gray. Dust curled around his boots, dry and restless, stirred by the faint breeze rattling the barn doors. The cattle were in the pasture, the chickens in the roosts, avoiding the day's heat. No dogs barked. There were no voices and no laughter from a little boy chasing after chickens. Everything was still. Silent. Exactly as it should be. *Had* to be.

He leaned against the porch's post, waiting for the vehicles Brando had told him were coming his way. He didn't move when he heard the low growl of engines grinding up the dirt road. He didn't so much as twitch when two blacked-out SUVs rounded the bend, tires kicking up long snakes of dust behind them.

He simply waited.

The vehicles rolled to a stop. The doors popped open, and four men stepped out. Not Simón this time. They were cartel soldiers, mid-tier muscle who would have been told of him.

They wore their guns low. Their fingers were loose, but Jinx saw how they watched him.

They were careful … respectful. Ah … there it was, he saw it. They were afraid of him.

Good.

One man broke away from the others. He was a wiry type with a scar splitting one eyebrow. The appointed spokesman stopped a few feet away and jerked his chin toward the lead SUV.

In a gruff voice, he stated, "Tomás wants you. Says you're in." He tossed the words out like a challenge, but his body echoed that tone. His weight shifted back, and he was ready to move if Jinx made any wrong move.

Jinx's mouth twitched, a slow, humorless ghost of a smile. He reached back, flicked the screen door open with a hollow creak, and turned the lock behind him. The soft *click* echoed loudly in the heavy air.

It was a final closing. A final goodbye to anything other than Mateo Rivas.

Without a word, he stepped off the porch, boots crunching over the dry earth, and slid into the back seat of the waiting SUV. The men around him seemed shocked as if they'd been warned he might not come willingly. What a crock of shit. Jinx waited while they got into the vehicle. The engine growled, and the convoy pulled away, leaving the farm behind. Z would tell the cousins that no one was available to do the chores. They'd take care of the animals, and Jinx would become one.

The drive was long and utterly silent. The slight man tried once to ask him a question, but the withering look he gave him shut him up. No others tried after that. It was what he wanted. Fear. Fear worked in his favor. The jungle started to close in tight around them. All twisted green with choking vines. Not the dusty farmland near the foot of the mountains any longer. No, from the direction of travel, it confirmed Tomás *had* taken over Montoya's compound. A place Jinx knew well. A place he'd occupied years ago. A place of death, drugs, and murderers. It was a fortress, and when he'd last been there, it had had enough supplies to sustain the men inside for over a year if someone were to try to take it.

The road narrowed to a battered track, potholes yawning under the tires. Jinx leaned his head back against the seat, eyes half-closed, body loose. Yet he missed nothing. He saw the gun placements on the lead truck. Noted the position of each soldier and the crude communications rigged up through ancient radios. These were the trucks of the work-force of Tomás's business. The drivers switched off with silent hand signals. One led for several miles before the next took over. They were professional to a point, but sloppy enough for Jinx to exploit later.

The SUV jostled hard as they rounded another bend, and the compound came into view. It hadn't changed. A fortress of concrete and rusted steel, rising out of the jungle like a rugged, ugly gouge in the miles of green. The outer walls were topped with razor wire, and two guards in mismatched body armor were posted outside the heavy gates, which were bolted shut from the inside.

Home fucking sweet home.

The SUVs rumbled up to the gate. After a brief check, the guards' rifles lowered, although more than one wary glance was thrown at Jinx in the back seat. After radio communication with the inside of the compound, the convoy was waved through.

Inside the compound, movement was everywhere, and Jinx absorbed the familiar and noted the differences between Montoya's operation and Tomás's.

As he exited the vehicle, Jinx watched as a convoy of soldiers formed. Armed men moved in tight clusters. Trucks were being loaded with crates. Shouts echoed off the walls, sharp and urgent.

Jinx took it all in and, within seconds, located Tomás. He hadn't changed, except for the haggard lines on his face and gray sprinkled in his hair. One hell of a lot of aging. Tomás stood stiffly near the courtyard's center, flanked by two men he clearly didn't trust. His stance was that of one who expected an attack, not respect. He held himself too still, too tight, like a man wearing armor he didn't believe in.

Jinx stepped forward slowly, stretching his arms, letting the others watch him, measure him, weigh their chances, and realize they didn't have any.

Tomás swallowed once, quick and nervous, then masked it behind a sharp chin jerk. Jinx walked over to him and stopped in front of him. Everything in the compound slowed as men watched what was happening.

Tomás glanced up at him. "You're with us now. Got plenty of work lined up for a man like you." His voice scraped across Jinx's nerves like fingernails on a chalkboard.

Jinx didn't react outwardly. Inside, he smiled. The man was terrified of him. He dipped his head once, a slow, deliberate nod. Quietly and respectfully, he responded, "Where do you need me?" His words were calculated to be simple and obedient, using Dr. Wheeler's information and advice immediately.

Tomás relaxed. Jinx noticed the smallest of physical movements, a tiny drop of his shoulders. Score one for the doc. Tomás motioned for him to follow. They moved deeper into the compound, the heat and the stink of oil, and men pressed close. The walls rose around them, caging them in. Exactly where Jinx wanted to be.

Tomás led him across the cracked courtyard, his boots striking sharp against the concrete.

Jinx followed two steps behind, hands loose, eyes scanning every angle without turning his head.

The building Tomás led him to was newly constructed, low and square, the door a heavy slab of reinforced steel. Two guards flanked the entrance. They were bored and inattentive, and no doubt

Tomás missed that fact as they pulled the door open when they approached it.

Inside, the air was cooler but stale with trapped cigarette smoke and old sweat.

Filing cabinets lined one wall, and a battered metal desk sat in the center. A single cracked leather chair sat behind it. There were no other exits, no windows. No way out, but more importantly, no way in if the door were bolted from the inside. A cage inside a cage, or perhaps a refuge inside the cage. Tomás's paranoia and fear were far beyond anything he'd seen in Montoya. Tomás moved behind the desk, gesturing Jinx forward with that tight jerk of his chin. When Jinx complied wordlessly, Tomás dropped a small folder onto the desk with a soft slap. "Got some shipments that need extra watching. Everyone says you're good with your hands. Prove it."

Jinx reached for the folder and picked it up. He flipped it open and saw coordinates, inventory lists, and names Jinx already recognized from Guardian's intelligence briefings. He didn't give any physical response to the information. He didn't show anything other than a dip of his chin. Slow and respectful before simply stating, "You can consider it done."

Tomás leaned back in his chair, studying him with hard, wary eyes. The man didn't know it yet, but the moment he'd handed Jinx that folder ... the moment he trusted him with *anything*, he'd already lost.

THE CONVOY WOUND its way through the weed and brush-choked jungle road. A line of half-assed armored trucks loaded with cocaine and cash trailed behind Jinx's lead vehicle. The late afternoon sun slashed through the trees, casting too many shadows to clear as he drove. In his profession, every shadow could hold a bullet. Tomás had revealed that the last four convoys had been attacked on this road. Two of those attacks were successful. The man's hands shook as he swiped his hair out of his face. "I can't afford another loss."

Jinx understood the assignment. He also understood that Esteban would probably take out Tomás before he could get to him. But that didn't matter. If Esteban knew he was being hunted, he'd become the ghost the assassin claimed as a handle and disappear. That would mean more death and needless violence that Jinx could prevent by playing his cards correctly. Two men would no longer live when he left this country. Tomás and Esteban's bloody reign in the territory would be over.

When the ambush came, it was fast and brutal. Two SUVs burst from the undergrowth, guns already firing. Jinx barely twitched. He swerved his SUV to protect the convoy in one fluid motion and leaned out the window. He extended his fully automatic M4 and laid down a spray of suppressive fire. His rifle sprayed death across the ambushers' hoods and windshields.

Jinx checked his six to ensure no one was coming from that direction before he got out of his SUV. Several bullet holes had pierced his SUV's exterior, but nothing that would stop him from leading the convoy. He moved to the trucks and opened the doors, making sure the men were dead. From the second vehicle, Jinx heard movement. One gunman scrambled toward cover. Jinx lifted his rifle and, with a clean, detached shot, drilled the man through the head.

By the time the dust cleared, the attackers lay dead, and the convoy rolled on without losing a single crate. Tomás's men shouted their thanks, some clapping Jinx on the back like he was already one of them. Jinx just reloaded in silence, eyes scanning the tree line. Protecting Tomás's empire wasn't loyalty. It was just business as usual until the real job could be done.

Later that month, Jinx dropped a bloodied duffel bag at Tomás's feet. Inside was a cheap burner phone, a thick stack of American dollars, and a flash drive containing shipping routes. Jinx had carefully planted every item. He picked the worst fucker in the compound and the one that consistently watched him as his target. Salazar was a bloody son of a bitch who killed for the joy of it and didn't care if the person were innocent or guilty. Blood excited the man, and he was more than verbal about his dislike for Mateo Rivas. Two birds, one bullet. Tomás would trust him more, and Salazar would be gone.

"Tomás," Jinx said quietly, "your boy Salazar's been talking to the military unit."

Tomás's face twisted in rage and then fear. "What did he say?"

"It's all on the phone."

Tomás yanked the burner phone from the bag, scrolling through the pre-loaded messages. It didn't matter that they were fake. To a man already steeped in paranoia, what he was reading was more real than truth could ever be. Tomás shook as he read through the messages. He slapped the phone down. "Lies. He told them I didn't have control of my house. Why? Why would he undermine me?"

"Advancement. He wants to be in your position." Jinx shrugged as if it didn't matter to him.

Tomás didn't hesitate. He barked orders, and minutes later, Salazar was dragged outside and shot in the courtyard. Jinx watched Tomás's silhouette against the setting sun. The man paced outside in the courtyard, running his hands through his hair and muttering to himself. No one approached him. Jinx was the only one to stay outside. He was Tomás's protection, and the man was realizing it. A sneer lifted the corner of his mouth. That card was played perfectly.

Two nights later, Jinx caught the scent of betrayal before the first shot was fired.

At a remote jungle airstrip, while Tomás's latest shipment was being loaded onto a plane, five of Tomás's men peeled off toward the cargo with stolen rifles and a getaway truck waiting nearby. The move was too obvious. Jinx moved like the shadow he was. By the time the traitors realized they'd been spotted, two were dead, their bodies crumpling near the plane's landing gear. Another screamed as Jinx tackled him to the ground, snapping his wrist before putting a bullet in his knee. He'd be the one he took back to Tomás to show him once again that he couldn't trust even his own men.

When they arrived back at the compound, Tomás marched up to him, flanked by guards. Jinx was cleaning his weapon, standing over the broken would-be thief like a grim sentinel. Tomás's eyes, wild and bloodshot, locked onto him with something close to awe, or perhaps desperation.

Jinx said, low and even, "Trust is the only currency that matters. Your men are traitors."

Tomás drew his automatic and shot the man without asking him a question. He looked at Jinx and turned, walking back into the compound. Jinx looked down at the dead man and shrugged. Two guards picked up the trash and pulled him toward the compound's entrance. Jinx started whistling a carefree little tune as he finished cleaning his weapon. It wasn't an act. He had just advanced his play without having to stage it. The fools were stupid to try when he was on the convoy. They learned that Mateo Rivas hadn't lost his honed edge. The men around him slowly left the area. Within two minutes, he was the only one in the courtyard. Jinx chuckled to himself. One step closer.

Tomás summoned Jinx to his private quarters

late that night. Jinx knocked on the heavy door, then tapped his earpiece.

“I’m recording,” Brando said without hesitation.

Tomás opened the door. A gun pushed through the chained opening in the doorway. Tomas looked past Jinx, ensured the area was clear, then snapped the door shut. The sound of the chain being removed preceded the door opening. Tomás motioned for Jinx to come in before he shut the door behind him. The room stank of sweat and expensive cologne, the air so thick with fear it was almost visible. Tomás moved in front of him and sat down hunched on the edge of his gaudy gold-framed bed. He ran a trembling hand through his hair. The nervous tic would make the man bald before it soothed him.

"They’re all snakes," Tomás muttered, staring at the floor. "Every last one of them."

He lifted his head slowly, bloodshot eyes locking onto Jinx with desperate intensity. "Except you," Tomás said, voice breaking. "You're the only one I can trust, Mateo. Without you ... I'm finished."

“The military wouldn’t dare make a move against you.” Jinx opened the proverbial door, wanting Tomás to walk through it.

“You have no idea. They would. *He* would.”

Tomás punched up from the mattress and started pacing again.

"Who?" Jinx asked, feigning ignorance. "No one would be so bold. You run the strongest cartel in Venezuela. People live because you allow it. People die because you order it."

Tomás nodded. "I tried to get Eira here to protect her." Tomás pulled on his hair with both hands. "She wouldn't come."

"She's safe." Jinx didn't even try to keep the growl out of his voice.

Tomás's head snapped up. "I didn't know you were involved with her. I swear. Once I found out, I stopped any type of courtship effort. I knew you'd be back for her. I wanted to protect her."

Jinx didn't move. He wanted to reach out and bitch slap the man. Instead, he nodded once slowly. "She told me. It's why I am loyal to you. You watched out for my family when I couldn't."

Tomás blinked and looked at him. "I did." He seemed to straighten, to stand taller. Thinking of himself as important to Jinx shifted the tables in Tomás's mind. Jinx could see his mind working.

Tomás dropped his hands to his sides and smiled. The first smile Jinx had ever seen on the man's face. "I need you to do something for me, Mateo."

Tomás's smile dropped as quickly as it had appeared. He paced in short, frantic bursts around his room, sweat glistening on his forehead despite the chill of the air conditioning. This was the only location in the compound with the luxury of a small air conditioning unit. Still, his silk shirt clung to him like a second skin, wrinkled and stained with the day's tension.

Tomás finally erupted. "You need to take out the person in charge of that military faction."

Jinx narrowed his eyes. "Why? They haven't threatened you. Even after Salazar gave information to them."

"You don't understand. You have to strike first," Tomás rasped, voice cracking under the strain. "Before he moves against me. Before he tears everything apart."

Jinx watched him quietly, arms folded, giving away nothing.

Tomás leaned in, close enough that Jinx could smell the sharp bite of cheap whiskey on his breath. "El Fantasma," Tomás whispered like the name itself was cursed. "He's the real power. The real threat. You kill him, and this empire *is* mine. I'll share it with you as a reward for your loyalty."

Jinx arched an eyebrow. "You want me to assassinate your ghost?"

Tomás laughed, a brittle, broken sound. "Not *mine*," he muttered. "He was never mine."

He didn't explain further, waving Jinx off with a trembling hand. "Find him. Kill him. Before he finishes what he started."

"How can I know who he is? El Fantasma has been whispered about for years, but no one knows who he is or what he looks like."

"You won't do it?" Tomás froze and looked at him like a deer caught by a spotlight.

Jinx frowned and extended his arms. "I would kill *anyone* for the man who cared for my family. I just don't know who the hell he is or how to get to him in that military compound he has at the base of the hills."

"Right." Tomás started pacing again.

Jinx gave him three or four minutes before he suggested, "If we could get him here, on our territory, we'd have the upper hand, and you'd witness me taking the man out."

Tomás stopped and stared at the floor. He nodded. "I can get him here. He's been here before."
Jinx said nothing, only inclining his head in a gesture

that could pass for an acknowledgment. Tomás had just handed him everything he needed.

CHAPTER 21

Jinx strolled through the compound. He poured himself a cup of coffee and stretched out in the courtyard. As Simón walked through the area, their eyes met. Jinx nodded to the man. Simón blinked, did a double-take, and then kept walking. He'd just given the man the notice he required. It might be more than a day before things came to a head, but at least Simón and his woman would be out of the area.

The day was long and heavy. Jinx loitered in the courtyard, catching the breeze the compound's interior areas didn't have. Brando's voice over his comms came about five hours after he'd given Simón notice to leave. "Z just reported Simón picked up his woman in the village, and they got the hell out of Dodge. Eira's mother is safe, as well as the rest of her family. Her aunt is slowly getting better. Panther Team was rerouted and has landed in country. They will ensure the war doesn't reach the village. Z is en route back to your location should you need the backup."

Jinx made a small sound in his throat to let Brando know he'd heard the communication.

Not more than an hour later, Jinx was summoned to Tomás's private office. He tapped his comms, activating them before he approached the little block building. It had heavy security posted outside this afternoon.

"Recording." Brando's voice was immediate and all business.

Jinx was let in immediately. "It's time," Tomás said after the door was closed. Jinx stood across the desk from the man, saying nothing. Tomás wiped the sweat from his palms onto his silk pants before he picked up the satellite phone. The signal buzzed faintly in his ear as he punched in the encrypted number, the one only a handful of men probably had.

Across the desk, Jinx stood silent, arms crossed, a stone monument of patience. Tomás shot him a quick, jittery glance. The look tried to be conspiratorial but landed somewhere closer to pathetic and pleading. "He won't see it coming," Tomás whispered, almost to himself.

The line clicked, then rang. Once. Twice. Then it connected as the dead air hummed between them.

Tomás straightened his spine, forcing steadiness into his voice. "Esteban," he said, all greasy charm. "Brother. We need to talk. I understand someone from inside this compound is telling you lies. I deserve the right to clear them up."

There was a pause. The kind of pause that made your gut twist. And Jinx watched Tomás drop into his chair as if the wait were too much for him.

On the other end, Esteban's voice slid through the speaker, smooth and cold as a mountain river stone. "What a surprise call," Esteban said. No warmth. Just a fact. "You think you deserve anything from me?" Esteban's voice held what Jinx thought was actual confusion, and that, too, followed what Dr. Wheeler had said when they talked. *Tomás was just a tool for Esteban.*

Tomás laughed too loud, too fast. "You and me, we've too much between us. I'm being reasonable. Let me explain. Come to the compound. We'll drink, talk. Set things right."

Jinx didn't move or react, but inside, he was

already cataloging the tremors in Tomás's voice and how his eyes flicked to the door as if expecting ghosts to walk through it. Another pause. This one was at least twice as long as the last. Tomás leaned forward to say something, but Jinx lifted his hand and shook his head. Tomás snapped his mouth shut.

Then Esteban's voice, low and amused, came across the connection. "Of course, hermano. I wouldn't miss your explanation for the world."

The line went dead. Tomás ensured the connection was severed by hanging up his line. Then the man exhaled a shaky breath and leaned back in his chair, forcing a grin at Jinx. "He'll come," Tomás said. "Walk right into his grave."

Jinx doubted it. Tomás was just trying to convince himself. The man was cunning and didn't tolerate people not following his demands. Tomás was unimpressive on so many fronts that Esteban had to be tired of the sniveling and whining.

"You'll be here when he comes?" Tomás shot the question at him.

"Of course," Jinx replied. "Let me know when he's at the gate, and I'll be by your side."

"Good," Tomás said and nodded. "You'll do what we agreed to do?"

"For you, I will do anything. I've told you this. Do you doubt me?"

"No." Tomás drew a deep breath and let it out slowly. "You're the only person I don't doubt."

Jinx smiled a mile-wide smile on the inside. Externally, he didn't move except to ask, "Did you need anything else?"

"No," Tomás said.

"Then I'll go clean my weapons and ensure they're in working order." Jinx was going to do just that. He had two bullets with names on them, and he planned on delivering them tonight. But just in case bullets weren't enough, he had a fail-safe option he'd bring along. A little help that would add a pop for the party, as it were.

JINX HEARD the first gunshots from the heart of the compound. They were sharp, controlled bursts that caused his instincts to kick in before his thoughts caught up. He spun toward the noise, hand snapping to his sidearm, already moving across the courtyard. Guards scrambled around him, shouting orders that made no sense, confusion splitting the night wide open.

He tapped his ear. "Brando!"

"Copy. Getting a satellite view. Z, what do you see?"

"Three SUVs are coming down the road. Do I take them out?"

The attack came from the inside. It was too clean. Happened too fast. This wasn't a random attack. This was an execution. Esteban was coming for Tomás. "No, don't stop them. It's the Ghost."

A body dropped to his left, the guard's mouth still open in a half-formed question, blood pooling across the stone. Jinx didn't stop. He sprinted toward the main hall leading to Tomás's office.

A figure loomed at the archway. He was a guard Jinx recognized, but something was wrong. The man's rifle wasn't aimed at the intruders.

It was aimed at Jinx. The traitor fired. Jinx threw himself sideways, the bullet grazing his ribs, the pain burning hot. "Motherfucker!" He hit the ground rolling and came up firing. Two rounds punched into the man's chest, dropping him like a sack of sand.

More footsteps were heading his way. Louder and heavier now. The men were coordinated in action and closing in on him.

Jinx cursed under his breath and pushed forward,

weaving through the open hallways, gun tight in his hand. Twice he had to fucking change course. The first time, a wall of gunfire pinned him down, forcing him to duck through a storage room thick with smoke. The second was when a locked gate sealed off the direct path to Tomás's inner courtyard and small building. Son of a bitch. He had to get to Tomás, not to save his ass, but to reach Esteban.

But for some reason, they were herding him. Keeping him away. By the time he'd cut through the servants' passage and emerged into the outer corridor of the main residence, the ground beneath his boots shook, and a deep, reverberating boom that rattled the walls.

The explosion ripped through the air like a thunderclap. Smoke and dust billowed through the compound. Jinx broke into a dead run, dropping his useless weapon. He'd fired all of his rounds and didn't have any for a reload.

As he rounded the final corner, he saw Tomás's heavy steel door blasted off its hinges, twisted metal hanging from shattered stone. Jinx sprinted to the empty doorway.

Inside the office, Tomás lay sprawled behind his wrecked desk, bleeding from a gash across his forehead, dazed and struggling to rise. And standing over him, calm as a man admiring a painting, was Esteban, with a pistol loose in his hand, a half-smile curving his lips.

Esteban turned slightly as if he'd been expecting Jinx all along.

"That didn't take you long, hermano. My men were poor at keeping you delayed," he said. "I'd hoped to finish this unfortunate business before we met. If you'll excuse me, this won't take long."

Jinx moved to position himself for the greatest access to Esteban. He glanced past the man to Tomás's shattered office. Smoke still curling through the blown doorway. Blood smeared the marble floor.

Tomás coughed wetly, dragging himself up against the ruined remains of his desk. Blood matted his hair, smeared across his face in streaks. He looked small. Broken.

Esteban stepped closer, movements unhurried, almost gentle. The pistol dangled loose at his side, forgotten for now.

"You should have stayed in your place, Tomás," Esteban said, almost pitying. "You must know you were never meant to be more than the face. The name."

Tomás bared his broken teeth, a low growl tearing from his throat. "*I* made this empire." He spat blood at Esteban's feet. "Without *me,* you'd be nothing."

Esteban smiled, a slow, indulgent smile, like a parent tolerating a child's tantrum. "Oh sweet, hermano. No, no, no," he said softly. "You made noise. *I made the empire.* You were just the puppet. A useful diversion." He knelt in front of Tomás, lowering himself to eye level. "You thought *you* could summon *me* here ...?" Esteban shook his head. "You don't have that power. You never understood, hermano. I've been holding your leash since the beginning."

Tomás lunged a weak, pitiful swipe at Esteban's face. Without even flinching, Esteban raised his pistol and fired once.

Tomás's body jerked, a single convulsion, and then he slumped sideways, lifeless. Blood pooled around his broken form, seeping into the cracked marble like ink staining paper.

Dead silence swallowed the room. Esteban stood smoothly, brushing dust from his sleeves. He turned, meeting Jinx's eyes across the wreckage.

The smile he wore wasn't cruel. It was welcoming.

"Now," Esteban said, voice calm and steady. "It's just you and me. So, you are *the* Mateo Rivas. I have had the most wonderful reports about you, your abilities, and your connections."

Jinx stood in the haze of gunpowder and blood, boots planted in the wreckage, body loose but coiled. He hadn't moved when Esteban pulled the trigger. One less life for him to take.

He glanced at Tomás's body lying crumpled near the desk. A crimson stain spread beneath him. His last gasp of outrage and fear was already lost to the night. Jinx hadn't lifted a hand to stop it.

Tomás was inconsequential. Weak. A loose end better severed by someone else's blade. And his end was one less obstacle between Jinx and his true target.

"My name is Esteban Ortega, his brother."

The man turned from Tomás's body, brushing a bit of dust from his jacket lapel, and smiled at Jinx as if nothing remarkable had occurred. As if his brother's life hadn't just been extinguished at his feet.

Jinx just stared at the man. No reaction, which Esteban seemed to love. He smiled. "I always knew you'd see the reason for my approach, Mateo," Esteban said, voice rich with satisfaction. "You had to have deduced this moron wasn't the leader of anything but peons."

Jinx's gaze was a mask, betraying nothing. Inside,

his mind mapped Esteban's movements, timing, and the feel of the razor-sharp blade hidden beneath his sleeve. The silence stretched between them, thick and electric.

“He was pathetic,” Jinx said in a deadpanned fashion. “It was only a matter of time before I killed him rather than listen to his whining.”

Esteban gave a wide smile and took a slow, measured step forward, hands loose at his sides. "He was weak. Emotional." Esteban shook his head, almost mournful. "He could never see the bigger picture." Esteban gestured to the burning world outside the shattered door. "This ..." he said, voice growing brighter, "this is an evolution. We are *the* evolved. The top of the hierarchy."

Jinx said nothing. His tension wound tighter. He held his poise as the tension strained to the breaking point. Mistaking his silence for agreement, Esteban waved a hand toward the guards lingering beyond the doorway.

"Leave us," he commanded, not looking back. Instead, he looked at Jinx and rolled his hand in a royal wave. “We are of one accord. We are the same person, the same intent.”

The guards hesitated.

“Now!” Esteban's authority cut through their

doubt like a whip. They withdrew into the smoke, leaving the two men alone amid the wreckage.

Esteban moved closer, his steps slow, almost reverent.

"You understand, don't you?" he said, voice low. "You and me, hermano. We are not like them." He circled Jinx slowly like a predator savoring the moment before the kill. "Lesser men have wasted your talents," Esteban said. "Sent you to kill, to bleed, to bury yourself in someone else's wars. But you were made for more. I see myself in you. I see our kindred spirit. You understand death, don't you?"

Jinx tracked him with his eyes, the gun still in Estaban's hand, loose but ready. "Better than anyone."

The man before him lifted a finger and moved it back and forth in a cautionary gesture. "Not better than me." Esteban stopped before him and removed a glove with a slow, deliberate motion, letting it fall to the blood-slick floor. He placed the gun down and took off the other glove. "That is a symbolic shedding. There will be nothing between us," Esteban said. "Complete transparency." He stepped into a thin shaft of moonlight slashing through the broken ceiling.

Esteban smiled wider, almost indulgent. "You've

been turning into me without even knowing it," he said softly. "It's only fair you finally see the man you could become." He paced the ruined room, movements fluid, unhurried. "You've been a tool all your life," he said. "Following orders. Killing for causes that were never yours." He stopped before the broken table, hands open in invitation. "I offer you something more. Something you've earned. *Power. Impunity.* Wealth and the respect of everyone." The man chuckled. "Whatever your vices, you'll have a bountiful buffet of extravagance. The only thing I need to make it happen is your connections. Your influence with the people in Europe. Then, we take over America."

Esteban leaned against the wreckage, casual and confident. "No more missions. No more lurking on the sidelines. No more men who see you as disposable. With me, you are an equal. A king."

He gestured toward the burning world beyond the windows. "The old order is dying. We will build the new one." He stepped closer. "I see you, Mateo. I see what you can be." He extended his hand, bare and unguarded. "Join me."

Jinx looked down at the offered hand. He thought of the blood soaking into the marble. He thought of what Esteban had destroyed and of what he had built on lies and corpses. Slowly, Jinx relaxed, and he took Esteban's hand.

Esteban's smile widened, triumphant. "I *knew* you would see sense," he said.

Jinx took a single step forward. An almost there smile on his lips. Close enough to strike.

Esteban's eyes gleamed with triumph. Insane triumph that encapsulated the feral sickness that lived within the man. Esteban squeezed his hand. "You and me," he whispered. "Unstoppable."

Jinx's voice was low, almost gentle.

"Never."

The blade slid free from Jinx's sleeve, a whisper of steel. He drove it into Esteban's side with brutal precision. Esteban gasped, body folding around the blade, hands clutching at Jinx in shock.

"You ..." he choked, blood blooming at his lips.

Jinx leaned in close.

"I'm nothing like you. I am the light for those in the darkness. I work for good, not self. I am your executioner. The world has deemed you guilty. Your sentence is death."

He twisted the knife sharply, severing arteries, breaking the future Esteban thought inevitable.

Esteban sagged, breath rattling in his chest. Jinx guided him down to the marble floor almost gently.

Esteban's eyes, wide and disbelieving, locked onto his.

"You ... could have ruled ..."

Jinx removed the blade and wiped it clean on Esteban's designer jacket. "And yet, *I chose* to serve," he said.

Esteban shuddered once and went still.

Jinx stood over the body, his breathing even. Slowly, he bent over and picked up Esteban's weapon. He checked the magazine. One bullet gone, one in the chamber.

Jinx turned toward the broken door, slipping the blade away, the compound's ruin unfolding before him. No ghosts left. No self-appointed kings.

Just smoke and blood and the endless work of cleaning the world.

Jinx didn't look back.

CHAPTER 22

"Both targets down." His voice was calm. Controlled. He glanced around the area. The guards wouldn't have gone too far. "Z, I need one hell of a distraction."

"Copy," came Z's gravel-coated reply, laced with barely restrained excitement. "I've been *dying* to light this place up, mate. You want chaos? I got you, all right."

Jinx's lips twitched. "Make it biblical."

"Fucking A, son. I'm letting it rip."

Outside, the first explosion shattered the air. The concussion felt like a five-hundred-pound bomb slamming into the earth. The detonation shook the ground under his feet. A fireball roared heavenward at the far side of the compound. Stored fuel in drums near the generator ignited in a tower of flame. Metal pieces of flaming barrels fell from the sky. Screams followed, garbled in Spanish over panicked radio chatter, Jinx could hear as the guards scrambled.

Jinx took the opportunity and sprinted down the corridor, weapon drawn and ready. The hallway flared red from the reflected fire outside, smoke already curling through the ventilation shafts.

Two armed men rounded the corner.

Jinx fired twice at center mass, double-tapped to the heart. The other received the same greeting before they could aim at him. They dropped, and Jinx didn't stop moving.

"Z, talk to me!" he exclaimed as he ducked into an alcove. Bullets pinged off the plaster wall behind him.

"Back gate's burning. Eastern wall's ready for breach. You've got about forty seconds before I blow the armor shed." The shed was directly outside the eastern wall.

Jinx waited until the bastards stopped firing, dipped out, and fired back. They may have been better than the cartel soldiers, but not by much. *Ever hear of cover?* Obviously not. He dropped both men and growled, "Make it twenty."

"You know I love it when you're bossy." Z laughed on the other side of the comms.

Jinx pivoted and fired off two shots into the shadow of a balcony. A sniper dropped like a rag doll, his rifle clattering down. Jinx sprinted to the man, grabbed his rifle and ammo before he booked ass to the east wall. Smoke from the first explosion rolled into the compound now, thick and choking.

He vaulted over a bench and ducked behind a stone planter. Another burst of automatic fire tore through the foliage overhead.

"You still breathing?" Z asked, voice tight with glee.

"Still alive. Little singed." Jinx reloaded the rifle with a fresh magazine. "Start your countdown."

"Going to stir things up a bit first," Z said. Immediately from across the compound, another blast ripped through the air, and it was a lot closer that time. Heat slugged him like a fist as a shockwave rattled the stone beneath his boots. A guard came screaming around the corner, half on fire, flailing.

Jinx didn't waste the bullet.

Instead, he ran toward the wall, veering off to the right where the wall was thicker.

"Ten seconds. East wall, charge two," Z counted. "Nine … eight …"

Gunfire erupted behind him from four men in matching tactical gear. These were Esteban's elite, and they advanced in formation.

Jinx dove through a blown-out doorway, rolled, and came up firing.

"Four … three … two …"

The east wall exploded in a shower of stone and fire. A twelve-foot gap tore open, framing the jungle like a blazing invitation to freedom. Smoke and dust billowed out like a living thing.

"Door's open!" Z shouted. "But you've got company inbound from the garage."

"Time to get dramatic," Jinx growled as he turned and pulled a small kit of C4 from inside his belt. He slapped it onto the compound's main fuel line, then primed it as gunfire raked the hallway behind him.

"Z, cover fire on the east breach."

"You got it, my man. Show 'em what heartbreak looks like."

Jinx bolted through the fire-lit corridor as Z opened up. The stutter of suppressed rifle fire cut down the guards near the breach. Bullets zinged past Jinx's shoulders as he cleared the wall in a leap and hit the ground in a crouch.

Behind him, the compound roared as the fuel line detonated. The eruption flattened him to the earth.

He scrambled away from the flames, keeping pinned to the ground. The sky turned orange.

Fire rolled across the roof. A tower cracked and toppled sideways in a cascade of sparks and steel. Jinx used the deafening noise to lurch to his feet and sprint away from the compound.

Z let out a low whistle as Jinx ran toward him through the smoke, wild-eyed and alive. "Damn," Z said, slinging his rifle. "You always make an exit like that?"

Jinx didn't stop moving. "Only when I'm feeling sentimental."

He grabbed Z's shirt, spinning him as he ran by. Z fell into step with him as they raced toward the vehicle. "No, this way!" Z shouted when Jinx veered the wrong way. They disappeared into the jungle. The inferno lit the sky behind them like a beacon formed in hell and sent straight from Satan himself.

Flames licked the sky as the compound collapsed. One explosion rolled into another like a storm gathering overhead. Trees shivered under the shockwaves, and the air was thick with smoke and the deafening sound of war.

Jinx sprinted through the undergrowth beside Z, his heart hammering and his lungs burning as they sprinted at full speed.

"We need distance!" Jinx barked as he ducked under a low branch while vines clawed at his shoulders.

"We'll get it," Z called, his grin audible even through his panting. "I gift-wrapped our exfil with surprises."

Behind them, engine growls echoed through the jungle. It was the distinct, grinding roar of armored SUVs barreling down the dirt road that flanked the ridge.

"They're moving fast," Jinx muttered.

"Yeah," Z said, swinging his rifle to cover their rear. "And in about ten seconds, they'll learn not to be so fucking dedicated."

They reached a jagged path cut through a thick brush. The trail was just wide enough to run through and just narrow enough to keep the enemy funneled in a straight line.

Jinx paused, eyes scanning the terrain. "How many charges?"

"Four. Pressure and remote triggers. Two buried, two in trees. That's why we veered." Z grinned and tapped a small control panel on his vest. "All timed to hit the sweet spot."

The rumble behind them grew louder. Headlights slashed through the thick jungle.

"They'll try to flank," Jinx warned. "We need to funnel them tighter."

"Already done," Z said, voice smug. "I dropped a cedar across the west bend. They've only got one way through now."

Just then, the first SUV came into view. Jinx glanced over in the darkness, but he could see the dark silhouette of a mounted gunner already aiming for the trees where they most logically would be.

"Wait for it …" Z whispered.

The vehicle hit the buried charge.

The jungle lit up in a white-hot flash. The SUV lifted off the ground, tires blown skyward, flames spitting from beneath its chassis as it flipped into a tree and exploded again on impact. The gunner never had a chance to scream.

"That's one," Z growled.

Another vehicle swerved hard, trying to break formation. It didn't make it far before a second explosion sent it sideways into a ditch, flames licking the canopy.

"That's two."

Bullets sprayed into the jungle as the third SUV's gunner opened up in panic, shredding trees and sending birds screeching into the sky.

Jinx returned fire from behind a fallen log, his

shots precise and controlled. The gunner dropped with a sharp cry.

More shouting. Another vehicle barreled through the smoke. "Time for the tree charge," Z said.

A massive tree trunk rigged with explosives snapped in half and crashed down directly onto the SUV's hood, smashing it like a tin can. The front axle crumpled like a paper cup, and the roof became one with the floorboard.

"Three and four," Z said with satisfaction, slapping Jinx's shoulder. "God, I love my job."

Jinx didn't reply. His eyes were already on the move while he scanned and calculated his surroundings. "They'll send a drone," he said. "We've got five minutes before air surveillance pins us."

"Already planned for that, too," Z said, pulling a small drone jammer from his pack and tossing it to Jinx. "Here. Don't push that until we need it, though. It'll cook their signal just long enough to get to out of the way."

They moved again, pushing deeper into the jungle.

Behind them, the trail was lit with fire and wreckage. The responding enemy was in ruin. What few guards were still breathing were probably too busy screaming, bleeding, or running for cover.

“You good?” Z asked, side-eyeing Jinx as they ran.

“Better than I’ve been in years.”

“Yeah?” Z grinned and panted, “Kinda sounded like you meant that.”

“I do,” Jinx said, eyes narrowing as they reached the next cover point. They vanished into the jungle, the night behind them still burning. Jinx and Z moved fast, dodging thorny vines and ducking under hanging moss. The thick, humid air stuck to their skin, oily and annoying.

"You boys made a mess," Brando’s voice crackled over comms, dry as ever. "Looks like a war zone from up here."

Jinx ducked a branch that about brained him and asked, "How bad’s the spread?"

"Half the compound’s gone. You clipped their communications tower. Good thinking, by the way. You’ve got a dozen survivors scattered through the jungle. Some look like they’re regrouping. Others … not so much."

Z laughed under his breath. "You’re welcome."

"Extraction?" Jinx asked, glancing up at the moonlit canopy.

"Confirmed," Brando replied. "A Guardian bird is already in Venezuelan airspace. You’ve got a clean zone about four klicks southeast of your position.

Look for the old hydroelectric clearing with big stone culverts, collapsed fencing, one rusted-out generator box. Touchdown in twenty minutes. You need to be there in fifteen."

Jinx swore softly and picked up the pace.

"They're deploying a UAV," Brando added. "Give me sixty seconds, I'll feed you a window to fire the jammer and blind it before it's overhead."

"Copy," Jinx said. He panted, hard and even as they bounded over a rocky ledge slick with moss. He slid down the other side, boots digging in.

Z landed beside him with a thump, grinning like a lunatic. "So ... want to do this again next weekend?"

Jinx gave him a flat look. "Only if I get to blow more things up next time."

"Fair."

Brando's voice returned faster now. "Okay, Jinx, that drone's coming in low from the north. Fire the jammer in three ... two ... one ... now."

Jinx pulled the device from his belt, flipped the cap, and pressed the trigger. A low hum vibrated the air, almost imperceptible, then it cut off just as quickly.

"Drone lost signal. They'll think it's an equipment

fault for the next few minutes," Brando confirmed. "Go now."

The two men raced forward, weaving through the trees, ducking under the low-slung limbs of malformed trees. Birds startled into flight from their movement shrieked above them.

"Satellite shows heat signatures converging on your six," Brando warned. "You're being tracked. Looks like three, maybe four, men. They're fanned out, moving fast. You need to disappear."

Jinx skidded to a stop near a narrow gully and motioned for Z.

"Down here."

They dropped into the wash, hidden from the sky. Z handed Jinx a smoke grenade. He pulled the pin and tossed it up onto the trail before they moved. Thick white fog floated out, masking their trail from any visual tracking.

"That'll buy us thirty seconds," Jinx said.

"Which is about twenty-five more than I need," Z replied, already priming a small claymore and placing it behind a log.

They moved again, cutting right through a shallow stream to break their thermal trail as much as possible. The jungle was a blur of filtered moonlight, ferns, thick roots, and hanging vines.

And then ... Light.

They emerged into a clearing. The moon broke free of cover to illuminate the abandoned hydroelectric site just like Brando said. Cracked cement channels, a fallen tower, and a half-buried generator box.

"We're here," Jinx panted.

"Bird's inbound," Brando said in their ears. "Ninety seconds. You'll hear her before you see her."

Jinx turned, eyes scanning the jungle. He crouched, rifle up. Z did the same on the opposite flank, laser sight sweeping the trees.

"We've got movement!" Z said breathlessly, finger tensing on the trigger.

The first of Esteban's surviving men broke into the clearing. Two came from the south, one circling from the west, lean and armed to the teeth.

They fired as one. Two bodies hit the ground in rapid succession. The third fired back, bullets screaming past Jinx's head as he dove for cover.

Then a low rumble filled the air.

Womp-womp-womp.

The sound of helicopter blades cutting through the night.

"Guardian has a visual," Brando confirmed. "Ten seconds to touchdown. Clear the pad."

A black silhouette descended through the smoke

like something out of a nightmare. The aircraft was sleek, unmarked, and the rotor wash kicked up debris.

The side door slid open, and a Guardian operator leaned out, waving.

"Let's move!" Jinx shouted.

Z tossed one last flashbang into the jungle as cover, the explosion lighting up the night. They sprinted across the clearing, climbed aboard, and the helicopter lifted before their boots were fully inside.

Below, the jungle fell away. Jinx looked down at the aftermath. The trail they'd run was flaming and broken. A scar on the country left by Esteban's demise.

Jinx exhaled as he dropped into a seat, body humming with adrenaline.

"Mission accomplished," Brando said through the headset, satisfaction in his voice.

Z clapped Jinx's shoulder and leaned close. "You know, for a guy who doesn't talk much, you throw one hell of a party."

IN THE CABIN of the aircraft they'd transferred to, the inside buzzed with low light and the faint hum of aircraft systems. Outside, storm clouds rolled beneath the plane, but inside, the air was charged with the weight of finality.

Jinx stood at one end of the mission table, arms folded, boots planted, blood and smoke still marking him. Across from him, Fury, their handler, could be seen on the monitor. The silence was sharp enough to draw blood.

Z, casually leaning in a chair nearby with his boots kicked up on a metal crate, chewed a protein bar.

"Esteban Ortega is confirmed dead," Fury said, breaking the silence. His tone was cool, clipped. "And with him, the man known as *El Fantasma* is gone, too. Tomás was also confirmed dead. The recording Brando sent us was enough to close the mission."

Fury tapped the edge of a tablet. Satellite images flickered across the center screen. They saw scorched jungle, cratered walls, wrecked SUVs.

"The aftermath," Fury continued. "Z, what you delivered was a full-scale incineration of a cartel stronghold and half its fighting force. Clean, yes. Loud as hell? Also, yes."

Jinx didn't blink. "We were thorough. Both targets are down."

"You were theatrical," Fury snapped, though a ghost of a grin twitched at the corner of his mouth. "Somebody will be cleaning up the political fallout for weeks."

Z raised a hand. "Just for the record, *he* pulled the trigger. *I* made the fireworks. And they were beautiful." He flicked his fingers into the air, mimicking an explosion. "Gorgeous, mate. Simply gorgeous."

Fury gave him a dry look. "I don't care if you wrote a sonnet while you were at it. What matters is the blowback." He shrugged. "Or so they told me to tell you."

He zoomed in on thermal satellite footage from earlier. "Half of Esteban's men are dead. The others scattered. Local militias are already poking around the ruins. Every cartel within a thousand miles now knows there's a leadership void. However, the government has taken the initiative to move their asses into the area to protect the route from being used again. We'll see how long that lasts."

"Until someone wants their palms greased," Jinx said.

Fury's eyes narrowed, and he studied Jinx for a long moment, then slowly nodded. "Esteban was the most elusive cartel tactician we've seen in a decade. Politically untouchable. Invisible on paper. You neutralized him and lit a fuse under his entire network." He paused, tapping the tablet again. "The Council is pleased. So is the brass." He exhaled. "Good work. Your report's due in twenty-four hours. The debrief file's already open."

The screen went black, leaving a charged silence in his wake.

Z pulled his boots down and leaned forward, elbows on his knees. "You know, for an op, that was kinda poetic. Big boom. Bad guy down. You get the girl?"

"Not yet," he said finally. "But I'm heading home, and I'm marrying her."

THE PLANE'S interior thrummed with a low, steady vibration. The quiet kind that seeped into your bones and dulled the edge of adrenaline, leaving only the fatigue beneath. Outside, the darkness was total. There were no stars, and no lights, just the long, invisible path home.

Jinx sat alone in the dim compartment near the rear bulkhead. His head was tilted back against the cool wall. He hadn't moved in almost an hour. His eyes were open, but he wasn't seeing anything.

"You know," a voice said from the aisle, "you missed one hell of a birthday party."

Jinx didn't turn his head.

Z dropped into the seat across from him, uninvited but not unwelcome. He set a half-sandwich on the armrest and leaned forward, forearms on his knees, elbows wide.

"The whole team was there. Specter even showed up and brought that spiked Russian punch he makes. Viper got so drunk he tried to arm-wrestle Phantom."

Jinx exhaled softly through his nose. "Hope someone filmed that."

"Oh, we did. Played it on loop until the comms guys threatened to break the monitors." Z's grin faded slightly. "But you weren't there."

A long silence passed between them. The only sound was the distant murmur of engine turbines and the occasional metallic creak of the aircraft hull adjusting to altitude.

"Didn't feel like celebrating," Jinx finally said.

Z nodded slowly. "I figured. Still, I noticed."

Jinx looked at him then. Not sharply. Just enough to acknowledge what wasn't being said.

Z leaned back, dragging a hand through his short hair.

"You've gone non-comm before, man. We've all been down that road. But this time … this time was different. You vanished. For years." He paused. "We all thought you were going to go dark on us."

Jinx looked away again, jaw tight. "I was close," he admitted. "Closer than I've ever been."

Z let that hang for a beat, then spoke softer.

"So, what pulled you back?"

Jinx stared at the floor for a long moment, the jungle's green flickering through his mind, the sound of Eira's voice, the weight of his son's small hand wrapped around his finger.

"Someone I never stopped loving. And someone I didn't know I had."

Z's eyes widened slightly. He straightened in his seat.

"Tell me about her. I met her for like ten seconds before Raven loaded them all on the plane."

Jinx smiled softly. "Her name's Eira. We were together when I was deep under. I left thinking I was keeping her safe. Turns out I left her pregnant. She didn't know until after I completed my mission and walked."

"Damn." Z ran a hand over his mouth. "Jinx as a daddy. Wasn't that a slap in the pants? He's a cute little bugger, too. Looks like his mother, thank God."

"Yeah." Jinx's voice dipped, and he smiled. "His name's Teo. He's got her eyes. Her stubbornness, too."

"No way that's a coincidence." A beat passed. "You're marrying her, right? Giving that boy a dad. It's fucking important. I know that better than anyone."

Jinx looked him dead in the eye. "I already said I was."

A slow smile crept across Z's face, not mocking, but genuine. Maybe even proud.

"Well, I'll be damned. Jinx the lone wolf, destroyer of drug lords, and now, a full-time daddy. Next thing you know, you'll go ranching full-time. I'm going to need a room at your place."

Jinx actually huffed a short laugh. "Why the hell is that?"

"Oh! I'm buying him a Nerf gun and teaching him how to short-circuit motion sensors by the time he's five."

Jinx chuckled softly, then fell quiet again. Z studied him for a moment, then said, voice lower now, serious, "I meant what I said back when we all thought you were gone. The team didn't just lose a sharp trigger. We lost a brother. You going off-grid … it shook us. It shook me."

Jinx didn't respond right away. But the way his posture softened just a little said he heard every word.

"I'm not gone anymore," he said finally.

"Good." Z nodded once. "'Cause I need you at my next birthday party. Rook swore he'd bring tequila, and I'm bringing the explosives." He leaned in. "I want someone sober enough to remember not to blow us all up."

Jinx looked over and finally smiled. Family, blood, and bond were the most important things in life. "I'll be there. You have my word."

CHAPTER 23

The wind rolled low over the open prairie, tugging at the edge of Jinx's shirt as he stepped out of the black SUV and looked across the land he barely knew as home. His boots crunched the gravel driveway, and the scent of sage and cattle hung heavy in the air. The ranch stretched around him, framed by distant hills and endless sky. He'd bought the place as a sanctuary for lost and mistreated animals, but it had become his sanctuary, too. The peacefulness and separation from the horrors of the world he protected covered him each time he stepped foot on his property.

The small house sat on a rise just past the barn. It was ancient by American standards. Painted white with a wraparound porch that the Macys cared for from where they lived just down the road in a house Jinx had built for them when he'd bought their land. A swing hung from one corner and creaked in the breeze. The sight of it, so ordinary, so untouched by violence and death, made his throat tighten.

His heart was here. His family, the land, and the animals. The simplicity of what made him happy had escaped him for most of his life. Not any longer. He turned to the house and made his way to the door. Jinx hadn't known what to expect. He'd sent Eira and Teo almost three months ago with nothing but a promise and an escort. The Macys were the quiet, salt-of-the-earth people he liked. They had no tolerance for laziness or cruelty. That was why when he'd purchased their land and home, he'd asked them to stay on and manage the place while he wasn't around. The house he'd built for them was Mrs. Macy's dream. A house with new floors and insulated windows. It was a small price to pay for the peace of mind that having them on the property gave him. He paid Mrs. Macy a generous monthly allowance to maintain the house, but she hardly touched it. He chuckled as he remembered the current state of the account. A major dent for women's clothes and all things Teo. His only regret was that he wasn't helping select what to buy for his woman and son.

His little boy. He was a father. The thought made him smile as he passed the porch steps and pushed open the front door.

Warmth met him. A soft, floral scent lingered in the air. A woven blanket of Teo's he remembered from Venezuela lay folded across the arm of the couch. A few toys were scattered across the floor near a colorful rug he hadn't bought. And on the mantel … was a photo. He and Eira. The one she'd taken of them together back at the farm in Venezuela after they'd first met. They were sunburned and smiling, and the camera angle was crooked, but it was a good picture. He stared at it, stunned.

Footsteps padded lightly behind him.

He turned.

Eira stood just inside the kitchen archway, one hand over her heart. Her dark hair curled softly around her shoulders. Her blue jeans were new and clung to her soft curves. She wore one of his old flannel shirts. It hung loose on her frame, sleeves rolled halfway up her forearms and tied at the waist. Her eyes shimmered. He wasn't sure if it was hope or disbelief, but he prayed her love was mixed somewhere within the visible emotion.

He didn't speak. He couldn't. His ability to say everything he wanted to say slipped away as the emotion of the moment throat punched him. She was beautiful and his.

Eira broke first, rushing into his arms, burying her face into his chest as she sobbed against him. Jinx held her, swearing he'd never let go again. His arms curled tightly around her, one hand cradling the back of her head, the other flat against her spine, memorizing the feel of her against him.

"I didn't know when I'd see you again," she whispered, her voice trembling.

"I promised I'd come back," he said, his voice gravel rough. "I'll always come back to you."

She pulled back just far enough to look at him, her fingertips brushing his jaw. His stubble was three days old and thick. "You look tired."

"I am," he admitted. "But seeing you, God, Eira... you are the reason I breathe."

Her lips parted, but a small, delighted shriek broke through the moment.

"Papi!"

Jinx turned, heart skipping.

Teo ran in barefoot from the mudroom door, jeans dusty, cheeks flushed from playing. Behind him, Mr. Macy called out an apology, holding the door open and waving once before vanishing with a knowing smile.

Jinx dropped to one knee just in time for Teo to launch himself forward, small arms flinging around his father's neck.

"Hey, pequeño caballero," Jinx choked out, holding him tight, burying his face in the boy's dark curls. "Did you take care of Momma? Did you take care of the cows?"

"New cow," Teo announced proudly, but it sounded like *nude dow*.

Jinx looked up at Eira, who was smiling through tears. "We bought a cow. For the raw milk. The thing you buy in the stores isn't milk." She shivered and rubbed her arms. "We got her from a dairy north of here. The Macy's son arranged it. She was very expensive. I told Mr. Macy it was too much, but he just laughed and said you could well afford it."

"I don't doubt it." Jinx picked up Teo and hugged him before draping an arm around Eira. "And it doesn't matter. If you or Teo need anything, it is yours."

"We don't need much." She put her hand on his chest. "Just you."

"Dow!" Teo said and pointed out the door. "See?" He looked at Jinx like he'd hung the moon and the stars. Teo tugged his hand. "See!"

"In a bit, hijo. I need to talk to Momma first."

Teo wiggled to be released and ran through the house toward the back hallway, yelling something about the *nude dow*.

When they were alone again, Jinx stood and reached into his pocket, while Eira watched him warily.

He took out the ring and dropped to his knee.

The ring wasn't large. It wasn't flashy. It was simple and solid. The stone was pale, almost translucent blue, set into a band shaped like three braided threads. One for each of them. "I know I don't deserve you. But if you let me, I'll spend the rest of my life trying to make up for our lost time. I want the rest of my sunrises, sunsets, and every damn star in the sky shared with you and Teo. Eira Isaacson, will you marry me?"

Her knees buckled. She grabbed his shirt and kissed him, fierce and trembling. He framed her ribs with his hands and held the woman as she gasped. "Yes," she breathed. "Yes, Mateo."

JINX STOOD behind Eira as they opened the door and peeked into Teo's bedroom. A nightlight illuminated the small boy in his bed. A stuffed donkey that had been washed too many times was clutched in his hand. Eira slowly closed the door and took his hand, leading him to the bedroom, and he shut the door behind her. She backed up, taking off her shirt as she stared at him. He lifted his shirt over his head and moved closer. He mimicked her actions, removing his jeans when she did and taking off his underwear when she slipped out of hers. He covered the few feet between them and drew her into his arms. The feel of her skin against his was incendiary, burning marks of possession into his skin with every touch. This woman owned him. He backed her to the bed and lowered them onto the mattress.

He trailed kisses from her jaw, down her throat to her shoulder. Her fingers trailed down his back, leaving gooseflesh in their wake. The feel of her hands against him was addictive and as necessary as oxygen. She made him feel alive and needed in ways he'd been afraid to imagine he could be.

When he rose over her, she placed one of his hands on her heart. "All I have is this. My heart. I don't have anything else to give you, Mateo. But what I have, I give to you, freely and with love."

He lifted their hands to place hers over his heart. "My heart, my life, and my love belong to you. I was insane to think I could stay away from you."

An eyebrow lifted, and she smirked. "Remember that," she teased.

He stared down at her, completely serious. "I will never forget it or the fact that you gave me a second chance." He lowered his lips. "You are my soul. You guide my life with your love. I'm lost without you. I love you."

He dropped down and kissed her long and deep. His tongue danced with hers as their hands traveled over skin that lay exposed to each other. Her legs curled around his as he centered over her. The need to be as close to his woman as humanly possible overwhelmed the want to be slow in the union.

Eira's nails along his back told him she wanted him inside her. He entered her and dropped his head to her shoulder, fighting back the urge to move faster. Instead, he withdrew and slid back in, going deeper. The feel of her body taking him in, moving against him, and pulling him back as he moved his hips was unquestionably destructive in the absolute best way. Rolls of electric pulses migrated from his limbs to the base of his spine. He moved with barely restrained control, keeping the build slow, which annihilated any possibility of coherent thought. But he *felt*. Emotions he'd bottled up for years, the love he assumed would fade, the woman he believed would forget him … he felt it all.

When Eira shattered under him, he dropped his head to her shoulder, and the guttural moan that erupted from him as he crashed over the edge cleansed that torture from his body. Love had won. It had made him whole and provided a way back to a life he thought he couldn't have.

* * *

"Absolutely not," Eira's mom declared, slamming her tea mug on the table. "I will not be hanging electricity from the barn rafters. That is senseless. I don't care what pin … pin …" She looked at Eira questioningly.

"Pinterest board," Eira informed her again.

"That … says. It doesn't make sense," her mother said and crossed her arms.

Eira, sitting in the middle of the table surrounded by a sea of wedding magazines, lifted her head from her hands. "It's just twinkle lights, Mom."

"You say that now," Raven deadpanned from her perch on the windowsill, cleaning her nails with a butterfly knife. "Until one string shorts out and the whole hayloft becomes a flaming death trap."

"Raven," Eira groaned. "We all know what you do for a living. You *can* handle fairy lights. I have faith in you."

Raven shrugged. "Well, in my defense, none of my jobs have asked me to coordinate floral arrangements with burlap runners and fairy lights."

"I am just saying," Eira's mom announced to no one in particular and everyone at once, "there will be no *fires* at this wedding." She glanced over to Raven. "And no boots with knives hidden in them."

Raven snorted. "So, that rules out half the guest list."

"I *heard* that," Eira's mom said from where she filled her teacup with hot water.

Eira sighed. She was unusually used to these types of conversations. Thank God they were speaking in Spanish. Otherwise, the Macys would think they were all insane. "This leads our conversation to the dress you'll be wearing as my bridesmaid."

"Oh, no. I wore a dress and heels on a mission once," Raven said, stretching. "Had to use one as a projectile to escape an elevator ambush. Almost took a guy's eye out."

"¡Dios mío!" Her mother gasped, clutching her chest. "You see? *This* is why I told Eira to marry a dentist."

"Mom," Eira said without looking up from her notebook. "He's better than a dentist." *He just turned out to be an internationally sanctioned assassin with a ranch and a collection of misfit animals and friends that were slightly off-kilter.* She snickered at her thoughts. "He has a ranch with a milk cow. Be happy." He had also changed his name. He still went by Mateo, but in the States, he was Mateo Dean, and she would become Mrs. Dean…soon.

Raven held up a finger. "Technically, it's two cows now. Mr. Macy bought another. Teo named her Moo Moo. Have you forgotten?"

"Impossible." Eira chuckled.

"That cow has opinions," her mother added, sipping her tea with a wry smile. "Loud ones."

"I need wine," Raven said.

"It's 9:03 in the *morning*," Eira pointed out.

"Flowers, fairy lights, and burlap, need I say more? I'm not wearing a dress, but I'll look good." Raven shrugged.

"I get approval of the outfit." Eira didn't even look up as she paged through the bridal magazines. She had a specific idea of what she wanted her dress to look like, and a seamstress in Hollister said she could help her make her dream come true. She had a meeting with her tomorrow and needed to give her a good idea of what style she wanted.

Just then, Teo came flying in from the hallway, dragging a stuffed donkey and wearing nothing but cowboy boots and pajama bottoms. "Moo Moo!" he said as he headed to the living room and his toys.

Raven muttered, "Miss Moo Moo's authority is expanding quickly."

"Chaos," her mother said as she followed Teo into the living room. "Next thing you know, we'll have a flower goat. Don't think I didn't hear Mateo say that."

"Could be," Eira said, laughing as she scribbled on her wedding to-do list. "Mateo already said if Teo wanted a flower goat, he'd rent a damn tux for it."

Raven leaned forward, voice low and wicked. "I could *train* the goat to deliver the rings. With a GoPro."

Eira lifted her eyes at a strangled gasp. Her mother stood in the doorway and looked one second from stroking out. "Ladies," Eira said calmly, "I love you. But if this turns into a barnyard battle royale, I'm eloping in Vegas with a bouquet made of antelope jerky."

There was a moment of stunned silence before Raven raised her tea mug. "To jerky weddings."

* * *

JINX STEPPED into the kitchen with absolutely no clue what he was walking into. At the table, Eira was surrounded by Post-it notes and something that may have once been a wedding seating chart but now looked like an explosion at a Crayola factory.

Raven was sharpening her throwing knives and watching *Say Yes to the Dress* on her phone.

Eira's mom was … praying. To whom, Jinx wasn't sure. But it sounded *serious*.

Teo, wearing one of Raven's tactical vests, was dragging a stuffed donkey around while mooing.

Jinx blinked. "Should I … come back later?"

Eira's mom turned toward him with the intensity of a soap opera villain. "*You.*"

Jinx took a careful step back. "Me?"

"You're the reason we are hosting a *barnyard wedding* with potentially armed livestock and assassin bridesmaids. You proposed. *You opened this portal to chaos.*"

Jinx slowly raised his hands. "Okay, that's fair. But, just for clarity…who gave Teo access to gear?"

"I did. Things are getting rough in here," Raven said without looking up. "And honestly, I respect that. Strong women, strong opinions."

Eira looked up at him and sighed, "What kind of cake do you want? You don't get to have feelings about color schemes, but I'll give you cake input."

"Chocolate," Jinx said automatically, eyes wide. "With caramel. Maybe whiskey glaze if no one's morally opposed."

"See? Now, that's a *man's* answer," Raven grunted and turned up the phone. "Oh, here, look, Eira, is this what you were talking about?"

Eira stood up, her eyes slightly wild, her ponytail halfway collapsed like a flag of surrender. She took the phone and jumped up and down. "Yes! Screen-shot that, please?"

"Got it, girl," Raven said and grabbed the phone back. "I love some deep research. I knew we could find it."

Jinx started to back out of the kitchen. Things were warped into a weird little wedding world right now. But Eira turned on him and pointed to Raven. "Did you *know* that if we invite your full Guardian team, we'll probably need security for the *security* if they are like my friend here?"

"Wait, are you inviting Phantom?" Raven asked, suddenly alert.

Jinx frowned. "Of course, I'm inviting him."

"Oh, good," Raven purred. "He owes me money. I'll make him wear a sash, too. He's gullible."

"No one's wearing a sash," Eira's mom thundered.

Raven laughed. "No promises."

Jinx slowly walked over to Eira and wrapped an arm around her, pulling her gently to his chest. She let out a sigh that was part exhaustion, maybe a small part exorcism.

"I love you," he murmured into her hair.

She leaned into him. "I just spent the last hour arguing about whether an imaginary flower goat should wear boots."

"Did you win?"

"No. He's wearing boots. They light up."

Jinx grinned and then laughed. "I'd call that a victory."

She tilted her head back and met his eyes. "This is insane."

"This is *us*," he said. "Completely nuts. Unexpected. Surrounded by armed women and mischievous toddlers. And perfect."

She smiled, slow and tired but real.

From across the kitchen, her mother hissed,

"Don't kiss her, you're going to smudge her makeup. We're doing engagement photos later!"

Jinx raised an eyebrow. "Engagement photos?"

Raven flipped a knife and caught it by the hilt. "You and her, field of wildflowers, holding crossbows."

"Never! Do you want this old woman to teach you a lesson, young lady? You're not too old to be taken to the woodshed." Eira's mom pointed at Raven. "No weapons allowed."

"... I'll allow it," Jinx said.

Raven and Eira's mom turned and looked at him simultaneously. "Which one?" Raven lifted an eyebrow.

"Figure it out," Jinx said and laughed when Raven bolted up and ran from the house. "I'm not going to the woodshed," she called out as the door slammed shut.

Eira shook her head into Jinx's chest. "I don't even care if the goat walks me down the aisle now."

Jinx kissed her temple and whispered, "No animals. Just us."

THE BARN at Jinx's ranch stood tall against the endless South Dakota sky, its weathered wood and dark metal roof softened by strands of fairy lights draped from beam to beam. Wildflowers, white daisies, purple coneflowers, and golden sunbursts lined the aisle between two rows of wooden benches filled with their Guardian family, the Macys, and a few others Eira had met in the local area. The scent of fresh hay and sweet clover drifted through the air, mixing with the faint sound of wind chimes that hung at the barn doors.

Inside, the space had been transformed. White muslin fabric swooped in gentle arcs between the rafters, and hanging lanterns cast a soft amber glow over the polished wood floors. A reclaimed wood arch stood at the far end of the aisle, twined with ivy and dotted with fresh blooms. Beyond it, the open barn doors framed the sweeping prairie beyond, filled with golden grasses swaying in the warm breeze. The Black Hills were just visible on the horizon.

Guests shifted and murmured in delight as the wedding party took their places. There was a sense of anticipation, and Jinx was as nervous as a long-tailed cat in a room full of rocking chairs. He watched the door open, and Teo walked out. The little boy waved at him and started down the aisle. But halfway down the aisle, a small disruption drew laughter. The two-year-old stood frozen in place, clutching the velvet ring pillow with chubby fingers, eyes wide as a fluffy brown-and-white puppy darted out from behind the rows and tumbled straight toward him. One of the rescues-in-training had wriggled out of the kennels near the stables. Teo, unimpressed by the formality of the moment, plopped right down on the aisle runner with a giggle and began patting the excited puppy's ears, forgetting entirely about the pillow and the crowd watching him.

From the side, Jinx's deep chuckle rolled across the space. In his tailored black tuxedo, which was modern-cut with a crisp white shirt, no tie, and just a small silver pin of a wolf's head at the collar, he broke rank from his spot at the altar and strode down the aisle.

He crouched beside Teo, murmuring something that made the little boy laugh and press a kiss to his father's cheek. Jinx lifted his son and the ring pillow, while the puppy scampered happily behind them.

"Guess the no animal policy was busted," he said as he returned to his place, setting Teo down gently beside one of the groomsmen with a wink.

And then the music changed.

Eira stepped into the light of the barn doors.

Gasps rose from the crowd. Her gown was breathtaking. It was a soft ivory fabric that clung to her curves before flaring slightly at the bottom. The hem was embroidered with delicate wildflower motifs that mirrored the ones blooming around the barn. When she turned to kiss her mother, he noticed the back dipped into a graceful V, and her shoulders were bare except for two sheer, off-the-shoulder sleeves that fluttered slightly in the breeze. Her dark hair was swept up into some kind of updo, loose strands curling around her cheeks. Tucked within the style was a silver comb shaped like flowers, which Raven had gifted her.

Escorting her down the aisle, Eira's mother wore a deep amethyst dress with lace sleeves and a gently flared skirt. The woman's proud smile shone brighter than the new jewels at her ears. She squeezed Eira's hand, whispering something that made her daughter laugh before stepping back to her seat.

As Eira walked slowly toward Jinx, the puppy gave a joyful bark, Teo clapped, and Jinx stood utterly still, his expression filled with awe and reverence. This was his world. The people he trusted, the woman of his dreams, and the son he loved more than he could imagine.

He offered his hand without a word, and she took it, their fingers lacing together effortlessly.

The crowd quieted.

The wind softened.

And beneath the open rafters of the barn, with the family, bonded and blood, that Jinx loved surrounding them, they promised forever.

The reception was in full swing as the sun dipped below the horizon, painting the sky in shades of lavender and autumn golds and oranges. Strings of Edison bulbs crisscrossed above the barnyard, casting golden pools of light over long wooden tables set with wildflower centerpieces and mason jars filled with sweet tea and beer. A live band played softly near the barn doors, their music drifting over the gentle hum of laughter and clinking glasses.

At one of the round tables near the edge of the gathering, the assassins had clustered like their own little lethal and low-key storm system, tucked just far enough from the dance floor to avoid being asked to waltz or, God forbid, polka.

Rook leaned back in his chair, boots crossed at the ankle, sipping from a dark bottle of stout. His sharp gaze scanned the crowd. It was instinct.

Phantom sat beside him, methodically disassembling and reassembling a silver cigar cutter he'd been given as a groomsman gift, his tie already loosened. Viper and Specter nursed bourbons with slow, calculated sips. Their silence was as comfortable as ever. Demon, in a dark charcoal vest and sleeves rolled up, had one arm slung casually over the back of a chair, chuckling at something Raven said.

Raven, the only woman among them, had traded her usual jeans for a slim black jumpsuit and boots that still looked like she could sprint a mile if necessary. Her messy bun hadn't survived the night, and a few strands framed her face as she laughed, sharp and genuine, at a memory one of them actually voiced aloud. Taboo, but they'd swept the area before the ceremony.

Berserker thumped a heavy boot on the table leg as he leaned in. "I'm just saying, if I ever say I'm thinking about getting married, someone better stop me. Like, physically."

"You'd terrify the officiant," Specter deadpanned.

Rook smirked. "Assuming you survive to the altar."

"Odds are slim," Phantom added, still fiddling with the cutter.

"Appreciate the support, assholes." Berserker

grinned. "With friends like you, I'll never get married. Totally fucking awesome."

Just then, Jinx walked over, his tux jacket unbuttoned, a dark smudge of icing at the edge of his shirt sleeve from where Teo had smashed a cupcake into his arm earlier. He looked relaxed, loose in a way only they would recognize. Tonight, he was finally happy. The evidence was everywhere.

"Well, look at this rogue's gallery," Jinx said, sliding into the open space beside Raven and snagging one of the bourbon bottles from the table. "We keep this table together too long, and someone will report an international incident."

"Only if Rook keeps talking about your dance moves," Demon replied with a grin.

Jinx groaned. "That was not a dance. That was Teo dragging me into a sugar-fueled stampede."

Raven tilted her head. "Looked like you were enjoying yourself."

"I was," Jinx said, quieter this time. "Never thought I'd get this."

For a moment, they all sat with that truth. The idea that any of them would live long enough for a day like this. A glorious sunset, vows, and peace, if only for a few hours.

Then...

Bzzzt. Bzzzt.

Berserker's phone vibrated against the table.

He grabbed it, eyes scanning the encrypted message. His entire body shifted instantly, the relaxed lines of a wedding guest sharpening into the ready poise of a killer.

He stood. "Got a call sign ping. Unscheduled."

Rook's phone lit up a second later. Raven's did, too.

Rook's voice was low as Ring's voice came over all of all their comms. He tapped his ear. "Where?"

"Madrid. Secondary target surfaced. High-level intel, time-sensitive. We have a primary for immediate extraction if confirmed hostile."

Berserker stood without a word, finishing his drink in a single swallow. He placed the glass on the table. Raven followed suit, pulling a tie from her hair and twisting it into a ponytail.

Berserker glanced at Jinx, one brow raised. "You good if we slip out early?"

Jinx gave a single nod. "Always."

Raven's gaze softened slightly. "Tell Eira goodbye for us."

"I will."

As they turned and walked away, slipping through the barn doors into the falling night, Jinx watched them go. Not with worry, but with understanding. It was the life. Always waiting, always watching. But just this once, for today, he wasn't part of it.

He turned back to the laughter and firelight, to where Teo was now sleepily curled on a blanket on Mrs. Macy's lap, and Eira dancing slowly with her mother.

His life was right here.

And it was good.

EPILOGUE

Talon King stepped away from the reception. Eira's mom had invited him. His team had watched over her as her sister recovered and ensured the family was safe from the cartel's blowback after Jinx's mission imploded the Venezuelan drug scene. Thankfully, the national government had stepped in, and the area was, for now, stabilized.

The drive back to his grandpa Frank's ranch was pleasant and quiet. When he pulled up, he was surprised to see his grandfather sitting on the porch swing. He dismounted the truck and walked up the huge flight of stairs to the porch. Sitting down next to his grandfather, he accepted the piece of taffy that was handed to him.

"Nice affair?"

"Yes, sir." Talon chuckled. "Seemed to be."

They sat in comfortable silence for a moment before his grandfather leaned forward. "Son, I don't offer advice often, but I'm going to give you a line or two."

Talon blinked and turned to his grandfather. He looked the same today as in Talon's first memories of the man. Tall, strong, sharp eyes that could look through a man and leave him bared to the world.

"What's that?" Talon asked.

"You need to drop your guard."

"What do you mean, sir?" Talon frowned. He wasn't on guard. Hell, he was just at a wedding.

"When was the last time you talked to a stranger?"

Talon cocked his head. "All the time. Grandpa, what in the hell are you getting at? Are you okay?"

His grandpa grunted. "I'm going to cut through the fat and get to the meat. When the Siege happened, it scarred you. Bad. You don't trust anyone."

"Not true. I trust family and my team."

"How long did it take you to trust your team and the new guy … will you trust him on your six without looking back?"

Talon sighed and leaned forward, placing his elbows on his knees, looking out into the darkness. "No, sir. Not yet." He had two new men on his team. Stryker and Jug were the only ones he trusted without hesitation. The other two were a work in progress … at least for him. They were good, but he didn't give anyone his trust without reason.

"And that's a problem." His grandpa handed him another piece of taffy. "When was the last time you talked to Wheeler?"

"Doc?" Talon's eyebrows shot north to his hairline. "Damn, years ago. I don't need a shrink, Grandpa. I'm fine."

Frank grunted again. "One day you're going to wake up and realize trust is as important as breathing." He stood up, fluid and strong. His grandpa made his way to the house's screen door before he turned. "It hurts your parents. They know how you close yourself off when you're not around family. Hurts me. We think we're responsible. You were just a kid."

Talon looked up at his grandpa. "No, you're not responsible, and neither are they. They didn't cause that damage. The Siege did. Yes, sir, I don't trust anyone for that reason. You know what happens when you trust blindly. Look at Foxtrot Team. They imploded. You know what I'm talking about." He shook his head. No one spoke of it, but the lack of trust and greed broke that team, and too many lost their lives that day. It was a textbook example, and he used it as proof of why he refused to trust anyone except his family.

"That was eons ago, son."

"Yeah, it was, but they still imploded. I see it on every mission. Trust is the way people take advantage of the weak or the foolish. Trust causes a person to turn a blind eye. Trust is a *weakness*. I've learned the lesson well. Trust no one with your life. And I don't, sir. I won't open myself or anyone I work with to that level of vulnerability. That is a personal choice I get to make. I will work to improve this world, but the people I trust are very few for many reasons."

His grandfather stared at him for a moment. "You'll be a very lonely man. Could die without knowing the love of a good woman or that of your own family." He walked into the house, and the screen door shut after him.

Talon leaned back against the bench and pushed off with his boot. He'd never let anyone get that close to him. Never. He stared into the night and said, "You have no idea how true that statement is, Grandpa. No idea."

TALON KING IS NOW the leader of his own team. He is thrust into a world where nothing is as it seems, a screwed up mission where love and family are used for profit and leverage. Come along as Talon navigates the razor-sharp edge of love and betrayal, and grab your copy of Heir of Honor now.

ALSO BY KRIS MICHAELS

Guardian Security Dynasty Series

Legacy's Call

Legacy's Destiny

Throne of Secrets

Echoes of Oaths

Heir of Honor

Heir of Courage

Heir of Shadows

Veil of Secrets

Kings of the Guardian Series

Jacob: Kings of the Guardian Book 1

Joseph: Kings of the Guardian Book 2

Adam: Kings of the Guardian Book 3

Jason: Kings of the Guardian Book 4

Jared: Kings of the Guardian Book 5

Jasmine: Kings of the Guardian Book 6

Chief: The Kings of Guardian Book 7

Jewell: Kings of the Guardian Book 8

Jade: Kings of the Guardian Book 9

Justin: Kings of the Guardian Book 10

Christmas with the Kings

Drake: Kings of the Guardian Book 11

Dixon: Kings of the Guardian Book 12

Passages: The Kings of Guardian Book 13

Promises: The Kings of Guardian Book 14

The Siege: Book One, The Kings of Guardian Book 15

The Siege: Book Two, The Kings of Guardian Book 16

A Backwater Blessing: A Kings of Guardian Crossover Novella

Montana Guardian: A Kings of Guardian Novella

Guardian Defenders Series

Gabriel

Maliki

John

Jeremiah

Frank

Creed

Sage

Bear

Billy

Elliot

Guardian Security Shadow World

Anubis (Guardian Shadow World Book 1)

Asp (Guardian Shadow World Book 2)

Lycos (Guardian Shadow World Book 3)

Thanatos (Guardian Shadow World Book 4)

Tempest (Guardian Shadow World Book 5)

Smoke (Guardian Shadow World Book 6)

Reaper (Guardian Shadow World Book 7)

Phoenix (Guardian Shadow World Book 8)

Valkyrie (Guardian Shadow World Book 9)

Flack (Guardian Shadow World Book 10)

Ice (Guardian Shadow World Book 11)

Malice (Guardian Shadow World Book 12)

Harbinger (Guardian Shadow World Book 13)

Centurion (Guardian Shadow World Book 14)

Maximus (Guardian Shadow World Book 15)

Hollister (A Guardian Crossover Series)

Andrew (Hollister-Book 1)

Searching for Home (A Hollister-Guardian Crossover Novel)

Zeke (Hollister-Book 2)

Declan (Hollister- Book 3)

A Home for Love (A Hollister Crossover Novel)

Ken (Hollister - Book 4)

Finally Home (A Hollister Crossover Novel)

Barry (Hollister - Book 5)

Hope City

Hope City - Brock

HOPE CITY - Brody- Book 3

Hope City - Ryker - Book 5

Hope City - Killian - Book 8

Hope City - Blayze - Book 10

The Long Road Home

Season One:

My Heart's Home

Season Two:

Searching for Home (A Hollister-Guardian Crossover Novel)

Season Three:

A Home for Love (A Hollister Crossover Novel)

Season Four:

Finally Home (A Hollister Crossover Novel)

STAND-ALONE NOVELS

A Heart's Desire - Stand Alone

Hot SEAL, Single Malt (SEALs in Paradise)

Hot SEAL, Savannah Nights (SEALs in Paradise)

Hot SEAL, Silent Knight (SEALs in Paradise)

Join my newsletter for fun updates and release information!

>>>Kris' Newsletter<<<

ABOUT THE AUTHOR

Kris Michaels' writing career is marked by 23 appearances on the USA Today Bestseller list and three on the Wall Street Journal Bestselling list for her full-length novels. As a writer, she is known for her compelling romantic stories set against military and law enforcement backdrops, as demonstrated in her series, The Kings of Guardian, Guardian Defenders, and Guardian Security Shadow World.

Originally from South Dakota, Kris's journey from a small-town high school to a twenty-two-year career in the military set the stage for her writing career, providing a wealth of experiences and backgrounds for her characters. Now living on the Gulf Coast, she writes full-time, focusing on creating stories that merge romantic elements with suspense and action. Kris explores the themes of love, duty, and bravery, which appeal to a wide audience.

Made in the USA
Middletown, DE
12 September 2025